THE
PEACE
MAKER

MICHELE CHYNOWETH

Michele Chynoweth

ND '83

Ellechor
PUBLISHING HOUSE

Ellechor Publishing House, LLC

www.ellechorpublishing.com

ACKNOWLEDGEMENTS

Thank you to all of the people who have helped me bring this story to you: to Robin Axtell, New Castle County Delaware Chief of Staff Dennis Phifer, Deacon Tommy Watts of St. Margaret of Scotland, Delaware, Carol Connolly, Mike Felker, Debbie Albano, my editor Veronika Walker, Ellechor Publishing — and to you, the reader for giving me the opportunity to share it with you.

To my best friend and biggest fan, my loving husband Bill.
Thanks for being my "giant," letting me stand on your
shoulders, and for keeping the faith with me.

"Blessed are the peacemakers, for they will be called the children of God."
— *Matthew 5:9*

AUTHOR'S NOTE

The Peace Maker is based on the story of David and Abigail in the First Book of Samuel in the Bible. To put the story in context, The Peace Maker covers most of the Book of Samuel I (from Chapter 8 up through the story of David and Abigail in Chapter 25) and includes many of the plot lines and characters from Samuel I. If you, the reader, care to refer to the characters in the Bible to see how they correlate to the characters in The Peace Maker, see the reference below – and by all means, I hope that the novel encourages you to read the original Book in the Bible!

The Peace Maker	**The First Book of Samuel**
Chessa Reynolds	Abigail
Leif Mitchell	David
Darren Richards	Nabal
Ray Silas	Samuel
Henry Mitchell	Jesse
Charles, William & George Mitchell	David's brothers
Martin Greene	Saul
Leon Slater	Goliath
Wendy Greene	Michal
Victoria Greene	Moreb
Jordan Greene	Jonathan

PART ONE

CHAPTER ONE

CHESSA

"He's gorgeous." Chessa Reynolds stared at U.S. Senator Darren Richards' photo on her laptop.

"He's okay." Amy Darlington peered over her college roommate's shoulder, arms crossed, unconvinced. "I don't see why you're so excited."

"Are you kidding? This is huge! I can't believe *The Spectator* assigned me the story. I think Senator Richards is going places. Not to mention I think I have a crush on him."

Amy shrugged, turned and went back to burying her head in the mountain of books on her desk.

"You're just jealous." Chessa looked at her watch. "Oh no, I've gotta run. The conference starts in a half hour, and it's clear across campus." She quickly packed her laptop, recorder and notebook into her backpack, dragged a brush through her unruly chestnut colored hair, and applied some lip gloss.

Senator Richards was scheduled to be the keynote speaker at the annual alumni conference at Columbia University, his alma mater.

As a junior enrolled in Columbia's College of Social Work, Chessa had lobbied to get the assignment for the school paper since she hadn't written any big articles in weeks, and she figured it would probably look good in her dossier when she went to apply for jobs after graduation. Plus she wanted to see the senator in person.

She had a good view from her seat in the packed auditorium's front row, which had been saved for dignitaries and the press. She listened intently as the Alumni Association chairman introduced the senator, who was going to speak on "Facing the Future with Confidence."

"Darren Richards is a New York native from the Hamptons who received his bachelor's degree from Harvard's Kennedy School of Government, graduated from Columbia Law School and served four years in the military—two of which were in active duty in the U.S. Marines," the chairman said. "Three years after leaving the military, he opened his own law practice and won his first bid for U.S. Congress. As a Democratic party leader, he then went on to win the U.S. Senate seat and has quickly become a champion of New York City's poor and homeless, education and the environment.

"Won't you help me give a warm welcome to one of our most notable Columbia alumni—United States Senator Darren Richards!"

Chessa couldn't help but notice how handsome the subject of her news story was as he climbed the stage and stood behind the podium to give his address. She felt herself lean forward slightly in anticipation.

After the applause settled down, Darren Richards addressed the crowd, starting with a humorous story about his life on campus, where almost all students, especially in the School of Law, had a fiercely competitive mentality and would do anything to get ahead. "Instead of saying my dog ate my paper, one time I told my professor my roommate set my paper ablaze over his Bunsen burner when he got mad at me for not helping him with his science project. Unfortunately, it was the truth. "

As the audience laughed, Chessa was mesmerized by the young politician's dazzling white smile. Craning her neck, she could see just a few flecks of gray in what was otherwise a perfect head of thick dark-brown hair that came just to his collar, blue eyes—yes, if she looked hard enough she could just see they were a gorgeous shade of blue that glittered with enthusiasm as he laughed—and… *was he glancing her way or was that just her imagination?* Her heart caught in her throat. She noticed how his dark-gray suit fit his tall, muscular frame and how he talked with his hands. They looked like nice, strong hands.

"…and in conclusion, as one of our wisest American leaders in history, President Franklin D. Roosevelt, who also happened to be a Democrat"—more laughs—"said: 'the only thing we have to fear is fear itself'." Thunderous applause erupted, and Chessa realized she had missed nearly the entire speech because she had become lost in stupid girlish desire.

Now what do I do?

She armed her way through the crowd, bounded up the steps of the stage, and stood in the long line that was forming to shake hands with Senator Richards. She fought to keep her voice from cracking and her knees from buckling when it was her turn to greet him.

"Hi Senator, I'm Chessa Reynolds, a reporter with *The Spectator*, and I know you're probably busy with all of the alumni events planned this weekend but I was wondering if I could schedule an interview with you to—"

He interrupted her with his magnetic smile, his blue eyes piercing her with curiosity and *something else*, and offered her his hand. "Of course, Miss Reynolds, I'd be delighted. Unfortunately I have to attend the alumni banquet tonight, but could I meet you afterward? There's a cozy pub near campus where we law students used to hang out called Rugby's. That might be a quiet enough place to meet. Is it still there?"

"Yes, um, okay, but I'm not quite twenty-one yet, almost, but—"

"That's all right, I'll get you in." He winked at her and grasped her hand—which he was still holding—a little more tightly before releasing it. "Let's say eight-thirty?"

"Okay." It was all she had time to say. An exasperated man in his sixties, standing close enough behind her that she could feel his foul breath on her neck, loudly cleared his throat with impatience.

Darren Richards politely turned and shook the man's hand and continued his banter.

I am a total idiot, Chessa chided herself as she walked in a fog off the stage. *I can't believe I stammered out that I'm not old enough to get in. Of course he'll get me in.* She felt her pulse quicken at the thought of sitting alone with Darren Richards. During her daydreaming she had done the math and reminded herself he was about twenty years older, and probably in a relationship (although she had glanced down at his hand and noticed he wasn't wearing a wedding band.) *Oh well, at the very least I'll walk away with a story.*

They met as planned at Rugby's, a dark, smoke-filled bar off Broadway. It had once been a popular hangout for students, but as a number of new establishments had opened over the years, it had become seedier and emptier and mainly catered to locals who came to hang out, get a good sandwich, drink cheaply, watch football, or play a game of pool. It was a Tuesday night and the place was nearly empty. No one bothered to even card Chessa, who slid into a booth, hoping she hadn't been seen. She felt out of place and waited fifteen long, uncomfortable minutes, ignoring a few stares from the scruffy-looking men who drank at the bar, before the senator finally entered. He was greeted by the bartender, who handed him a tumbler filled with ice and some type of amber liquid—probably bourbon or scotch. He approached her with a huge grin, and seeing she had no drink before her, asked if she wanted a glass of wine. She nodded, wanting to appear experienced and nonchalant. Chessa had drank on a few occasions at college parties, but didn't really care for the taste or the effect. Almost immediately a waitress placed a glass of white wine before her.

"Thank you for meeting me, Senator Richards."

"You're welcome, Miss Reynolds. But this is only going to work for me if you call me Darren. Can I call you Chessa?"

Chessa could feel her cheeks blushing. *He remembered my name,* she realized.

"I'm sorry we didn't meet somewhere nicer," Darren whispered across the table. "This place used to be quiet and classy when we law school students hung out here. I had no idea it had deteriorated like this."

"That's okay; at least it's quiet." Chessa pulled out her reporter's notebook and a pencil, deciding not to bring out her tape recorder. *Stay casual, but remember you're on duty,* she told herself.

The rest of the evening was a pleasant blur. Darren was easy to talk to and made her feel comfortable, peppering their conversation about the state of New York and its future with funny stories about his life as a student at Harvard and Columbia, and the challenges of his first political campaign.

Chessa hadn't had much for dinner and started feeling a little tipsy after her second glass of wine. She held up her hand when the waitress delivered their third round of drinks. *I need to stop before I make a fool of myself,* she decided. She noticed that, meanwhile, Darren drank her glass of wine and his third martini, but she wasn't concerned. *He can obviously handle his liquor, unlike me,* she thought. She reminded herself that she also had to walk the two miles back to her dorm room in the dark. She checked her watch, and must have looked panicked, because Darren spoke up.

"Don't worry, I can drive you back," he said. "I've got to make sure *The Spectator's* ace reporter gets back safely to write a good story about me. I need all the positive press I can get." He laughed softly, and Chessa wondered if he might be flirting with her.

He stood and offered his hand to help her out of the booth, then held her coat for her. He waved to the bartender and patrons who recognized him, then opened the door and led her out into the blustery night and quickly into his sleek black sedan. Chessa was nearly as impressed with the car as she was with the man. She looked around its interior, admiring the soft leather seats and new car smell, which mingled nicely with the scent of his cologne.

The ride seemed to go by too quickly, and within minutes the sedan pulled up along the circle in front of Chessa's dorm. She thanked the senator as he opened her car door and again offered his hand to help her out of the vehicle.

"You know, Miss Reynolds, this has been the most delightful interview I've ever had, and I've had a lot of them," he said, holding her hand in his. "Perhaps I could have the pleasure of your company again soon? Could I get your number and give you a call next time I'm in town? I have to go to D.C. for the next few weeks on business, but I'll be back in New York for the holidays, and I'd love to take you out to a much nicer place."

Chessa's heart hammered in her chest as she wrote her number on a page in her reporter notebook, ripped it out, and handed it to him. *Can he really be interested in me? He's a man of the world and I'm just a schoolgirl, just a...* As if to answer her unasked question, Darren leaned over and kissed her on the cheek, bidding her goodnight.

She smiled as she walked dreamily to her dorm room. *Amy won't believe this one.*

Being a reporter and writing for the paper was Chessa's second love. Her first was her mission to help underprivileged women who were victims of domestic violence or abuse.

She wasn't sure how she'd developed her career goal. Perhaps it started around the time her parents divorced when she was twelve. She remembered attending group counseling sessions for students in her grade school in Greenwich Village who were children of divorced or widowed parents, and admiring the woman who had led the group, thinking she'd like to be a counselor like her someday, helping others.

Chessa recalled the intense anger she had felt when her alcoholic father left her mother for the last time. Even though Stephen Reynolds had walked out the front door dozens of times over the years after the many shouting matches he had with his wife, he always returned. Sometimes it would take a day or two, but he always came back. Until the last time.

Often Chessa would try to intercede between her parents when they argued, if the argument wasn't too intense or violent. She would play peacemaker by standing in between them and trying to divert their attention, asking them for a snack, to help with homework, anything she could think of. One time she even brought home a stray cat and hid it in her bedroom until she heard the yelling start, and then brought it out to show them. That time, the yelling only got louder, and the cat was booted out the door and she was sent to bed early.

Theresa Reynolds got full custody of Chessa in the divorce proceedings. Chessa was never asked her opinion and later in life she would wonder if her father ever argued for custody, but was too afraid to hear the answer.

Her father would pick her up at the door on his obligatory semi-monthly visits and take her to the movies or the park, bowling, fishing, or out to eat. Often she had wished her dad wouldn't take her anywhere but just sit in the car and talk to her. They always had a good time, but she just never really felt like she came to know him that well. He was never the hugging, affectionate type.

Still, she had adored her father and like most children, blamed herself and her mother for his leaving. *If only I had been a good girl,* she had chided herself. *If only Mom had loved him better.*

Chessa vowed that she would marry someone just like Stephen Reynolds one day and that she would love him enough so that he would never leave her.

The self-pity she wallowed in for years as a teenager had waned some when she eventually became wrapped up in the lives of those less fortunate whom she read about in the news while doing research for her sociology paper in her sophomore year. She had read about rape victims in the Congo, some not even teenagers yet, who were held hostage and often violently abused by enemy soldiers, sometimes whole armies of them. Some were so severely sexually abused that they ended up physically and emotionally scarred for life, unable to bear children, or were forced to become prostitutes or sex slaves.

While feeling sorry for these girls halfway around the world made her feel less sorry for herself, Chessa also struggled with her faith. She would weep for hours after reading the stories, lying on her dorm bunk bed unable to sleep at night, wondering why humans inflicted such pain on each other, trying to make the torment of those mental images go away.

Chessa had always believed in God, although her parents rarely took her to any formal religious services growing up, but she started to wonder how a God who was all-loving and all-powerful could allow suffering of such magnitude. The only thing that helped her cope was her decision to do something about it. She hoped to graduate from Columbia's School of Social Work and become a counselor. Perhaps she would never get the opportunity to visit the Congo, but she realized she could at least help on a local level. She knew that women in the United States, right here in Manhattan, suffered abuses, perhaps of a lesser degree, but painful and degrading all the same. She felt in her gut that she was meant to help.

Between her studies, her job at the paper, and volunteering at the local women's shelter, she had little time for anything else, including a boyfriend. Chessa had only had a few dates since she had attended Columbia, and she had made just a few close friends.

Her best friend was Amy Darlington, who had been assigned as her roommate freshman year.

Chessa remembered the day she met Amy as if it was yesterday.

The two girls had just stared at one another that first day in their dorm room on campus—the tall, skinny white girl with long, light-brown hair and green eyes, and the short, heavyset black girl with short, curly, raven-black hair and black-brown eyes. The first one smiled shyly and said hello. The second one just kept staring in disbelief.

Amy didn't like most white people very much. Her parents' agenda was to get ahead, get their fair share when she was growing up as a child, and white people seemed to be the 'enemy.' So Amy was wary of whites, even at an early age, and she figured Chessa Reynolds was no different than the rest.

Chessa hadn't liked Amy at first either, but it wasn't because she was prejudiced. Being raised in Greenwich Village by parents who were middle-class bohemian scholars, Chessa had grown up open-minded about a lot of things, and had been taught to be tolerant and nonjudgmental about other races, creeds, nationalities, and the like. But Chessa had detected a negative vibe and defensiveness almost immediately upon meeting her roommate. It was an imperceptible feeling that turned into the discovery that Amy felt she had something to prove as a female African American.

She had tried, introducing herself with a big smile and an outstretched hand that fateful day.

But her hand was left dangling.

"This is just great," Amy had said sarcastically, walking right past Chessa to head out of the room. "I'm going to have to make a change."

Chessa was hurt but persistently optimistic. "What's wrong?"

Amy stopped in the doorway, turned around and looked at Chessa with a scowl. "Well as you can see we're totally different."

"Is it because I'm white or because I'm beautiful?" Chessa folded her arms defiantly.

"Hah, you wish!" Amy crossed her arms too and they both glared at each other for a moment longer before bursting into laughter. "Well, no one else will probably take you in so I guess we can give this a try." She held out her hand to Chessa, who shook it, and then gave her a hug.

The two had somehow learned to like each other over time despite their differences. Amy's judgmental attitude would often infuriate Chessa, but when she did her dead-on comedic impressions of other students or teachers, or used her exaggerated "poor Negro" tone, or even sometimes when she got really angry, Chessa would laugh so hard that the two would forget what made them mad in the first place.

Eventually they came to love each other as friends.

Chessa helped Amy become more tolerant and patient. Amy helped Chessa become more outgoing and confident. They balanced each other out in a good way, and found out they had more in common than they'd originally thought, including a mission to help the oppressed. Amy also worked at *The Spectator* and wanted to become an investigative reporter when she graduated.

Darren had returned to New York as promised just before the Christmas holidays and had called Chessa, asking her out to the swank and expensive Boathouse restaurant in Central Park. He was funny, intelligent, charming, and a gentleman the entire evening, and Chessa felt herself falling for the handsome senator. She loved the idea of dating an older, wiser man. Compared to Darren, all of the boys she had dated before now seemed immature. She still wondered a bit why he would be attracted to a schoolgirl so many years his junior. She knew it certainly wasn't to con her. She had already written her article on his speech at the university with a lengthy sidebar about the senator himself. Both sang the praise of the alumnus who had made a name for himself, yet continued to give back to the university and society as well.

Chessa did her homework and found Darren was from the very wealthy Richards family whose patriarch had cofounded RA Technologies, a leading Fortune 500 company that was on the cutting edge of biotechnological and pharmaceutical manufacturing. Darren had only worked briefly with the firm to handle some corporate legal matters to cut his teeth in the business world before entering government affairs. Since he was the only son, and his older sister had chosen to become a nurse, he had at first disappointed his father by not entering the family business, but was eventually supported by his family both with money and connections.

Yet, despite his privileged upbringing, Darren exuded a "common guy" appeal to the people and really did display a desire to help the underdogs of the world and do his share to help save the planet. His military service in the Marines cemented that.

Chessa had described Darren Richards in glowing terms in her article. She had quoted him when he said he wanted to go "all the way to the top" if he had to, "to make sure the world would one day be a better place."

If the date was out of gratitude, Chessa figured he could have sent her a thank-you note instead of taking her out to one of the city's most prestigious restaurants.

She realized she was prettier than the average young woman, with eyes that ranged in color with her emotions, from sea-green to turquoise to dark jade, doll-like features and a tall, shapely figure that made some other girls jealous. She had been told a few times that she looked like Maria Shriver in her youth or like a young Brooke Shields. In fact, many of her friends had encouraged her to go into modeling. *Still, Darren Richards could have his pick of pretty women in New York or Washington, DC*, she thought. After enough second-guessing, she decided to give up questioning why and enjoy herself.

He kissed her for the first time on her doorstep when he took her home after dinner at the Boathouse.

They filled the following Christmas week with romantic dates: they went to see the Rockettes at Radio City Music Hall, went ice-skating in Rockefeller Center, watched the sunset from the top of the Empire State Building, and took long walks holding hands through Central Park.

But Chessa had made a promise to herself that she would wait until she got married to make love. She didn't want what happened to her to happen to her child.

Darren said he had respect for her wishes…although he did try to change her mind one night in his penthouse condo in Central Park West.

They wound up sharing a pizza and a bottle of wine after a sunset walk through the park on their fourth date. Like all of their dates, it had been romantic, magical, amazing, and especially hard that night for Chessa to say no.

She and Darren had been lying facing each other on the plush bear rug in front of the roaring fire, sipping wine and staring into each other's eyes. Darren leaned over and kissed her, and she kissed him back hungrily.

The next thing she knew, his hands seemed to simultaneously be unbuttoning her shirt and her pants. "Darren, stop, remember…"

He silenced her with his mouth and she had to push against his chest with her hands, using what little strength and willpower she could muster through the wine-induced fog that had clouded her senses.

At that instant, Darren froze, then suddenly sat upright, clenching his hands into fists. "This isn't working," he said angrily, not looking at her.

Chessa started to cry. "I don't understand. I thought you said you loved me."

Darren took a deep breath, visibly controlling his temper. "I do. But I don't understand why we have to wait."

"I've told you…"

"I know what you've said." He stood up, his tone a little softer but still tinged with resentment. "Maybe you should go. It's been a long day and I'm tired. I'll call you a cab."

Chessa fought not to cry any more tears, stood, gave him a brief hug and when the taxi arrived minutes later, left without saying any more.

Of course Chessa put a slightly different spin on it when she told Amy about her date the next morning as the two sat on their beds in their dorm room eating apple slices and peanut butter. She left out the part about the argument at the end of the night.

"So you really love him?" Amy asked with more than a little incredulity in her voice. "Do your parents know about all of this? Do they even know how much older he is?"

"They know we've been seeing each other, not about—you know—how serious it is. Dad hasn't met him, but I brought him by to meet Mom and she seemed to like him all right. They're both a little concerned that he's older and more worldly-wise, but they like his political views, the causes he's working for, and the way he treats me. You'll have to meet him, but now that he's back in DC, I'm not sure when we'll see each other again." Chessa sighed. *It would be another long semester.*

"And how does he feel?"

"He said, and I quote, 'I think I'm falling in love with you, Miss Reynolds.' That was the night we watched the sunset from the top of the Empire State Building. I must be the luckiest girl alive!"

"I think I'm gonna be sick." Amy pretended to gag, which sent Chessa into a fit of laughter.

For the next two months, Darren called her almost every night, occasionally sent her notes and flowers, and promised as soon as he could to visit her in New York once Congress let out.

Then a week passed with no calls, mail, or flowers. And then another. Chessa called Darren a few times but was met with his voice mail. Like her calls, two of her letters went unanswered. *Something was up.*

She finally got through one day to Peggy Lee, his secretary, and asked if Darren was planning to return to New York for the upcoming recess. Peggy had always been nice to Chessa when she called but was strangely silent for a few moments.

"He's seeing someone else, isn't he?"

Peggy's continued silence was enough of an answer.

Chessa thanked the secretary and hung up, in tears. *He could have at least had the decency to let me know,* she fumed.

CHAPTER TWO

LEIF

The strawberry roan horse lay on her side, her massive chest heaving up and down in pain. She had splintered one of the bones in her ankle while cantering along in her paddock. No one had noticed the large divot that caught the thoroughbred's right front hoof, sending her down, in moments ending her previously glorious destiny as Little River's next hopeful for this year's Kentucky Derby, which was less than four months away.

"Darn shame." The vet sent in to administer the lethal injection that would permanently take the filly's pain away stood over her, sadly shaking his head.

"Yeah, but nothin' more we can do 'cept put her out of her misery." Hal Baker, a big cowboy who had grown up helping in the stables at the Little River horse farm and eventually become a successful trainer, knelt beside the horse, stroking her head.

"Wait." A man's shadow fell over the horse next to those of the other two men.

Leif Mitchell suddenly appeared, stopping the vet from reaching further into his big black bag for the needle.

Hal looked up at his boss but couldn't see his expression. The noon sun glared white behind Leif's cowboy hat.

"I think we might want to save her." The vet and Hal looked at Leif in astonishment. Rarely was a horse, especially a filly, spared with a broken leg, no matter how great a racehorse it had been or might promise to be. If it had been a colt, it could possibly be put out to stud. But a filly...

Leif knelt gently next to the horse's thick neck; she was lathered in sweat from the pain. She whinnied in recognition. Leif had cared for her since she was born.

He felt along her flanks until she neighed and almost bit his hand when it came to rest on her belly. "Easy, girl." Leif spoke soothingly, pulling his hand out of the way just in time. Then he turned to the men. "I think she's pregnant."

"That's impossible," the disgruntled vet said.

"Tell that to her."

It had been a long, cold day, and it was far from over. Despite the chill in the air, Leif wiped the sweat from his forehead with his shirtsleeve as the late January sun started slipping close to the horizon.

His father wanted an appraisal of the situation with Little Sally, which would now be scratched from the upcoming Derby race. The owner of Little River would also need to arrange a press conference. The media would have a field day with this—a pregnant horse should never have been entered into a race, and a racehorse in training would normally never be allowed to get pregnant.

Although he preferred to lay low and just tend to the horses, Leif and his three brothers were all expected to rally behind the family horse farm when it came to matters of great importance. Plus, he cared deeply about animals, particularly horses, and especially Little Sally. So despite his inclination against it, Leif decided to get involved.

To make matters worse, he had just heard that his family was having company that night for dinner, some political head honcho who wanted to meet him and his three brothers to talk about the possibility of "helping out" the Republican Party on the local level by running for office. As a business owner, his father had been a staunch Republican and fairly big party supporter.

"Well, it won't be me," Leif said softly to Little Sally. After being administered some heavy duty painkillers, the filly was resting comfortably in her stall. Leif stepped into the stall and sat down next to her. The smells of the barn – a unique mix of fresh cut hay, saddle soap and leather from the hanging tack – immediately calmed him, and, taking a deep breath, Leif reached for his guitar, which he had left in the corner of the stall the night before.

He absentmindedly strummed the old redwood instrument he had received when he turned sixteen. Like Sally, it was also an old friend.

Leif had an hour before he was due in his father's office and then expected at dinner, which would give him enough time to rest for just a few minutes before showering and dressing in appropriate dinner clothes. *Might as well sit a spell,* he ruminated, laughing to himself that he couldn't help but rhyme sometimes. His passion, besides horses, was music. Leif had been told he had a knack for songwriting. Just poetry put to music, really.

A warm breeze blew into the stall, seemingly out of nowhere. The stable door was open and Leif could see the sun, big and orange, almost touching the pasture beyond, where it would soon dissolve into the land. The spring sky was bright with the sunset, a canopy of feathery cirrus clouds reflecting hues of coral and russet.

Leif was inspired and sang as he strummed, making up the words as he went along.

> *"You never know what the day will bring,*
> *Which way the winds will blow,*
> *When the sun goes down and the darkness falls,*
> *And the embers start to glow.*
> *You're left with having done your best*
> *And the rest is up to God.*
> *You can't change it now,*

It's what's meant to be,
So rest your head, little girl
And dream for me
Of what tomorrow holds;
Don't worry about days gone by,
Just stay with me now
In the miracle of this Kentucky sky."

Henry Mitchell was a no-nonsense man who, together with his wife Elizabeth, had raised four sons in their small log cabin on an acre of land in Shepherdstown, Kentucky while working as a farmhand at a huge Lexington thoroughbred ranch about two miles away. Many nights he came home too dirty and too tired to eat or do much more than wipe off the day's grime and crawl into bed, only to start all over again at dawn. But somehow he and Elizabeth managed to keep the boys fed, clothed, educated, and indoctrinated in the Catholic faith by going to church every Sunday.

When Henry learned that the small horse ranch nearby called Little River was being put on the auction block, he had scraped together every cent of his life's savings to buy it.

Little River had come with three horses at the auction. Henry had always dreamed of one day entering his own horse in the Kentucky Derby. With a lot of time and effort, eventually he turned the small horse farm into a thoroughbred racehorse breeding farm. Little River had entered horses in at least a dozen stakes races at Churchill Downs, and a few had won. But the filly was his first hope at having a Derby contender, so he wasn't in the mood to entertain anyone after finding out Little Sally had come up lame and pregnant.

Still, he had promised Raymond Silas he would have him over for dinner one night soon. Unfortunately, that night was tonight.

Arguably the wisest and most influential leader of the national Republican party ever and the current Republican National Committee chairman now serving a second term, Silas had surprised the Mitchell family by asking if he could visit them, including all four sons, about a political matter of urgency. The former senator and Speaker of the House had watched as the Little River ranch made national headlines with its Derby contender as the big race grew near, and he was on a mission.

Silas had a problem: the empty Kentucky gubernatorial seat vacated by Governor Nicholas Ramone, who had been impeached after being indicted on money laundering and fraud. Ray Silas needed to fill the position with a candidate who could stir up some good press for his party, and help him turn this debacle around as quickly as possible.

He didn't have time to waste; the special recall election was scheduled for that October, only nine months away. Since the lieutenant governor had also been involved in the scandal and was facing jail as well, there was no incumbent, nor any readily viable Republican candidate, in his opinion, to run for the seat.

Silas had thought long and hard, and realized he needed to find a man completely outside of politics who would be well liked by the people of Kentucky once he was introduced to them. The governor's fall had tarnished nearly everyone around him, and the people's faith in their state politicians was waning fast. The best candidate for election would be one of their own, Silas knew—a man who was educated yet down-to-earth, smart yet compassionate, easy on the eyes but not too much of a ladies' man and, obviously, a Republican.

It was a difficult combination to find, but Ray Silas was never one to give up without a fight. He had research done on the Mitchell boys, found they all had become self-made men (which the people of Kentucky would appreciate), made sure each had a spotless reputation, and watched on television as they, along with their father, adeptly fielded the media as their horse farm was put in the spotlight with the upcoming Derby. He felt in his gut at least one would be a good choice. He had prayed about it. And between his gut and what he heard when he prayed, Silas was usually right.

He just needed to pay them a visit and choose wisely.

As the sun set in a glorious sky that late January evening, Ray Silas paused before ringing the front doorbell of the Southern plantation-style house, hearing men's voices raised in debate from within. He stood on the wraparound porch with its white columns, glanced around to make sure no one was watching him, and strained to hear what they were saying, but couldn't make out the words. The front door suddenly opened, startling him before he had a chance to ring or knock.

He was greeted by a short, rotund woman of Spanish descent in her fifties, dressed in a typical maid's outfit replete with starched black dress and white apron, her curly black hair cut short. She smiled tersely, asked if he was Mr. Silas, and opened the door wider, asking him to please come in.

Henry Mitchell and three young men who Silas figured were his sons quickly hid their startled expressions, their frowns instantly turning to smiles. Henry strode across the oak parlor floor and warmly shook his guest's hand.

"I hope I wasn't interrupting anything; I know I'm a few minutes early. You know airlines these days—they want to get you on and off the plane as quickly as possible."

"No problem; we were just finishing our discussion." Henry Mitchell shot a look of admonishment to his three sons, whom he then introduced one by one.

Ray Silas rapidly sized up all three young men, making mental notes.

"This is my oldest, Charles, who is the vice president of Farmers National Bank in Danville. He was hired right away after graduating with a business degree from DeVry. Of course, I get free financial advice when I need it for helping him pay back all those student loans."

Henry and Silas chuckled as Charles Mitchell firmly shook his hand. "It's an honor to meet you, sir."

"And this is William. He graduated summa cum laude from Louisville and went on to get his law degree at the Brandeis School of Law. He's with a law firm right here in Lexington and hopes to make partner soon."

"Hello, Mr. Silas. You can call me Will."

"Only if you don't call me Mr. Silas. It's Ray."

George Mitchell beat his father to an introduction. "Hi Ray, I'm George. I wanted to introduce myself, since I'm in the field of public relations and can probably do a better job at it than dad." He winked at his father, who gave him a mock frown. "I also attended the University of Louisville, where I starred as Hamlet before graduating with a degree in mass communications. I am currently the PR director with a big ad agency in Owensboro. Charmed to meet you."

"Likewise," Ray Silas said, smiling.

"Always the actor," Henry said jokingly with a broad smile. It was obvious he was quite proud of the sons he had raised.

Silas frowned.

"Is there something wrong?" Henry asked him in a worried tone.

"Well, it's just . . . I thought you had four sons. Where is—"

"Leif? You're right; he should have been here by now." Henry didn't fully mask the slight irritation in his tone.

"I thought his name was Phillip . . . that he was named after a king like your other sons?" Silas was perplexed. His researchers were experts. He was sure they had done their homework correctly.

"He was. Phillip Leif Mitchell. He chose to be stubborn and go by his middle name when he became a teenager."

"Hmmm."

"Well, I'm sure he's on his way. I'll go ahead and tell you about him anyway. Like my other three boys, Leif also made a name for himself at a young age. He graduated from Thomas More College with a degree in theology. I'm not sure what he plans to do with it, but meanwhile, he is becoming known as a country-rock singer and songwriter. I don't know if you've heard his songs on the radio, but it looks like they're climbing the charts. He's a big help around here since he has a knack with horses. He's helped train some of our best."

"That reminds me—we haven't even gotten Leif's opinion yet on what to do about Little Sally." The statement was out of George's mouth before he could take it back. His father glared at him with disapproval, his mouth set grimly, hoping Ray Silas wouldn't notice the family secret had just slipped out.

But it was too late. Silas was very perceptive, and curious to start them discussing a matter of importance to see their various opinions, which might offer him a clue as to which one to select. "By all means, now you have my curiosity raised. How is your Derby filly doing?"

"We have a small issue with her health, but it's nothing to worry you about, with everything you already have on your plate," Henry told his guest, trying to redirect the conversation. "You're here to discuss which one of my sons might possibly interest you as a candidate for a political office within the party, right?"

"Right. But first, maybe I can help with your issue. I'm known to give sage advice from time to time." Silas winked at the brothers, who nervously laughed. "Tell me what's up. I promise I won't spill the beans to anyone outside this room."

Leif entered the back door of the house into the kitchen and stopped to give his mother a hug as she was putting the finishing touches on the dining room table. His hand had been ready to open the door to the adjoining parlor when he overhead Ray's comments. Intrigued, Leif paused and stood with his ear to the wall, putting his finger to his lips to caution his mother not to speak.

Elizabeth Mitchell loved all her children, but Leif knew she was fondest of him. They just seemed to have a special bond since both of them were musically talented and loved to sing together. Maybe it was also because he was the baby of the family. While her other sons were all gifted and special, Elizabeth secretly believed that Leif would someday go the farthest in his life's journey. So she stood still and quiet, watching helplessly while her youngest son's expression turned from interest to perplexity to an angry mask of fury.

Henry recounted how his prize filly had not only come up lame but was discovered to be with foal. She was resting in her stall for the moment, but they were all undecided as to her eventual fate. "We're just not sure whether it will be a lot more costly to keep her alive than it will be to put her down."

"Costly in a monetary way, or for the reputation of Little River?" Silas asked.

"Both."

"It could become a public relations nightmare," George chimed in, now that the matter was going to be openly discussed. "I've been trying to tell Dad that I know this won't bode well for any of us, and could have enormous ramifications. The media, animal rights' activists and the like will all probably deluge us with protests if they find out that Sally is pregnant and we were running her to get ready for the Derby.

"I say we put her down and tell the press she broke her leg trotting around in the paddock, which is the truth, and we'll conduct an investigation into how it happened, which of course will show it was simply an act of Mother Nature," George continued. "The media will cover it and it will be over. They'll never know about the pregnancy. If we go the other route, there's no telling how long the media will hound us."

Leif shoved his hands in his pockets and angrily pursed his lips. He wanted to punch a hole through the door but decided to listen to the rest of the conversation.

"Not to mention the attorneys." Leif heard Will speak up. "We'll probably be the target of a bunch of lawsuits by everyone from the ASPCA and PETA to our competing Derby entrants, who could jump on the bandwagon claiming we had an illegal entry. It could be financially disastrous."

"What about the foal? Won't it be worth something?" Silas asked.

Leif nodded to himself, remaining quiet.

"That's a possibility, given her mother's excellent breeding, but not knowing what horse sired it, we'd have to look into it," Henry said. "Even if one of our prize colts had, uh, had his way with Sally, the percentage would still be small that the offspring will be thoroughbred racing material. It's just the nature of the business. It doesn't begin to offset the costs of vet bills, nursing a lame horse during her pregnancy, the delivery—and of course the financial tornado that could hit if what Will and George are predicting actually happens. It could bring an end not only to Little River but the careers of each one of us. And of course it would not look good for you to have a Mitchell running for political office in the middle of all that."

Leif had enough. He banged open the parlor door and stormed into the room, his face red with anger. He faced all of them staring at him. Dismissing with any pleasantries, he directed his raised voice at his brothers.

"How dare you talk about Little Sally like she's a piece of merchandise we can just throw away? You're talking about killing an innocent animal, a member of our family, no less, who ran her heart out to make us all richer, just so you can save face with the media or avoid some stupid lawsuit. I'm ashamed of you! I love that horse, and I'll do what it takes to save her and her foal. You can say the whole thing was my fault that she got pregnant. I'll say the horse belonged to me alone, disassociate myself from the rest of you, and say the decision was mine. They can all come after me and sue me."

"Calm down, son." Henry crossed the room and put his hand on Leif's shoulder. "We were merely having a discussion about the matter while we were waiting for you. No decisions have been made yet."

"Why are you all discussing it with this man anyway?" Leif shrugged off his father's hand and glared at Ray Silas warily. "No offense, but you're not even a part of our family."

"Because he happens to be wise in these matters and has promised not to let it leak out before we do," Henry said.

"And he's a politician?" Leif barely held back a sneer.

"Correction. A political and government advisor. Name's Raymond Silas." Ray held out his hand and, after a brief moment of hesitation, Leif shook it. "Your father invited me to dinner at my request to meet all of you in hopes that I might find the next Republican candidate to run for the highest office in Kentucky—that of governor. But clearly I've come at a bad time . . ." Silas let the bait hang out for a moment before turning to go.

Upon hearing that the office in question was that of governor, Leif's brothers started to grumble and object.

"Wait." Leif took a deep breath and walked over to Silas and shook his hand again. "I'm Leif Mitchell and I'm sorry. That was very rude of me. I had no business taking my anger out on you, or eavesdropping like I did. It's been a very rough day, and I apologize for being late. Can we all start over? I'm sure part of my problem is that I'm starving, and I'll bet you're all hungry as well. Why don't we have dinner and talk more about this afterward?"

Conversation during a spread of homemade chicken and dumplings was kept to small pleasantries about the weather forecast for the Derby, gossip on the other contenders and Elizabeth's homemade apple pie.

Afterward, Ray asked if Leif could take him to see Little Sally in her stall, saying he had never seen a racehorse up close.

Leif agreed to walk him down to see her. His brothers, meanwhile, said they needed to get home; Charles had two children below the age of five and wanted to get home in time to tuck them in, George had an infant and needed to get home to help his wife, and Will said he had a big court case the next day for which he still had to prepare.

After Ray took a peek at the peacefully sleeping horse, he lit up a cigar outside the stalls. Leif pulled up two chairs and the two of them sat to talk.

"So you want to be a singer?" Ray sat back in his chair, taking a long draw on the cigar.

"I am a singer." Leif stressed the word 'am,' a little perturbed. "Actually I don't know what I want to be. It seems God gave me a few talents. I'm good with animals. And I like to write songs as well as sing them."

"So you believe in God?" Ray puffed on the cigar, its tip glowing red in the oncoming dusk.

"I do. Don't you?"

"Yes of course. It sounds like you believe in yourself and your convictions too."

"I believe that God has big plans for me. I'm just not sure what they are yet. I believe in doing His will. Today, that was saving Little Sally."

"You were very…passionate when you came in." Ray looked at Leif and started to chuckle. Leif joined him, and the two sat laughing until they had tears in their eyes.

After their laughter subsided, Ray looked at Leif thoughtfully for a moment. "I like your spunk, kid, and the fact that you can laugh at yourself. That's a good thing. I also like your ability to stay rational, despite the fact that you were so angry. But most of all, I like your compassion for your horse and the fact that you think God has big plans for you." He took another puff, blowing smoke into the night air. "You know, I think He does too. And believe it or not, I hear God talking to me sometimes. And right now He's telling me He wants me to choose you to run for the Governor of Kentucky.

CHAPTER THREE

CHESSA

Chessa strained to see past the common street sights flying by outside the bus window until she finally caught a glimpse of what she was looking for. *Wow. There it is. The Capitol.* It was miles away, but she could see the white-domed building gleaming, just like it did in the brochures she had seen.

As soon as she had noticed the fliers posted all over campus announcing the bus trip to DC for the Human Rights Rally, Chessa had started saving every dime of her meager income from the paper, as well as from a part-time waitressing job, to make the trip. She had even managed to sign up to attend the Senate hearing and vote on Bill 928, the new International Violence Against Women Act. The volatile bill had been indefinitely tabled in Congress several years earlier but had been redrafted and brought successfully before the House Foreign Affairs and House Armed Services committees. A victory in the Senate would mean the bill would go to the president for his signature, while a defeat would probably kill the measure altogether.

The bill aimed to make violence against women and girls a US foreign-policy priority. It would create a five-year strategy to combat such violence, supplement research and reporting standards, take emergency measures to respond to critical outbreaks of violence against women and girls in situations of armed conflict, and increase humanitarian funding to support the policy to over ten million dollars. The funding, in the wake of the US recession, was the hot issue of debate.

Chessa believed the funding was nominal if it meant the US would take the lead with the United Nations on stepping in and protecting women in the Congo and other Third World countries from more brutal mass rapes like those they had suffered in the past by warring soldiers.

Since she had written several papers on the topic, Chessa was glad she now had the opportunity to see her government in action on an issue so dear to her heart.

Amy sat beside her on the bus. She had signed up to cover the hearing for *The Spectator* in hopes her article would help land her an intern job at *The New York Times*. Plus, neither girl had ever been to Washington before, and they were excited just to visit the nation's capital.

Once they made it through the long security lines and into their seats high up in the Senate chamber of the Capitol reserved for the public, Chessa and Amy listened attentively as a hush fell and roll call was taken.

While Amy wrote furiously in her reporter's notebook, Chessa sat back to observe, soaking in all of the goings-on, trying not to miss anything. But the beat of her heart seemed to catch in her chest when she recognized a familiar face in the crowd on the Senate floor below.

Darren Richards had turned to speak to a colleague on his left and she could see his perfect profile. *He looks good*, she couldn't help noticing. *Even more handsome and distinguished than before in his suit and tie.*

She wordlessly clutched Amy's forearm with her hand when Senator Richards' name was called.

"Oh my God." Amy's words spilled breathlessly out in a whisper as Chessa motioned toward Darren. "Did you know he was going to be here?"

"Of course not!" Chessa lowered her voice, not wanting to annoy the nearby audience members. "I'm just as surprised as you are."

The Speaker of the House announced the bill and discussion ensued. Chessa sat back to listen and felt a small smile cross her lips despite herself as fond memories started to seep into her consciousness.

"Snap out of it." Amy brought her back, actually pinching her leg. "He's about to speak."

". . . couldn't be prouder to be added to my fellow Senators as a sponsor of the bill." Darren was standing, his back to them, as he addressed the Senate Majority Leader. "I firmly believe that the United States needs to stand up and be a leader in this crucial fight for the basic rights of women and girls. They are victims of war, just like the Jews were in the Holocaust. If we look the other way, then we're sending a message to the women and girls of our own country that they are second-class citizens. As Edgar Burke said, 'All that is necessary for the triumph of evil is for good men to do nothing.' And as Winston Churchill said, 'The price of greatness is responsibility.' I know we've just come out of a recession, but if we continue to use that as a cop-out, millions of innocent girls will continue to be raped, mutilated, forced into prostitution, and killed. Think about your wives, sisters, mothers, and daughters. It is our responsibility and duty to pass this bill into law."

Chessa found herself clapping along with the crowd. She forgot about the unanswered letters and phone calls. This was her hero.

Amy stopped writing furiously in her reporter's notebook, glancing with amazement at her roommate, and shook her head.

After the Senate let out, Chessa scrambled to meet Darren to thank him. *I'll keep my personal business out of it*, she thought, craning her neck to try to spot him amid the hundreds of legislators, lobbyists and guests. *This is like trying to swim against the tide.* She walked against the stream of humanity trying to exit the Capitol while Amy waited for her outside.

Her roommate was a little miffed when Chessa told her she was going to look for him but wasn't about to wait with her. "I'm not going to waste my time in here talking to a politician." Amy frowned. "Especially one who broke up with my best friend. But you do what you want. I know you will. It's nice out there, and I'm starving. I'm going to get something to eat and do some sightseeing. See ya."

After the majority of people had vanished and she was just about to give up, Chessa heard her name, and her heart stopped.

"Hey, Chessa, I thought that was you. Wait up." Darren looked even more handsome close up as he caught up to her, out of breath. "It's so good to see you. I've tried to reach you but you never returned my calls."

Chessa was confused. "What calls? I never got any. I thought you . . . we were over." She tried to fight to keep her voice from quivering with anger and hurt.

Darren smiled, shaking his head. "That Peggy! She's had a crush on me since she started working for me and tries to keep away all other young females—especially those I'm interested in or who seem interested in me. I should have known. She probably was nice to you on the phone, but it's all an act. Meanwhile, she just screened your calls, deleted your messages, and threw away your letters. This hasn't happened for a long time. I haven't been dating for a while, so I forgot . . . can you forgive me? I'm telling you, if Peggy wasn't such a good secretary, I'd…"

"You're forgiven." Chessa wanted to believe him and found herself shoving any doubts to the back of her mind. She felt herself basking in the warmth of his smile.

Like Prince Charming in a fairy tale, Darren gallantly took her hand and kissed it. "May I take you to dinner?"

Chessa hesitated. "I can't. I came on the bus from school with Amy. In fact, it will be picking us up soon."

"Then how about tomorrow night? I can take the train up to New York."

Chessa recalled she had plans to go to dinner with the staff of *The Spectator*. *I don't want to appear too eager*, she thought. "I can't—"

"The next night then?" Darren grinned.

"Okay. But how can you . . . aren't you still in session?" Chessa was delighted in his persistence, but still a little bit skeptical.

"It's the weekend and I don't have anything pressing. I will fly around the world in a day just to make this up to you and spend time with you, Chessa Reynolds."

She beamed.

Three months later, Darren proposed.

And it was as romantic as any fairy tale. They spent that cloudless Saturday afternoon roaming around Central Park, walking and talking, taking in the sights. Darren retrieved a picnic basket from his car, which he had packed with supplies for an early dinner.

After spreading a blanket beneath a tall oak tree on the fringes of the park, he pulled out the bounty: a bottle of cabernet, a small loaf of French bread, an assortment of cheeses, a pâté spread, a garden salad, and for dessert, chocolate-covered strawberries. He actually brought real wine goblets and china dishes and a vase with roses for a centerpiece.

After they had finished their meal and sat lazily soaking in the July sun, Darren suddenly knelt and started rummaging through the empty basket.

"What are you looking for?" Chessa was only mildly curious, content with the day. She was half lying down, leaning up on her elbow, dressed in a short-sleeved white blouse and lightweight yellow skirt, with her long wavy hair held off her face with a yellow headband.

"I can't believe I forgot to bring it out."

"I can't eat another bite." Chessa tilted her head back, her eyes closed, her face soaking in the day's last rays. *I feel like a contented kitten.* She sighed.

"It's not something to eat. It's to wear. Here, I found it."

Chessa's curiosity was piqued, and she opened her eyes and sat upright to see what Darren was talking about. And then she felt her mouth drop open.

Darren was up on one knee, and in his fingers he held out to her the most gorgeous diamond ring she had ever seen.

"Chessa Reynolds, will you marry me and make me the happiest man alive?"

Chessa was truly stunned, so it took her a minute to answer. *Isn't this what I've always wanted? To marry the most handsome, successful, intelligent, philanthropic man in the world? It's just that I'm surprised . . . it's so soon. But why wait?* "Yes!" She knelt and held out her hand, letting him slip the ring around her finger. It fit perfectly, and she put her arms around his neck, kissing him.

"I have another surprise. Come on." Darren quickly shoved the dishes and empty bottle into the basket, helped Chessa to her feet and led her down the sidewalk toward the north end of the park.

As the sunset started to color the sky, a horse-drawn carriage pulled up along the street where Darren and Chessa exited the park. Darren smiled and shook hands with the driver, who helped Chessa into the carriage. Seemingly out of nowhere, Darren brandished a single white rose tied with a ribbon, which he handed to her, and a bottle of champagne with two flutes. While Darren climbed onto the seat next to her, the driver wordlessly popped the cork and poured the champagne into their glasses, then took his seat and gave the horse the order to take off.

I feel like Cinderella, Chessa thought.

Amy was waiting up for Chessa, studying, when Chessa excitedly returned to her dorm room later that night.

"Uh-oh, what did he do this time?" Amy didn't hide the fact she wasn't keen on Darren Richards. She confided in Chessa that she had never really trusted members of the opposite sex to begin with, and hadn't entirely bought the story about Peggy the receptionist. But Chessa appreciated that her roommate tried to keep her mouth shut to keep the peace in their friendship.

"Look." Chessa twirled around and then held her arm straight out, dangling the ring in front of Amy's face.

"Oh my God. You didn't . . .?" Amy sat rigid behind her desk, staring at Chessa, stunned.

Chessa felt like a balloon that had just been punctured. She had expected her best friend to be excited and happy for her, to leap up and hug her. "You could at least say 'congratulations.' And yes, I did say yes. I'm sorry you don't approve." Chessa couldn't hide her disappointment.

"Congratulations." Amy remained seated, the word she uttered as forced as her smile. "It's just that . . . well, you're my best friend, and I don't want to see you get hurt. I think you should maybe wait longer, get to know him better. Maybe date other guys first. He's just so much older and more experienced. I guess he knows what he wants. But do you? Are you sure?"

Maybe she's just jealous. She could at least try to be happy for me. Chessa crossed her arms defiantly. Yet beyond the hurt, she felt a deeper uneasiness churning in the pit of her stomach. *This is all so sudden.*

"You don't need a man to make you happy, you know," Amy continued. "You have so much to see and do before you settle down, right? I know I do. Maybe you should get to know yourself better, spend some time apart from him. Maybe we could go on a trip after graduation, then if he's still interested—"

"I do know myself, and I want to be with him," Chessa interrupted. "I don't want to end up alone. I'm not like you."

Chessa instantly regretted her words as she watched a pained expression fleetingly cross her friend's face before she turned back to her books.

"Whatever. I was just looking out for you. Do what you want."

Chessa flopped onto her bed and closed her eyes, but it took hours before she finally fell asleep once they turned the lights off. She mulled Amy's words over and over in her head. *What if she's right? How well do I really know Darren?* His speech before the Senate played back in her mind and she answered her own question. *Enough to know he is championing a cause I believe in. Enough to know he's really handsome, successful, and a great catch. Enough to know that if I say no, he may not wait for me.*

She fell asleep with a vision of Darren dressed like a prince, waltzing her around a dance floor as a crowd of ballroom guests looked on. She was wearing Cinderella slippers and a white princess gown.

Chessa set her sights on planning the perfect wedding.

She and Darren picked a Saturday in early August the following year after her graduation from Columbia while he would be on congressional vacation. They agreed to get married in New York, since they were both natives and most of their friends and family lived there and wouldn't have to travel. Since Chessa had grown up Methodist, they agreed to get married at Christ Church United Methodist, one of Manhattan's most beautiful and historic churches located on Park Avenue. Darren said he didn't mind. His family was Lutheran but he had never practiced nor seemed to care much about religion.

But the reception was a different matter and caused their first wedding argument.

Money was not a problem since the Richards, Chessa learned, were multimillionaires and agreed to pay for everything. The only dilemma was where to have it. Chessa wanted to hold the reception at the Central Park Boathouse. But Darren preemptively told her he had the Delegate Dining Room of the United Nations in mind.

Not to be deterred, Chessa argued her case as they walked along Columbia's campus talking about the wedding plans. "The Boathouse is so beautiful and romantic, looking out over the lake at Central Park."

"The UN building is gorgeous and looks out over the whole city," Darren said.

"But the Boathouse has special meaning."

"What do you mean?"

Chessa started feeling angry, and tried hard not to sound childish. "Darren, it was the restaurant where you took me on our first date! And of course, you, proposed in Central Park. Besides, the Boathouse is on the city's top-ten list of wedding reception locations and it's close to the church."

"Well, the Delegate Dining Room is also on the top ten list. Besides, everyone will be really impressed if we have it there. It's not every day a US senator gets married in the United Nations building. I'm sure we'll get our pictures in all the papers—"

"I could care less about that. And you should care more about what I think than all of your buddies in the legislature or the public for that matter." Chessa sulked, and then felt guilty for feeling that way. She finally decided it wasn't that important after all. Even though the choice of a reception hall was one of the biggest decisions an engaged couple usually made, she would let him have his way to keep the peace. She told him he could make the final decision.

Darren took Chessa to see it one night. With the UN's entrance flanked by its 191 member flags, and the dining room's floor-to-ceiling windows providing a panoramic view of the city skyline and the East River, Chessa couldn't disagree that it was a reception site fit for a king, or at least a United States dignitary.

Another argument arose, however, when it came time to discuss their selection of a best man and maid of honor.

Chessa had no problem with Darren's choice of Pete Connor, his campaign manager and closest confidante. Chessa had only met Pete once and considered him nice enough, although a little standoffish. She guessed it came with the territory of being protective of his candidate.

But Darren had a big problem with her choice. Since she didn't have any siblings, Chessa told Darren she had decided to ask Amy Darlington, to which her fiancé balked.

"My sister will be offended I'm sure," Darren said, disgruntled. "And my parents won't be too happy either."

"Why do you care what your parents think?"

"They are paying for the whole thing, don't forget."

Chessa's parents didn't have much money, so she had thus acquiesced to Darren's offer that his parents pay for everything. She realized now with regret that this would probably continue to come back to bite her.

"But she's my best friend, and I don't have any sisters or brothers." Chessa switched tactics.

"That's not my fault."

It dawned on Chessa that perhaps her future husband was prejudiced. "Is it because she's black?"

"Of course not!" Darren seemed offended by her questioning him but he cut her off from further probing. "Fine, do what you want."

Darren's parents were not only unhappy about their daughter-in-law's choice for a maid-of-honor; they apparently weren't happy about their only son's choice for her as their future daughter-in-law either.

Darren took Chessa to meet his parents two weeks after they were engaged. Donald and Dorothy Richard had asked them to their estate for dinner to celebrate.

Chessa marveled at the huge stone mansion in the Hamptons as they walked up the drive. She found it slightly disconcerting when Darren rang the doorbell and a male voice came over a speaker. "Who is it?"

"It's us dad." Darren seemed to find it amusing that his father had answered the door over an intercom. Chessa found it odd.

They were served drinks before dinner in the "receiving room." Chessa asked for a soda and felt awkward toasting with it as Darren and his parents raised martini glasses of gin and vermouth. These were quickly followed by a second round.

"So dear, do you need any help with the wedding plans?" Dorothy smiled sweetly. She was impeccably dressed in a pencil thin navy skirt and white blouse, and her honey colored hair was coifed and shiny.

"My mom is helping so I think I'm okay." *Oh no, that wasn't a good thing to say.* Chessa agonized over every word that came out of her mouth. *Maybe she wants to help and I just shut her out.*

But Dorothy interjected as if she hadn't heard the response. "Of course you need all the help you can get. I'm in between charity work now so it will be the perfect time for me to help you shop."

Over dinner, Dorothy chatted like a bird, giving Chessa advice on everything from food choices for the reception to picking out a china pattern for her gift registry.

"I'm not much on shopping," Chessa said, again without thinking. Dorothy looked at her like she was an alien.

"So tell us about yourself, Chessa," Donald interjected, breaking the tension.

When Chessa said she was a senior at Columbia University, she saw Dorothy frown.

"You robbed the cradle, boy," Donald said a little too loudly. Chessa had lost count of how many drinks he had downed but she guessed it was at least four or five.

When Chessa said she grew up in Greenwich Village, she saw Dorothy's frown deepen.

"So were your parents the hippy type?"

"Donald, that's not appropriate!" Dorothy chided her husband.

"Actually, yes they were," Chessa said, trying to lighten the mood. But her husband and his parents just stared at her, realizing she was serious.

Donald Richards excused himself to go to the "little boys' room." But when he got up from his chair he nearly tipped over a vase on the table, slurring an apology and then laughing. Both Darren and his mother looked embarrassed but didn't say a word, ignoring the situation as though it hadn't happened, continuing to talk about the wedding.

Chessa was mildly concerned but shrugged it off. She'd seen her parents drunk before, although she was still a bit surprised at how quickly her fiancé's father seemed to get inebriated.

Like his dad, Darren had a lot to drink that evening, but managed to talk more succinctly. When he brought her home later that night, though, he tried with more libido than ever before to engage her in making love while they were parked in front of her apartment building. Chessa brushed his hands away when he groped her more aggressively than usual, and she finally had to push him off her. He protested and got mad at first, sitting upright in the driver's seat red-faced and silent. But seeing her upset, he had apologized, saying the stress of having his parents meet his fiancée had caused him to get a little tipsy.

The whole scenario—not only the drinking, but the way the Richards had made her feel so inferior—sent alarm bells off inside. But Chessa decided she was probably being an overly sensitive bride-to-be.

Besides I love Darren and that's what's important, she concluded, trying to banish thoughts of the evening from her mind.

Christ Church was ablaze with candles. *Oh, God, please help me through this,* Chessa prayed as she approached the start of the runner down the long aisle.

She felt overwhelmed with anxiety as the organist started playing the processional music, the ornate cathedral's huge arches and domed ceiling towering above her as she began the very long walk down the aisle.

She gripped her father's arm tightly. Stephen Reynolds' health was faltering; his liver and kidneys were almost shot due to his heavy drinking over fifty years, and he had suffered a heart attack as well. But Chessa wouldn't take no for an answer when she asked her dad to give her away, so it was she who helped her father down the aisle that day. *He's still my daddy and I love him,* Chessa thought, fighting back tears.

A few steps down she looked up and saw Darren's broad smile and her fears melted away. He looked perfect, standing tall in his navy Brioni tux, starched white shirt, and pink satin tie which matched the flowers she carried. Seeing his adoring gaze, suddenly Chessa felt like a princess in her wedding dress, a full-length white satin gown that flowed from a beaded form-fitting bodice. She hoped no one would guess her mom had helped her find it in a secondhand store.

Cameras flashed and Chessa smiled and nodded. Finally she let go of her father's arm and joined hands with her betrothed.

The rest was beautiful but fleeting: "Love is patient, love is kind...wives, submit to your husbands...do you Chessa...promise to love and honor him...in sickness and health...and forsaking all others remain faithful to him all the days of your life...with this ring I thee wed...you may kiss the bride..."

After hundreds of photos were snapped, the bridal party was transported by limousines to the United Nations, causing many tourists and bystanders to wonder what famous dignitaries were in town.

Most of the guests were amazed at the lavishly decorated Delegate's Dining Room, and again with the feast of delicacies that had been flown in from around the world and expertly prepared: an assortment of caviar, wild Gulf shrimp, smoked Atlantic salmon, filet tournedos with fois gras, roast breast of Magret duck, New Zealand rack of lamb, Chilean sea bass, Maryland lump crabmeat and sautéed Diver scallops, along with all the accoutrements. A large variety of intricate desserts accompanied the five-tiered wedding cake, and the finest wines, champagnes, and premium liquors flowed.

A gifted speechwriter, Pete Connor gave an entertaining wedding toast at the reception, telling a story of how he had gone to see a fortune-teller earlier in the day to help him prepare. ". . . I foresee great things in your future; perhaps even the White House one day. How can you miss when the most charming man in America weds the most beautiful woman...in the United Nations building, no less."

Halfway through the night, Chessa was in the ladies' powder room adjusting her makeup when she heard voices from the adjoining bathroom.

". . . going to have a rude awakening. He's probably on the same path as his father." The voice sounded like it came from an older woman, although Chessa couldn't place it.

Another unfamiliar woman's voice answered, "Poor thing, she's in over her head. She's probably not ready for the cutthroat world of politics, much less all the drinking and womanizing that goes on down there."

"She is very pretty though," the first voice chimed back. "I guess I can see why he chose her."

"I just hope she didn't choose him for his money. Oh well, it will serve her right if she did."

"She's so shy though! I don't see her fitting in with the rest of us. And can you believe she didn't ask Deborah to be her maid-of-honor? I bet Dorothy had a cow!"

"Especially when she saw that, instead, her new daughter-in-law picked a *black* girl!"

The voices must be family members—maybe aunts or something. Chessa felt a knot of anger and fear growing in her stomach and started to feel as if she might throw up. She didn't want the two women to discover she had been listening, so she hurriedly finished putting on her lipstick and exited into the hallway leading to the dining room. She almost smacked right into Darren's cousin-in-law, Stephanie.

"Whoa, what's wrong, honey? You look like you've seen a ghost. Do you need to talk?" Chessa didn't know what to say and didn't see a way to escape even if she wanted to. A plump woman in her forties with a friendly smile and kind eyes, Stephanie Richards stood before her, filling the hallway.

"Actually, yes, I do." Chessa felt like she couldn't keep her emotions in check any longer and needed to confide in someone. She had met Stephanie twice before—once at Christmas and again at lunch.

Stephanie was a sociology professor at Columbia University and had offered to meet Chessa at the cafeteria one day, telling her she would try to help make her transition into the Richards family a little easier. Chessa had discovered from that one meeting that she and her future cousin-in-law had a lot in common; they were both from similar modest backgrounds, and they were both civic enthusiasts determined to help make the world a better place—Chessa through social work and Stephanie through teaching. Both women were also married into the Richards dynasty; Stephanie was Darren's cousin Bob's wife. Chessa had also learned Darren's cousin-in-law was completely unlike the rest of the family. In fact, Stephanie seemed to enjoy making fun of them a little, which made Chessa laugh and put her immediately at ease.

So Chessa decided to take a leap of faith and pulled Stephanie into an adjoining hallway off the main floor of the reception to tell her about the bathroom talk.

"Oh, honey, I'm sorry." Stephanie put her hand on Chessa's shoulder in a gesture of compassion. "As far as your new mother-in-law and sister-in-law go, don't worry about them; they'll always be the way they are, all prim and proper. But I think they'll warm up to you. It's just that their precious baby boy has found another woman. As far as the other issue the women are referring to…shall we say, the propensity some of the Richards family members have for alcohol… well, most have never admitted it, but I would venture to say a few are full-blown alcoholics—including my husband, who's in recovery, by the way."

Chessa felt her mouth drop open at Stephanie's candor.

"Now, I'm not saying your Darren is, but just in case you have a problem down the line, you call me. I go to Al-Anon and I'd be happy to take you along. It's been a big help to me, and none of the rest of the family needs to know. Thank God it's anonymous."

"What is Al-Anon?

"It's a twelve-step program to help family members of alcoholics deal with the fallout of the disease and help them maintain some sanity and serenity despite the alcoholic's behavior, whether he's drinking or not."

"Well . . . I don't think . . ."

"You don't need to let me know if you're interested tonight, honey. It's your wedding night, after all. I'm just telling you there's help out there if you ever do need it. Now, you go dance with your husband and have fun." Stephanie gave Chessa a hug.

Chessa began to wonder if Stephanie could really be trusted or if she should just steer clear of the whole Richards family if at all possible.

Then she heard her name being called over the microphone by the bandleader. Walking back out with Stephanie into the large reception hall, Chessa stole a sideways glance over at her husband, who was laughing, fifth or sixth drink in hand. He seemed to be flirting with the ladies who surrounded him, hanging on his every word. She didn't recognize them, but then again, she hadn't known half of the people Darren invited from his political enclave. *It's just part of the territory*, she reminded herself, trying to ignore her feelings of jealousy. *He is a senator after all, and his charm is part of what captured my heart.*

Amy walked up to her. "Hey girl, they've been asking where you are. It's time to cut the cake." Amy noticed Chessa's expression. "Why the down face?"

Chessa nodded in her husband's direction. He was still laughing, his perfect white smile dazzling all the way across the room on his tanned, handsome face. He leaned down on his elbow, resting it on the back of some red-haired woman's chair, and whispered something in her ear. Chessa and Amy watched as the beautiful young woman's red lips parted into a grin, and they both laughed, heads bent together as if sharing a private joke. The woman wore a red rhinestone-studded dress to match her hair and lips, revealing a lot of cleavage that was just inches away from Darren's face, which in Chessa's opinion, lingered there a minute too long.

Amy caught her friend looking down at her wedding and engagement rings. Chessa had received hundreds of compliments on them. Her engagement ring held a three-carat marquis-cut diamond encircled by another two carats in tiny white diamonds.

"Come on, let's go get him," Amy said, grabbing her friend's hand and yanking her in his direction.

She's such a good friend, Chessa thought, sighing. *She could have said 'I told you so.'*

After a final dance, Chessa braced herself for the onslaught of cameras and microphones that would surely be thrust in their faces once they exited the UN building. Hopefully the limo would park just a step or two from the door. It had been a long day. A great one to be sure, but exhausting.

Chessa gave Amy a hug and peck on the cheek. "Thank you for everything."

"Ah, just doing my job. I want you to be happy."

"I am—deliriously." Chessa heard Darren calling her. "Gotta run."

She ducked into the limo as the crowd of guests cheered them off to the start of their lives together as man and wife.

CHAPTER FOUR

LEIF

Leif had prayed long and hard while considering Ray Silas's invitation to run for governor. He was flabbergasted that he had been chosen over his brothers, who he thought were more qualified, and who seemed to want the job much more than he did.

But Ray was unwavering in his choice. Either Leif Mitchell would run, or Silas would have to search elsewhere.

A heated debate among his family developed once Ray made his choice known, and Henry called another family meeting the following Sunday after church to discuss it. Leif only had until Monday to give the Republican National Committee chair an answer.

"I think we should be proud of Leif and support him," Henry Mitchell said.

"I just don't see why he picked Leif. No offense, little brother." Will had been the most disgruntled at having not been selected and was the most outspoken. "I'm an attorney, for God's sake. I've actually been considering running for office. Everyone knows attorneys make good politicians. Leif is a horse trainer. What does he know about government and politics?" Brothers George and Charles nodded in agreement.

"You forgot I'm also a musician," Leif said, trying not to grin at the ludicrousness of it all.

"I should have been asked since I'm the oldest," protested Charles. "Leif's barely old enough to run." It was true. The minimum age to run for Governor of Kentucky was thirty. Leif had just turned thirty-years-old the previous November.

"Well, Silas made his choice and that's that," Henry said. "You heard him. It's either Leif or nobody. So what's it gonna be, son?"

Leif looked into his brothers' angry, jealous faces.

"Who will take my place to help you on the farm, Dad?"

"Don't worry about that. I think this is a higher calling and maybe a once-in-a-lifetime opportunity. The farm will always be here waiting for you."

Leif got on his knees that night and prayed about it.

He gave Silas the answer he was looking for the next day.

Leif invited his three brothers to help with his campaign, but they all said they were much too busy. So Leif asked for help from his childhood friend Logan Reese, who at the time was unemployed after being laid off from his public relations job with a local advertising agency that had gone out of business.

Although most people, especially women, looked at Logan as somewhat of a nerd, Leif considered him a savvy marketing strategist and brilliant writer. Leif had often turned to Logan to help him with the lyrics to some of his songs, and had asked his advice on promoting his music tours before signing with his record label, which now handled all his affairs.

Growing up, Logan was like Robin to Leif's Batman. In fact, as young boys they would often play "superheroes" and Logan would always vow to fight by Leif's side to beat the criminals of the day at large. Of course they would always win, no matter how tough their make-believe assailants happened to be.

Leif and Logan set up a little campaign office in a vacant strip center store in Louisville, hanging a red, white, and blue banner over the door that read "Leif Mitchell for Governor."

For weeks it was just the two of them working long hours developing a database and website, printing and delivering fliers, sending e-mails and making phone calls.

Then they had their first visitor. It was none other than Leif's opponent, Leon Slater.

Everyone in the know, including Ray Silas, predicted it would be a tough race. The Democratic Party not only had the upper hand with the incumbent's bad press, but an extremely popular candidate lined up.

Leon Slater was a retired local prizefighter and war veteran whose mother named him after the famous world heavyweight champion Leon Spinks, who had gone down in history by defeating Muhammad Ali.

The South had long cried for a black man to finally win a major election. If Leon Slater won, the governor's seat in Kentucky would afford them their opportunity.

Leif and Logan watched out the storefront window with incredulity as the huge black man, dressed impeccably in a dark-gray suit, white collared shirt, and red-and–navy-striped tie, approached their campaign office door, two television news crews in tow. He entered alone, after apparently asking the TV crews to stay outside. Their cameras were mounted, however, and Leif could see the two reporters each talking into a microphone about ten feet apart from one another.

Slater flashed his trademark white smile and removed his sunglasses, blinking in the semidarkness of the office.

He looked straight at Leif, who was sitting on a desk in his jeans and a ragged T-shirt. He hadn't shaved that morning in his hurry to get to the office, and had covered his unruly hair with one of his cowboy hats. He hadn't known he was going to be filmed that day.

On the other hand, Slater had known, and had taken full advantage of the opportunity.

"Just stopping by to see how it's going and to say hello," his bass voice boomed, filling the tiny office.

Leif stood up and approached him, looking up. Slater was a giant compared to most men, with his bulky, muscular frame measuring six foot nine to Leif's five-foot-eight. "Well thanks, we're doing just fine. Welcome to our humble abode."

The fighter grabbed Leif's hand and shook it. His back was to the camera crews outside, so they could neither hear nor see what he was saying. He bent down and whispered into Leif's ear so even Logan couldn't hear him. "If you even think you stand a chance against me, you are sorely mistaken, Cowboy. If I was you, I'd get out before it gets ugly and you ruin what little reputation you have. Why don't you go back to your horse farm and stick to playing your guitar?"

Without giving a stunned Leif a chance to reply, Slater turned, smile intact, and headed for the door.

Once outside, he began signing autographed photos for a gathering crowd of kids who had lined up to meet the great Leon Slater.

The reporters, who had multiplied as word had quickly spread to their dispatchers, stuck microphones in his face for a comment.

"Mr. Slater, why are you at your opponent's campaign headquarters today?"

"I just wanted to tell Mr. Mitchell, 'may the best man win' and let him know that even though I can look pretty mean in the ring, I'm really a friendly guy and it will be a clean competition." More smiles and a few laughs. More autographs.

"And what was Leif Mitchell's response?"

"You'll have to go in there and ask him yourself. But he seemed much obliged."

Leif had gone to the only place he knew he would find refuge and solace that night—to the stables at Little River, where he worked out his aggravation after watching the six o'clock news by grooming a colt and two mares.

He had watched the news with his parents in their den. The cameras had zoomed in on his scruffy face looking like that of a deer caught in headlights, then cut to the proud Leon Slater politely answering the reporters' questions and signing autographs in front of their puny campaign headquarters. It then showed Leif caught by surprise as he opened the headquarters' front door, squinting in the sunlight and uneasily holding up his hand, refusing to answer any questions, and turning around to go back to work, while Logan shuffled paperwork in embarrassment.

"Apparently Mr. Mitchell has no comment," the reporter on the local news station said. "I guess he wasn't prepared for his opponent to be so friendly."

"If they only heard what Leon really said." Leif told his parents the whole story. "The guy actually threatened me."

"Let it go, son; there will be other battles," his father said. "You may have lost this one, but it doesn't matter, as long as you win the war."

"Dad, I know it sounds cocky, maybe even crazy, but I just know I will win. Most people would question why I'm even running against him and say I don't stand a chance. But even though Leon Slater is more experienced and way bigger, not only physically but in the public eye, I just have a gut feeling I can do this. I've been praying about it and I think God is on my side."

Vice President Martin Greene stood alone in his office in the West Wing, looking out the window over the White House lawn and gardens.

But the vice president didn't really see the varying bright shades of green, the vivid pink tulips, nor the happy yellow daffodils just starting to bloom.

His mind was sharply focused inward on the turmoil that he faced, and he felt like a man obsessed. His bid for election to the highest office in the country was only a little over a year away. It would be the end of President Thomas Stone's second term, and Martin, who had served him and the country faithfully as vice president for the past six years, would be running for President. The nation's economy had finally recovered following the past recession. It had been a long climb and the recovery had been slow and modest.

Still, for most leaders, any economic incline during their tenure normally came as good news.

But not for Greene. As was typical, Americans—aided by their window on the world, whether it be a tablet, cell phone, laptop or television set—just shifted their focus onto another area of bad news the media covered. Their attention had veered from the local economy to the situation in the Middle East which, unlike the economy, had only gotten worse for the current administration.

Greene thought the President had made fairly good strides in the past few years to develop more allies among the Arab nations, hold the Islamic extremists and terrorists at bay, and keep gas prices from climbing any higher. Another 911 had never materialized. The wars were all but over. And while internal skirmishes still cropped up from time to time, the US was helping maintain a tenuous truce of sorts there. Still, despite the fact that he and President Stone had fought and won several battles both in the Middle East and back home with Congress, the president and vice president had a lower popularity rating than ever.

His advisors told him it was because of Israel. Martin Greene had worked closely with the Secretary of State to keep peace in the Middle East by providing aid for war-torn Arab countries, but his critics claimed that he had virtually sacrificed Israel, putting the small country in a precarious and isolated position. Jews in the United States were increasingly holding protests, carrying signs that proclaimed slogans like "Peace at What Cost?" and "Save Israel, Get Rid of Stone and Greene."

In addition to most members of the cabinet, Ray Silas had warned the President that he had gone too far in supporting the Arab countries, particularly Palestine. Usually not one to admit mistakes, Martin Greene prided himself that he had at least finally listened to Silas, realizing perhaps the administration had gone overboard to please Americans by making deals with the oil-rich Arab countries to bring gas prices down and bring US troops home to their families.

He had tried in vain to impress this upon the President, who apparently wanted to coast out of office without any major upheaval. Martin just hoped it wasn't too late to promote striking a better balance. It had been impossible to distance himself from President

Stone, but Martin had managed to rearrange his platform and he was leading, just barely, in the polls.

At least Silas had brought him back good news about the Republican candidates running for state offices in the upcoming elections. Martin would need strong support from his fellow Republicans.

Silas had seemed particularly interested in one candidate he was grooming for the Kentucky gubernatorial special recall election in October. His name was Leif Mitchell.

The vice president had read Silas's briefing and couldn't quite comprehend what his trusted advisor had seen in the cowboy turned budding country rock star. He had thought the other Mitchell boys had far greater potential on reading their dossiers. But Silas was the National Republican Party leader and expert in all things politic so he decided not to argue with him.

Suddenly a brilliant thought crossed the vice president's mind as he continued to gaze out of the windows of his West Wing office. He picked up the phone and called Ray Silas. He decided it was time to hold another benefit concert at the White House. And he would include the Kentucky candidate, since he was a singer. Perhaps it would help the kid win the governor's seat. After all, he was up against formidable competition. Either way, it would draw some good press, which Martin knew he sorely needed. And it would once again show Americans that the Republicans could be charismatic and entertaining and still get the job done. They had loved Ronald Reagan, after all.

Leif's mouth hung open in awe as he stared at the invitation from President Stone to perform in the Fourth of July show, "In Performance at the White House PBS Special."

He called the president's press secretary to accept and was informed he would join a variety of country-rock singers and bands like old-timers Bon Jovi and Martina McBride and hit sensations Lady Antebellum, Carrie Underwood and Taylor Swift.

The special was aired on July Fourth in conjunction with the fireworks on the Mall in DC. The actual concert took place a few days prior on a Friday night in the East Room of the White House. Afterward, a special dinner was hosted in the State Dining Room by the president and vice president and their wives for all the performers and a select group of family, friends, and dignitaries.

The Greene's children were in attendance as well—their twenty-nine-year-old son Jonathan, and two daughters, Victoria and Wendy, ages twenty-six and twenty-four respectively. None of their children had dates, as none were in serious relationships with significant others at the time.

Leif was dressed more formally than normal for the dinner, in a white starched shirt and dark-brown suit that accentuated his golden-brown hair and light-blue eyes. He had gotten a tan, both from working on the farm when he could, and on the campaign trail attending picnics and going door-to-door to meet and greet potential voters.

He was pleased with his performance; he had chosen to play his two top songs acoustically, since he didn't have his backup band to accompany him. One was more of a fast-paced rock song about being on the road, both as a performer and politician, called "Trail to Somewhere," which had recently hit the charts, and the other was an older, soulful blues-and-country ballad about his love for fillies, called "Love You, Girl," which many of his female listeners loved, interpreting it as a personal message.

After the dinner, Wendy sidled up to Leif and asked for his autograph, then strategically sat entranced across from him at dinner. Unfortunately for Wendy, Victoria sat right next to her and Leif had to divide his attention between them.

Both girls were beautiful but strikingly different from each other. Except for her brown eyes, Wendy had her father's Aryan looks with her fair skin and straight sandy-blond hair, while Victoria looked exactly like her mother, who was descended from the Mediterranean region. Wendy was bubbly and outgoing and went on at dinner about how well Leif sang and how she so enjoyed his performance. Victoria, meanwhile, was noncommittal and mostly listened, seemingly lost in her own thoughts.

Leif was flattered, although a little uncomfortably, by Wendy's obvious adoration. It was so evident that Vice President Greene noticed it out of his peripheral vision as they bade farewell to the stars and other guests that evening.

Despite the televised concert and all of the hard campaigning Logan had forced him to do, Leif was still down by a whopping twenty points in the opinion polls heading into the election, and most political pundits predicted he didn't stand a chance.

According to them, the only people who were going to be casting votes for Leif Mitchell were staunch white Republican men who were casting a vote against having a black man as governor of their respected Southern state.

It didn't even matter to the electorate majority that Leon Slater had been caught partying with a harem of young girls one night, some of whom looked barely eighteen. It didn't matter that his campaign pockets had been filled to the brim with illegal corporate donations, and that he would probably never fulfill all the promises he had made in return for all those sizeable sums. It didn't matter that the fighter had attacked his opponent with low blows about his Derby horse being pregnant and being pulled out of the big race, accusing Leif of poor handling and a lack of judgment. Just as the Mitchell boys had predicted, the matter had come to light and had resulted in a few lawsuits they had fought and won. But the press coverage had faded—that is until the heavyweight candidate resurrected it again. "How can such a poor businessman, who can't even manage a horse, manage the great state of Kentucky?" one commercial repeated over and over again.

Those commercials had been aired along with others that showed Leon being decorated upon his return from the Iraqi war, Leon's glove-clad fist being held up in victory in the ring, and Leon holding a small black child in his arms with the words of Martin Luther King Jr.'s "I Have a Dream" speech being played in the background.

Appearance was everything, and it didn't look good for Leif Mitchell, despite his performance in the White House PBS special.

The special election day dawned cool and dreary as a fine mist blanketed most of Kentucky.

Leif showed up early at the local elementary school to vote after having breakfast with Logan, a handful of campaign workers, and his parents at Little River.

Then he went to visit his opponent, with television news crews in tow, just as Leon had done months ago. Only this time, it was Leon who was taken by surprise.

When Leon Slater, dressed in his finest suit, showed up in all his glory to vote at his local polling place, FBI officials pulled up in *Dragnet* fashion to the curb of the school building turned polling place, hopped out and put handcuffs on the prize fighter. Then they led him to a waiting squad car and pushed him into the back seat, stuffing his head down like he was a common criminal.

Leif Mitchell was waiting at the door of the school, watching the scene unfold, a half-dozen camera crews behind him.

The media assaulted the hulking black man as he was shoved into the police car with a barrage of shouted questions and accusations. Leif stood to the side and simply watched his opponent's face contort in anger and his lips tighten in defiant silence.

When Leon's dark eyes found and locked with his, Leif thought he saw murder in them.

The story went viral via YouTube and the Internet by noon.

After a tip from Martin the night of the concert, Leif had spent countless hours looking into the financial disclosures, background documents and life history of Leon Slater, praying each day for God to guide him, constantly wondering if he was doing the right thing by prying into his opponent's campaign, trying to win by bringing him down. But the more he found, the more justified he felt in digging further to do what was in the best interests of the people.

And then he hit the mother lode. Just a week before the election his small team of investigators, including Logan, his brother

Will, and two hired hands, had amazingly found a financial trail officially linking the former heavyweight champion to the Muslim Brotherhood.

Following weeks of research and phone calls to the CIA, NSA and FBI, reading documents and news clippings, watching hundreds of newsreels, and putting together the pieces of the puzzle, Leif had discovered the truth: that the big Leon Slater had received funding from an extremist wing of the Muslim Brotherhood for his campaign. Leif discovered that the Brotherhood had also invested in Leon so he would support their terrorist activities domestically.

Leif had taken a big risk by waiting until Election Day to make the scandal public. But he had to make sure his investigation was as complete as possible and decided to rely on the element of surprise, afraid that if Leon had been alerted any sooner he would have either fled the country or found a way to deny the charges.

Many had already voted on election day, but the story spread so rapidly that enough people found out in time to change their minds.

The votes seesawed back and forth as each district's results came in.

Leif won the election by a scant two percent of the vote. After waiting for the final tally that cast him as the winner, Leif gave a victory speech to his small but elated campaign crowd that had gathered at the local VFW hall to await the results.

The national news crews not only covered Leif's discovery of his opponent's shady dealings, but the election results, dwarfing the other political races and turning Leif into a political icon.

With just a few hours of sleep, Leif was on a plane to New York City to appear on various talk shows over the next few days. The boy from Kentucky had gone from being a barely discovered country rock singer with two hit songs and an unknown candidate for governor to an overnight sensation.

CHAPTER FIVE

CHESSA

After working as a writer for an online New York City entertainment website and then as a reporter for New York *Daily News* online, Chessa finally found a job in her chosen field of social work at the local Safe Horizon center for domestic violence and rape victims in Manhattan. At the age of twenty-three Chessa had discovered that the reporter's life was not for her. She especially disliked working at a computer for long hours, doing research and feeding stories into online newsfeeds. She needed human interaction, and a more concrete knowledge that she was touching someone's life and making a difference—even if it was only in a small way.

She and Darren had settled into somewhat of a routine in the year that followed their wedding, Darren flying back and forth between his apartment and Senate position in DC and their new house in the rich Manhattan suburb of the Upper East Side to be with his wife on the weekends, and Chessa keeping busy during the week working at the center while he was in Congress.

Chessa became increasingly fascinated by her husband's growing political aspirations, which he shared with her when they were together over cocktails, dinner, or even before or after making love.

But sometimes he could become derisive over members of the Republican party, whom he seemed to despise. And if he was drinking, he sometimes became moody, argumentative or even nasty.

Lately, there were times when Chessa was glad she didn't see her husband more often than she did. Over the short time they had been married, his usual glass or two of wine during dinner on their weekends together had gradually started turning into several drinks before, during and after. His occasional golf outings with his buddies once every few months had lately turned into a regular occurrence nearly every Saturday and he almost always came home drunk.

It didn't matter how many times she scolded or chastised him, pleaded with him or gave him the cold shoulder. He would apologize the morning after and try to moderate, or even curtail his drinking for a time, and Chessa would hope that he had changed.

And then his drinking would resume.

Chessa bolted upright when she heard a glass smashing against the wall.

She scurried out of her warm bed and went downstairs and into the living room, where she saw Darren plopped on the couch watching the news blaring loudly from the TV screen.

"What's wrong with you?" Chessa blinked in disbelief, shaking off the veil of slumber that had cloaked her. She had fallen asleep while watching the network news coverage in bed, waiting for Darren to return from his rounds at the various campaign parties in New York. It wasn't his year to be re-elected but he was obligated to support his Democratic colleagues that were up for election.

He didn't return to their Manhattan condo until close to one in the morning.

She could smell the stench of stale liquor coming from her husband's breath several feet away.

A news anchor was on the screen still talking about the close race for governor in Kentucky, which had finally just been decided.

Darren had evidently hurled his glass half full glass of whiskey toward the TV set and just missed.

He stood and turned around to face his wife. His words came out in a slur. "I'm dishgusted with my party," he said, swaying a bit on his feet. "That stupid Democrat is an idiot. That singing cowboy Leif, uh, what's his name?"

"Mitchell."

"Yeah, he didn't deserve to win, but the Democrats managed to mess up again."

"But I thought Leif Mitchell did America a favor by uncovering that boxer's ties with the terrorists the last time he ran. The news said he's done a good job as governor his past term and that he deserved to win again. According to the news…"

"News, schmooze. Don't believe everything you hear." Darren rudely cut her off, pacing back and forth on the living room carpet.

"Are you blaming the reporters now?" Chessa suddenly didn't feel tired anymore. She knew she should just ignore her husband, go upstairs and go to bed and let him sleep it off. But he had not only woken her physically, he had roused something inside her emotionally. She was sick and tired of him dismissing her like some dumb schoolgirl. Darren always thought he was right. And he always blamed everything and everyone else for his problems—her, his staff, the Republicans, the Democrats, the weather, the media.

If he wants a fight, I'm ready this time, she thought, her anger rising within her like steam inside a kettle. *I'm right and he's wrong, drunk or not, and I'm not going to give in like I do every other time.*

"Yeah, you're all part of the problem." Darren was red-faced and belligerent now. "If the media wasn't so biased, we would have won more seats tonight. But they're itching to latch on to this backwoods cowboy out of nowhere, making him to be some kind of hero. He's as bad as Reagan or Arnold Schwarzenegger."

"You shouldn't judge him just because he's a Republican or an entertainer." Chessa felt her self-righteousness mount along with her anger at her husband's drunken state. "As long as a man does what's good and right for the people, that should be all that matters."

"You're an idiot. You have no idea what you're talking about."

That hurt. Even though Chessa's brain kept sounding *he doesn't make sense, he's drunk,* her heart was still wounded and she suddenly felt a sharp pang of doubt. *I don't know why I even married this man. I didn't even know him well enough. I don't really know him at all.*

Chessa couldn't help her pride from getting in the way, so she blurted out, "well you're just a mean drunk who thinks the whole world revolves around you." She immediately regretted engaging with him but it was too late. She couldn't take her words back.

"Obviously I know a lot more than you do when it comes to politics. I know who's good for our government and who isn't. I was going to wait to surprise you and tell you my good news when I was in a better mood but since you think you're so smart, how's this for who's smarter—the National Democratic Party leader called me tonight with a proposition. He wants me to start thinking about running for president."

"President?" Chessa's voice rose with incredulity.

"As in, of the United States of America." Darren gave her a superior smile. "I've got five years to prepare for it. Our candidate doesn't stand a chance against Martin Greene this time around. So the Democratic party is already looking ahead to the next election and they think I'm their man."

Chessa knew what her husband meant, but she couldn't believe it. She stared at him for a moment, trying to wrap her mind around what he had said. *Great,* she thought, not saying a word. *Now he'll never be home, and we'll never start a family.*

Chessa shocked herself with that last thought. But she realized in that moment that she wanted with all her heart to have a baby, to start a family. *To change our life around and be happy again.*

"What's wrong, aren't you happy to hear your husband might become the next president of the United States?" Darren asked impatiently, jarring her out of her trance.

Here goes. Chessa took a deep breath and exhaled. "No, it's just that . . . well, I was hoping, now that this election is over, you would start spending more time at home with me, especially with the holidays coming up. And I was hoping we could work on starting a family."

Darren's face turned a deep shade of red and his eyes flashed with anger as he stood just inches away from her, his six feet of height towering over her smaller five-foot-five frame. "You are the most selfish woman I have ever met!" He practically spit the words at her. "All you think about is yourself. Just because you don't have a big career like I do doesn't mean we don't have a lot going on. We've only been married a year, for crying out loud. I don't want a baby now or any other time soon. I thought I married a girl who was smart and who would be a good partner, who would appreciate being the wife of a US Senator, not to mention a possible president. But she's just some dumb girl who wants to go around barefoot and pregnant. Here I thought you'd be proud of me." His voice trailed off with a pout.

Chessa smarted from his words, but felt guilty that she hadn't been happy for him.

She approached him to say she was sorry and give him a hug, but he roughly shoved her away. Her back hit a wall corner and she felt a sharp pain between her shoulder blades.

"Get away from me." Darren turned and grabbed a bottle of whiskey sitting on a nearby service bar and poured some into a glass, spilling half of it.

Chessa stood silent for a moment choking back tears, her back and her heart aching, and quietly retreated upstairs to try to go to sleep. *I'm not going to let him see me cry.*

The next day, sitting at her desk going through a pile of paperwork at Safe Horizon, Chessa still felt a dull ache in her upper back and was reminded of her husband shoving her.

Could it be that I'm a victim too? She couldn't help but wonder. But then she thought of the many victims who came to them— women who were battered, bruised, or bleeding, with eyes swollen shut, broken teeth, or broken bones. *I'm not as bad as they are,* she reasoned. *Darren just had too much to drink. He didn't mean to hurt me.*

Tonight will be different. She willed herself to think positively. Darren had decided to stay in New York the day after the elections to make some local congratulatory rounds and start to garner support for his potential presidential bid. *I'll cook him a nice dinner to celebrate his news, and we'll spend a quiet, peaceful evening together. Maybe we'll even be intimate.*

When she got off work, Chessa stopped at the grocery store and then came home to prepare a special dinner to celebrate her husband's good news. By six, she had carefully set the table in their cozy dining room, lit a few tapered candles, and took the roasted duck out of the oven. It was one of Darren's favorite dishes.

Darren had told her he would be home by six. When seven p.m. arrived and she didn't receive a call, Chessa started to worry and tried Darren's cell phone. It went to voice mail. She kept the duck in the oven on warm, blew out the candles, and turned on the television to distract herself from thinking the worst.

Another hour passed, and still she received no phone call. Now her worry was turning to anger. *How dare he not show up for dinner and not even bother to call?*

Too upset to eat, Chessa just turned the oven off leaving the duck in it, turned out the lights, and went to bed to read herself to sleep.

She must have finally dozed off because the sound of footsteps in the bedroom awakened her. It was dark in the bedroom, but she could just make out Darren's form by the light of the moon coming in between the slats in the blinds. She looked at the nightstand. It was one in the morning.

Darren clumsily removed his clothes and shoes, almost tripping into one of the bureaus. He crawled into bed beside her, lying on his back. Chessa could smell traces of whiskey and the faint smell of perfume—definitely a woman's scent she didn't recognize.

She knew she wouldn't be able to sleep, so she decided to test him. She rolled over and started stroking his chest with her fingers.

"Hi, honey," she whispered sweetly. "I cooked a roast duck for you to celebrate your good news, but you didn't show up for dinner. What happened?"

"Hmmm, what?" Darren was obviously pretending he had already started to fall asleep. "Oh, I'm sorry, I got caught up at work and lost track of time."

"But usually you call me when that happens."

"I know. This time I was hit so hard by a last-minute problem that came to my attention that I had to really focus on solving it, and I guess I left my cell phone turned off so I wouldn't be interrupted. I'm sorry."

Chessa felt her anger rising but fought to keep it at bay for the moment. Darren always told her she'd get more with honey than vinegar. It was one of his favorite sayings.

"You smell good, but a little feminine. You didn't get new cologne, did you?"

"Uh . . . no. But this woman in one of the offices I visited was wearing something really strong today. It must have sunk into my clothes." Darren shifted away from her, rolling onto his side. "Look, the stress today took a lot out of me. I am really tired. Can we talk tomorrow?"

Chessa didn't give up. She pressed her body up behind his, the thin silk of her nightie not concealing her womanly curves. "But, Darren, I'm in the mood. And you won't be home tomorrow night." Actually, she really was in the mood, her urges and needs defying her. She wanted him to please her the way he had probably pleased someone else.

Darren shifted from her further, his voice taking on a hard edge. "I said I'm too tired. Good night."

Chessa rolled away from him onto her other side, hot tears stinging her cheeks.

He's not only drinking. Now he's fooling around. She felt helpless and trapped in despair. She prayed long into the night for God to give her the blessed relief of sleep, but it seemed to take hours before she finally drifted off.

When Chessa awoke, sun streamed through the blinds, illuminating the bedroom. Darren was gone.

She sat up groggily. She felt like she had been hit by a Mack truck. Her head and body ached. She went into the adjoining bathroom and looked in the mirror. Her eyes were swollen and her hair was a tangled mess.

Just as the memory of last night started to permeate her morning fog, Chessa heard pots clanging and smelled bacon and coffee wafting up from the kitchen below.

She stumbled down the stairs of their two-story town home and looked at Darren with confusion from the kitchen doorway. "I thought you were going back to DC today."

"I decided to stay in New York the rest of the week so I can spend time with my beautiful wife."

He looked handsome, dressed in a white polo shirt and khakis, and was at the stove cooking breakfast. He nonchalantly moved a glass on the counter back a few inches in an apparent effort to conceal it, but not before Chessa saw it was half full with amber liquid.

"Are you drinking already?" Chessa stood in the doorway in the sweat suit she had donned, her arms crossed. Gone was her façade from the night before. *I'm not buying any more of his lies,* she thought. *I want some answers.*

Darren feigned innocence, picking up the glass she had already seen. "Oh, this? It's just a little hair of the dog that bit me." He threw the contents down the sink. "But you're right, it's a little early. Although, it's almost noon, sleepyhead. I feel bad about last night, so I made you some breakfast. Your favorite—a bacon and cheese omelet with hash browns."

Chessa felt her stomach turn. "I'm not hungry. And you can't just sweep away what happened last night by acting like it didn't happen."

"What are you talking about?" Darren didn't look at her, continuing to stir the potatoes on the stove.

"You know what I'm talking about. You came home five hours late last night. Five hours! With no phone call, nothing. And you smelled like another woman. Don't tell me it was through osmosis. We've been married for only a year and already you're having an affair." Chessa choked out the last words, a sob catching in her throat. *I'm not going to let him see me cry,* she decided, holding back her tears.

"Honey, that's not true." Darren turned and approached her, his arms out to give her a hug, but she recoiled at his touch. "I told you what happened. That's the truth. I'm sorry, it won't happen again. Now come on, let's eat some breakfast."

"I'm not hungry."

Darren turned and went back to the stove to finish cooking, talking to her with his back turned. "Fine, have it your way. Be stubborn. I'm going to eat, and then I have a golf match with some big shots in an hour. For your information, it's work-related. Don't hold dinner for me tonight."

"You're leaving?" Chessa hated the shrill tone of her voice, but couldn't hide her emotions. "We never spend time together. And what kind of way is that to make things up to me?"

Darren slammed the frying pan of hashed browns down on the burner and turned around to face her. His face had instantly changed from the look of a sweet, cajoling husband to a mask of fury. "You should have known what you were getting into when you married me!" he yelled. "Grow up!"

And with that he wiped his hands on a dishrag, left the kitchen, and headed into the garage to get his clubs, leaving breakfast on the stove.

Chessa stood frozen in place for what seemed like an hour, leaning against the door frame, paralyzed with disbelief and fear. She thought back to her wedding day, and how beautiful it had been. But now she realized it had all been a charade. *I can't believe I made such a huge mistake*, she thought to herself. *I should never have married him.* She thought back to when they had first started dating, how her calls and letters had gone unanswered for months, how she had confronted him after her strange conversation with Peggy and how he had denied that he was seeing someone else, dismissing it by saying his enamored secretary was just protecting him. She could see it all more clearly now. *He had been lying. He* was *seeing someone else when we started dating!* Then the memory flashed back to her of the 'lady in red' Darren had been flirting with at their wedding reception. *At our own wedding!*

She started trembling and clutched her stomach to keep herself from crying out loud. She had never felt so alone or lost. *There's no one I can even talk to about it! No one who won't go blabbing it around and get me in trouble. No one who will understand.*

And then she remembered Stephanie. Something about her being able to help if she ever had problems with her husband being drunk. *I wonder if she really could help. Lord knows I have to talk to somebody before I go crazy.* When her foot started to tingle indicating it was falling asleep, she came out of her trance and decided to take action. She picked up her cell phone and called Stephanie.

That night Chessa found herself sitting on a metal folding chair in an Al-Anon meeting in a nondescript church hall in Manhattan. *This is a big mistake*, she told herself. *I should not have come. I don't think I belong here.*

She was the wife of a United States senator, and if anyone recognized her she figured it would most likely make the morning headlines or stir some type of trouble.

She confided her fears to Stephanie when her cousin-in-law picked her up from work.

"You aren't the first well-known or famous person to enter the rooms," she explained. During the twenty-minute ride to the meeting, Stephanie had assured Chessa that it was an anonymous program and no one would give up her identity. She had explained that Al-Anon was for friends or family members of alcoholics and wasn't designed to help them "cure" or "fix" the alcoholic but to heal themselves. "We get sick too, even though we're not the ones drinking," she explained. "We get sick with worry, anger, regret, fear, low self-esteem, self-pity, guilt, and a lot of other emotions. If we don't get well, we end up making ourselves sick or crazy."

"Well, I am starting to feel some of those things," Chessa confided. "But I'm not willing to leave Darren. Maybe I'm exaggerating this whole drinking thing."

"It doesn't sound like it. And nobody says you have to stay or go, honey," Stephanie said soothingly. "We don't give you our opinion on anything. We just help you to vent and hear yourself think, and let you know you're not alone. Whatever you decide, you will be okay. All we care about is you." Stephanie further explained that the program worked by members attending meetings, listening to each others' stories and sharing their pain. Members also worked through the twelve-step program of Alcoholics Anonymous, usually by getting a sponsor who was available to guide them through it.

"Why would I have to go through an AA step program?" Chessa asked defiantly. "I'm not the one who's drinking too much."

"You'll see how it works eventually. But when you have nowhere else to turn, you have to trust something. It's really worked for me, and not just because Bob is in recovery. Unless you can get Darren to go to AA—which, if I know my cousin-in-law, is out of the question right now since I'm sure he doesn't believe he has a problem—you should do something that makes you feel better. Why don't you just try it and see how you like it?"

Chessa was ready to beg Stephanie to turn the car around before they were halfway to the church. Now it was too late; the meeting was starting and she didn't want to draw attention to herself by standing and walking out. There were about thirty people in the small room; about three-fourths of them were women. Chessa sank low in her seat, pulled up the lapels of her raincoat, and left her sunglasses on. *Maybe I can at least be inconspicuous,* she hoped.

Stephanie sat next to her, patting her back periodically to try to comfort her.

Fortunately, Chessa was not called on to share, and when they asked if anyone was new, she merely had to give her first name. She remained quiet throughout the meeting and they respected that. After the meeting, a few women approached her, introducing themselves and offering their phone numbers if she'd like to call. *They really are nice,* she thought. *I just don't know if this is for me yet.*

When Stephanie dropped her off close to eight o'clock, Darren was sitting there on the living room couch waiting for her.

"Where have you been?" he asked her bluntly.

She realized she couldn't lie to him. "I was with Stephanie."

"Stephanie? My cousin-in-law? Don't tell me you went to one of her Al-Anon meetings?"

"I did, and—"

"Are you out of your mind?" Darren jumped to his feet and cut her off, practically shrieking at her. "Do you know that if this gets out, I could be ruined? If people think I'm an alcoholic, they will never vote for me again. I don't care if I'm running for president of the Central Park Middle-aged Men's Society!"

"It's an anonymous program," Chessa protested. "Plus, I kept my coat and sunglasses on and introduced myself by my first name only."

"And how many women do you know who are named Chessa?" Darren yelled. "You are a moron. So help me, if this gets out, I'll . . ."

Chessa tried to step past him to go upstairs and escape any more verbal abuse. She had noticed out of the corner of her eye the half-empty bottle of Jack Daniels on the living room end table.

Her husband grabbed her by the arm to stop her, pressing his fingers into her flesh. She tried to pull her arm away, but he held tighter.

"Darren, stop, please. You're hurting me."

"I'm not done with you yet." He gripped firmer. She couldn't help it. She slapped him in the face with her free hand.

Chessa heard the blow to her own cheek before she felt it, like a resounding crack. Darren let her go, watching her stumble backward. She stared at him, rubbing her jaw in disbelief.

He only sneered at her. "You hit me first. People always say, 'never hit a girl,' but my mother always said, 'if she hits you first, then she deserves it'."

Tears of pain – emotional more than physical – welled up in Chessa's eyes.

"Oh, now you're going to cry. That figures. Well, you're hurting me and my candidacy. I better never hear that you go to another Al-Anon meeting again." He picked up his cell phone. "And I'm calling Bob to tell him to warn that stupid wife of his not to meddle in our affairs."

CHAPTER SIX

LEIF

President Martin Greene sat alone in the Pressroom of the White House watching various news stations on the monitors before him.

It was seven a.m. and all of the stations were covering the state elections from the day before. The top story involved Leif Mitchell's brother Will winning the election for Maryland's governor and recounting Leif's own former "heroic win" against Leon Slater and subsequent re-election into office three years ago.

Good Morning America actually had Leif sitting in the studio doing a live interview.

The president sat incredulous as the smiling cowboy—he was dressed in jeans, a plaid shirt, boots, and a cowboy hat—strapped on his guitar and sang "Trail to Somewhere." The tanned, handsome thirty-three-year-old from Shepherdsville was still single, the young female anchor chirped, dubbing him the newest "Most Eligible Bachelor in America."

After his ditty, Leif thanked the viewers and congratulated his brother. But William Mitchell's win wasn't what captured viewers.

The anchors on CNN, MSNBC and the network news channels still focused on Leif's bold move to uncover the terrorist backing of his opponent in his first bid for governor, and how it had led him to become one of the most visible and adored politicians in the country.

"Leif Mitchell has certainly remained popular following his re-election, and his brother's win only brings the story to the public mind all over again," one anchor said to a panel he was interviewing. "No one can forget Leif's efforts to not only uncover the terrorist backing of his opponent, but to stop what might have become another 911. And yet, the White House administration has not seemed to be able to capitalize on any of this."

The president leaned forward in his chair, turning up the volume.

"I believe the administration is going to have to finally step it up a notch in doing more to protect Israel from being invaded from terrorists in the future," a gray-haired political scholar from Georgetown University sternly said. Greene flipped from that screen to another, turning up the volume.

". . . I hope it lights a fire under the president, and that he finally gets something done over there to fortify Israel," Democratic Senator Mike Meese from Indiana said. "It's about time. Leif Mitchell has been called a hero, and rightly so. He got the ball rolling but it doesn't seem like Martin Greene has picked it up and run with it yet. Now that his first term in office is half over, let's see if he can finally take some action. It's my opinion that the President needs to wipe out our enemies over there and stop them once and for all, instead of wheeling and dealing with them all the time like his predecessor did."

After about a half hour of watching the various television stations, the president wearily left the room and headed out to his private chambers for breakfast with his wife. He needed the comfort and support of the one person whom he trusted. He needed to vent. Not one announcer or political "expert" had asked how Leif had gotten his information behind Leon Slater's terrorist connections years ago in the first place. If they had asked, Leif must have remained mute on the issue, just like Martin had asked him to do.

Unbeknownst to the American public, Vice President Greene had pulled Leif aside after dinner the night of the July Fourth benefit concert in which he had performed and spoke to him privately for a few minutes. The vice president had given Leif some invaluable advice on his opponent Leon Slater: that he was suspected of possibly having terrorist backing.

Martin Greene handed Leif a piece of paper that night telling him to open it after he left and was alone. On the paper was a list of sources within the CIA, NSA, and FBI that he had cleared to talk to Leif about Slater.

It was up to Leif to do the digging, but the cowboy singer would have never known to even begin searching, much less where and how, without Martin's help.

And now the whole thing had backfired. Leif Mitchell was a hero and he, the president of the United States, would sink even lower in the public eye until he took action against the Palestinians and Islamic extremists—or at least punished another major terrorist leader.

If he didn't, he probably wouldn't get reelected to another term. It seemed to him that the American people were reaching lynch-mob fervor and all eyes were on him. He may even be impeached.

Martin knew his mind was wandering in a dangerous direction, and he was becoming paranoid. He needed to talk to Carol and get some relief.

He met her in their private dining room. She looked like a butterfly in a light yellow suit, which contrasted with the dark ringlets that framed her face.

He kissed his wife on the cheek and sat across the dinette table from her. Before he had a chance to unload his resentment about Leif on her, Carol started the conversation.

"Our youngest daughter has asked me to ask you a favor," she said, her eyes twinkling with merriment.

"Why wouldn't she just ask me herself?" Martin took a big bite of the turkey sandwich they had just been served. He was starving.

"Because you're always busy, understandably so, and she just hasn't seen you. Besides, it involves a young man, and I think she could talk about it more easily with me."

"So what does she want?" Martin asked absentmindedly, savoring his sandwich, his mind elsewhere.

"She wants to invite this young man here to visit her," Carol said, smiling. "It seems she's developed a crush on him."

"Do I know him?"

"In fact, you do. It's Leif Mitchell."

It was a good thing Martin had swallowed the last bite he had taken or he probably would have choked. He gasped, grabbed his glass of iced tea, and gulped it down, regaining composure. "You've got to be kidding me."

"Why, what's wrong with Leif Mitchell? I just saw on the news how he helped his brother win the governor's seat in Maryland. I would think you'd approve. You seemed to be friendly enough with him when he was here to do the benefit concert. I thought he was a perfect gentleman and would be a wonderful suitor for our Wendy."

Martin left the remains of his sandwich uneaten and rubbed his temples. He had suddenly lost his appetite and had a headache. He knew what his wife meant when she said that Leif would be good for "their Wendy."

Their youngest daughter was known for her wild, impetuous streak. She had partied through college out at Stanford University, being caught on camera at various bars with dozens of men, despite her father's constant warnings. It hadn't helped his presidential candidacy any.

Wendy was a natural beauty, although she was constantly "updating" her appearance, as she would say, adding highlights and extensions to her naturally long blond hair and wearing a variety of outfits, some a little revealing or risqué in Martin's opinion.

Ever since she had come back home to DC about a year ago, she had calmed down a bit under the threat from her father that he would cut her off financially if she didn't shape up. She got a job as a bank manager, which forced her to wear more conservative clothing, didn't frequent many bars or parties, and had only dated one young man for about a month before breaking it off.

". . . don't you think, dear?" Carol brought her husband out of his reverie.

"I think it's a terrible idea."

"But, Martin, this young man is a hero."

"Yes, only because I made him one." Martin's blood pressure started to rise hearing the word 'hero' for the umpteenth time that day, and he finally told his wife what he had wanted to tell her all along: how he had set up the victory for Leif Mitchell the first time and how it had eventually backfired when the young Republican had turned around and stolen his glory.

Martin mulled over his wife's suggestion. His daughter could be a potential embarrassment to the White House if she was "out there" in the news. And he didn't want to swell Leif's ego any further by matching him with the daughter that obviously adored him.

But the more he thought about it, the more he realized a match between one of his daughters and Leif Mitchell might actually be a good thing. If Leif became a suitor and thus, frequent visitor to the White House, he would attract the media along with him. The favorable limelight that seemed to follow Leif Mitchell would be cast on all of them, just like it had been with the benefit concert. And his eldest daughter wouldn't be as likely to cast any shadows once in that limelight as her younger sister might.

"Like they say, hold your friends close and your enemies closer."

"What, dear?" Carol was confused.

Martin didn't realize he had spoken the words out loud. "I'll talk to Victoria."

"But I don't think she's even interested in Leif Mitchell." Carol was perplexed, as she was often lately by her husband's brooding and seemingly rash decisions.

Martin smiled. "We'll see."

"But what about Wendy?"

"She'll get over it and find another young man in a heartbeat. There are plenty, I'm sure, just standing in line."

Carol started to object again but was met with her husband's deep frown. So she kept quiet, knowing once her husband had made up his mind it was futile to try to change it.

Victoria had thrown a fit when her father sat her down to talk to her about having Leif visit more and possibly court her. Martin had lied, saying Leif was interested in dating his oldest daughter.

"Well, I'm not interested in some cowboy rock singer, even if he is a governor," she protested. "I'll find my own man when I'm ready, thank you very much, but right now I'm only interested in getting my master's degree and furthering my career."

Victoria was extremely smart like her mother, and goal-oriented and driven like her father, and right now she was only focused on climbing the corporate ladder at one of DC's biggest marketing firms.

When her father pushed a little more, she pushed back. "There is no way I'm going out with Leif Mitchell and that's final," she said. So Martin gave up.

Fortunately his wife wasn't one to say "I told you so," so he went back to tell her she was probably right and he was willing to give her idea a try with their youngest daughter.

Martin watched his wife smile triumphantly when he told her Victoria had said "no way."

"Don't worry, dear, I'll handle this one," she said.

As Leif had quickly learned, in politics there was no rest for the weary. Once his brother was elected, it was time to turn his focus once again on his own campaign for gubernatorial re-election coming up the following year.

Still, he managed to take time off every once in a while and when he did, he turned his sights back home to Little River for some much needed rest and relaxation. His parents had assembled the family, the farmhands, and everyone at the ranch for a family feast to celebrate Will's victory.

Leif took advantage of the opportunity and, after everyone left, lingered until dusk settled on the farm, breathing in the familiar barn smells that for him were like aromatherapy, helping him focus and maintain his feeling of serenity amidst the rapidly changing world around him.

After spending the night, Leif took Monday off, and visited the stables, cherishing the rare moments to be around his favorite thing in the world—his horses.

He expelled some pent-up energy by taking a ride on one of the newer colts in the stable. The animal was almost untamed and galloped for nearly an hour through the pastures and woods until both horse and rider were exhausted and covered in sweat, despite the winter chill.

Leif needed a shower and was removing his dust-caked boots upon entering the mud room in the main house when his father walked in and handed him the phone.

"Dad, can't you take a message?" Leif was disgruntled. He had come to the farm for some peace, hoping to escape the madness for a little while, and wasn't ready to give it up and face the real world just yet. He had been looking forward to just sitting before the blazing fire. Besides, he was covered in grime.

"I don't think so, son. It's the president."

Leif listened as President Greene invited him to the White House for a weekend stay to discuss an "objective" he said he wanted to talk to him about in person.

"Of course Mister President, I'll be there this Friday," Leif said, winking to his dad, who stood watching him, smiling proudly.

When the limousine dropped Leif off at the White House security entrance, a press mob was waiting. Thankfully, three Secret Service men shielded him from the barrage of microphones and questions, so the media had to be satisfied with photos and video footage.

When he had come to the White House the first time, Leif had been escorted right to the East Room to set up for the concert. Today, he had been told the president's daughter Wendy would be giving him a full tour and would meet him in the Blue Room. He would then meet with the president over a private dinner.

He remembered Wendy because she had sat across from him at the White House dinner following the benefit concert he had given.

She was pretty, he remembered. Still, Leif had had so much on his mind that night that he really hadn't paid her too much attention.

But he couldn't help noticing her now as she walked toward him in a smart, form-fitting royal-blue dress cut mid-thigh level with a scoop neckline. Her smooth blond hair was hanging down below her shoulders, pulled playfully back on one side with a matching blue barrette. She looked even more stunning now than she had in her full-length gown the night of the concert, carrying herself with more poise and confidence than she had years ago.

Her eyes sparkled as she extended her hand to shake his. Leif suddenly felt like a bumbling teenager instead of the governor of the state of Kentucky, and he was tongue-tied.

"Hi Governor Mitchell. Welcome back to the White House." Her genuine smile was radiant.

Leif finally snapped out of his reverie to answer her. "It's good to be back. And it's nice to see you again." He took off his cowboy hat and gave her a slight bow.

"So are you ready to see our humble abode?"

Leif looked around him at the anything-but-humble surroundings. Even on a non-holiday, the Blue Room, where she had received him, was ornate with its blue-and-gold trim. It looked out on the South Lawn, which was presently covered in a blanket of snow that had fallen the night before, and glistened as if covered with millions of diamonds in the midday sun.

But since it was December, the Blue Room was adorned with the official White House Christmas tree. The Christmas theme this year as planned by the First Lady was called "Birds of a Feather," and the twenty trees throughout the White House were decorated with handcrafted birds, each from various states, that looked and even felt real. The eighteen-foot-tall Douglas fir in the Blue Room was the biggest and most beautiful, trimmed with white doves to symbolize national unity and peace, captivating the hundreds of thousands of visitors that were lucky enough to schedule a Christmas tour.

Leif was mesmerized for a minute, then turned to his hostess. He knew she was just teasing with her choice of words; still, they were evidence of her education and upbringing and piqued his interest in her.

"Lead on, Miss Greene," he said, and crooked his arm, through which she slipped her hand and led the way.

"Please, call me Wendy."

"Only if you call me Leif."

"Deal." He felt an instant comfort and warmth between them as she led him through the elaborate halls decorated with enormous wreaths made of a variety of evergreens, flowers, berries and pinecones.

She showed him all of the main rooms and some of the residence rooms, which were off-limits to the public, then the indoor and outdoor recreational facilities, including the bowling alley, movie theater, tennis courts, track, and swimming pool.

They passed by the White House kitchen, which emanated the smell of fresh-baked breads, roasted lamb, and apple pie. A half-dozen cooks, led by three chefs, were scrambling about and didn't even notice them.

"The kitchen is extra busy this time of year," Wendy said, glancing at her watch. "Wow, it's going to be dinnertime soon. This was so much fun I didn't realize what time it was. Do you want me to show you to your room so you can relax a little bit before meeting my father?"

Wendy led Leif down a long hallway to the guest rooms. "We have a total of 132 rooms in the White House. Which one would you like?" She smiled teasingly.

His room had already been chosen. When they arrived at his door, Leif faked a frown.

"What's wrong—you didn't like our tour?" Wendy asked, concerned. "You don't like the White House?"

"Well, there are no horses. I'm used to sleeping in a stable." Wendy's eyes opened wide, and Leif burst out laughing. "I'm kidding. This has been great. You have been. . . a wonderful tour guide. It's just all so overwhelming. But I guess a guy could get used to it."

Wendy laughed with him, and then pouted. "I'm sure you and Dad have lots of important business to discuss. Will I get to see you again?"

"I don't leave until the day after tomorrow, and yes, I'd love that. It looks like there's so much to do right here we won't even have to go anywhere. Although maybe you'd like to get out of the 'House'?" He grinned mischievously. "Since you're such a good tour guide, how about if you show me the sights in DC tomorrow after I'm done with whatever your father has planned for me? That is, if you have his permission. I wouldn't want to get in trouble with the boss."

She grimaced. "Oh please, I don't need Daddy's permission. But I do like that you're a gentleman," she added coyly.

"Then it's a date." Leif bowed and bid her farewell. "I'm an early-to-bed, early-to-rise kind of guy, but I'm sure dinner won't run so late tonight that we couldn't do something afterward—maybe get a cup of coffee or something?"

"How about bowling? Let me know when you're done and I'll beat the pants off of you." Wendy smiled suggestively.

"I'm sure you will." Leif detected her double meaning and realized he was probably playing with fire. "You have a lot of practice, I bet."

"I guess you could say that." And with that, Wendy said good-bye and walked away, strutting casually down the hallway.

That same friendly ease interspersed with sexual tension pervaded their bowling match, and Leif found himself irresistibly drawn to the president's daughter, yet realized he was on new and probably dangerous turf.

So he continued to behave like the utmost gentleman, trying not to stare as he watched her from behind in her tight black jeans as she approached the alley, bending over to release her ball.

In the end, she beat him, but just barely. He was a good all-around athlete, but she had obviously had lots of practice with a bowling alley in her own house.

They kept their conversation light, talking about college, being the youngest among their siblings, and their mutual love of music. Although he obviously liked classic songs and she favored more popular music, they had some common ground in country-rock. And while she had never been horseback riding, she said she enjoyed watching horse racing. It was a start.

Leif found it very hard to part ways with her that night but did so, keeping his affection to a hug and kiss on the cheek. She had gazed into his eyes with longing, but remained a lady, accepting his kiss and wishing him a good night's sleep, telling him she was looking forward to the next day.

Leif didn't have too much time the next day for fun.

The president had briefly explained the purpose of his trip during the previous night's dinner. He wanted Leif to head up a governors' advisory task force on US relations with the Middle East.

"Since you were so adept at uncovering Leon Slater's terrorist backings, I'm confident you can lead the other governors I've selected to start looking at finding a real solution to the mess over there," Martin Greene told Leif. "I've chosen governors who are popular among their constituents and who are doing the best job at running their states. I want you all to show the nations in the Middle East, including Israel, how they can govern their own people and yet work together with each other—like the United States do—to form a peaceful union, whether they agree on various issues or not. And who better to lead the group than the most popular governor of all?"

Leif hesitated before accepting Martin's offer. "I like the idea, but Mr. President, I am still relatively new in office. Perhaps I could be part of the team and let one of the other, more experienced governors take charge?"

But the president shrugged that off. "Some people are just naturally gifted at diplomacy and relations with people, and I think you're one of them."

"Thank you, sir." Leif shook the president's outstretched hand and grinned. "I can't very well say no to the president now, can I?"

Greene told Leif that he had lined up a press conference that afternoon to introduce the new task force. "This will boost your profile and popularity even further," Greene said. "It's a win-win."

Unfortunately for President Greene, his scheme once again ended up being more of a win for Leif Mitchell and loss for himself.

In a one-o-clock press conference in the White House Press Room, the reporters attacked the president for wasting more taxpayers' dollars by having a bunch of governors try to solve the Middle East problem.

"Instead of putting this off on other elected officials who should be running their own states, shouldn't you be tackling the problem yourself, Mr. President?" one gutsy reporter asked.

Another was equally brazen. "President Greene, are you just using Governor Mitchell and his recent popularity and notoriety to deflect the negative press you've been receiving?"

"Of course not!" a red-faced President Greene sputtered into the microphones, becoming visibly indignant.

"Governor Mitchell, what do you think of this whole plan?"

"I think it makes complete sense," Leif said in his slight Kentucky drawl, naturally radiating his cowboy allure. "And I am offended y'all think the president is using me or any of the governors he's chosen to be on the task force. I am honored to be part of this project, and I think you have it backwards. I am lucky to be in the president's company and to benefit from his leadership and knowledge." He shot them all a big grin. "If anything, he's helped me, not the other way around."

Martin Greene appeared to relax as Leif spoke, relieved that his plan hadn't totally backfired.

Leif didn't walk out of the press conference and meetings that followed until close to five p.m. He was supposed to have met Wendy hours earlier for their tour of DC but had gotten word to her through one of her father's assistants that they were running extremely late.

She was waiting in the limo that met him in the high-security underground garage so they wouldn't be bothered by the press. He sidled next to her in the backseat and the limo took off.

"I'm so sorry things took so long," Leif told her. He noticed she looked beautiful in a mid-length red dress and white faux fur coat.

"It's not your fault," she replied, rewarding him with her beatific smile. "I'm just glad you're finally free." She put her hand on top of his. He turned his over so he could hold hers and glanced up. She was staring at him with a look of passion glinting in her eyes, and he felt as if a volt of electric coursed through his body.

The limo pulled up as close as it could to the Washington Mall, about halfway down its length. In one direction they could see the Washington Monument, backlit by a breathtaking sunset. In the other, they gazed at the Capitol bathed in a rosy glow. Both looked magnificent, surrounded by the newly fallen snow.

Leif felt another surge of adrenaline course through his veins, this time prompted by the realization that he was sitting at the core of the most powerful country in the world. It seemed like God was smiling on His kingdom, at least for the moment.

After a riding tour past the Jefferson Memorial, the Lincoln Memorial and several war memorials, Wendy directed the limo driver, and in a few minutes they pulled up in front of an obscure little restaurant tucked away on one of the side roads.

"I don't know about you but I'm starved," Wendy said.

The Red Moon Café was no more than the basement of a townhouse. Wendy had reserved the entire restaurant, although there were a dozen tables inside.

Leif and Wendy shared a bottle of cabernet and an assortment of appetizers she had ordered ahead of time. After sharing an entrée, they split the restaurant's famous tiramisu.

They chatted and laughed throughout dinner, but decided not to linger too long. Even though they knew the owner wouldn't take any chances on offending his star diners by alerting the media, they also realized reporters always had a way of sniffing them out, so, limo waiting, they managed to ride back to the White House, sight unseen.

A full moon lit up the clear night sky, and the air was unusually warm, so Wendy suggested they take a stroll through the Rose Garden before retiring.

"Isn't it beautiful?" Wendy walked ahead of him, stopping to smell some of the winter roses that bloomed year-round.

"It's not as beautiful as you." Leif stood there in his black suit, red tie, and black cowboy hat, the most eligible bachelor in the country. "Thank you for a wonderful time tonight."

She had turned around and their eyes locked for a moment. "You're welcome," she said, taking a step closer until their bodies were almost touching.

"Will I get in trouble if I kiss you, or will the SWAT teams shoot me down?" Leif teased.

Wendy put her arms around his neck, and he kissed her slowly, passionately.

"I better get you home," Leif said.

"I am home, silly."

"You know what I mean." They went back inside and parted to go to their separate rooms, darting glances over their shoulders and smiling at one another like two swooning school kids.

Leif had just changed out of his suit and tie into a comfortable pair of lounge pants when he heard a light tap on his door.

He opened it just a few inches, enough to peek out and see it was Wendy.

"Can I come in?" Her voice seemed shy and small.

He opened the door and she stepped into the dimly lit room, still in her red dress and heels.

"What's wrong, Wendy?" Leif asked, flustered. He closed the door behind her and frantically looked around for his shirt.

"I knew I wouldn't be able to sleep without another kiss." Her teasing girl voice had deepened into a woman's, husky with desire.

And in seconds, her dress fell to the floor, revealing lacy black lingerie. She kissed him, her arms wrapping around his bare shoulders, and they fell backward onto the bed.

"But what about . . . ?" Leif's head was spinning.

"No one will hear us; we're almost a half mile apart from my parents." And she kissed him again hungrily, silencing his protests.

CHAPTER SEVEN

CHESSA

It should have been a joyful day, standing by her husband's side as he publicly announced his candidacy for president of the United States.

If not for what she had learned in Al-Anon, she probably would have hid in a closet or run away screaming. But instead, here she stood, the dutiful wife, putting on a smile for the cameras.

"This too shall pass," she kept reminding herself. *They're watching. Keep smiling.*

It was warm for a January day in New York, with temperatures in the fifties. Darren was making his announcement at the recently completed Franklin D. Roosevelt Four Freedoms Park on Roosevelt Island on the East River.

Thousands of supporters carrying "Richards for President" signs cheered in the open tree-lined triangular garden that was at the southern tip of the park, bordered on either side by water and panoramic views of Manhattan and Queens.

On the large platform constructed at the garden's narrow tip, Darren stood with Chessa on one side, Pete Connor on his other, and dozens of aides and other campaign advisors behind him, as well as his parents and sister. They were separated from the media hordes by a wide podium. Behind them was the concrete contemplative square plaza, on which hung an enormous American flag. And behind it the expectant crowd had a view of none other than the breathtaking city skyline.

"We are standing here today, on this historic spot, for this historic occasion. It will be historic because it will hopefully be the beginning of a new leadership that will transform a weary America into a nation that is bolstered again by pride in itself that shines a light of truth and justice out to the rest of the world." Darren had hired one of the country's best speechwriters to work with Pete.

"As Franklin Delano Roosevelt, one of the greatest presidents—who was also from this great state of New York—once said in his famous 'Four Freedoms' speech, 'I address you at a moment unprecedented in the history of the union. At no previous time has American security been as seriously threatened from without as it is today.'

"Back when he gave that speech, we were facing World War II, a war against dictators who were threatening the democracy of other nations, a war that threatened our very own democracy. I believe the same is true in a very real sense today as we continue our war against an equally dangerous foe: the terrorists of the Middle East. And we need a new, stronger leadership to take charge and destroy this threat to democracy, and to our very peace and safety right here in America.

"As President Roosevelt said: 'We are not at peace so long as those dictators and terrorists are out there.' Those four basic freedoms he addressed—freedom of speech and expression, freedom of worship, freedom from want or economic insecurity, and last but not least, freedom from fear—are our rights as Americans. The terrorists seek to eliminate those very freedoms. Since the current president and his administration are doing little to nothing to protect them, we are becoming precariously close to losing them."

The breezes off the water did little to quell the uproarious cheers coming from the crowd. Chessa had to fight from rolling her eyes. *He loves to quote old FDR.* She remembered his speech at Columbia University, the first time she met him. She thought he was so attractive, so smart. *My hero.* Looking out over the sea of admiring faces, she reminded herself that everyone saw him that way. *If they only knew the Darren Richards I know now. But of course, they never will.* She clapped like the rest of them. She had to.

"Ladies and gentlemen, the current administration has failed in its promises and its mission to ensure peace and prosperity." Darren spoke in a compelling, authoritative voice. The audience was riveted. Chessa realized that she could hear the wind whistling in the trees and on the water, everyone was so quiet and attentive. "They have tried and failed to work with the Middle East countries that still are backed by terrorist regimes. I say it is time that Americans face reality. It's time for a new age; one that looks back to the pioneers who circled their wagons to protect their families and hard-earned possessions. I say when you can no longer work with the enemy, then stop trying and start working within your own country to make it stronger."

Darren went on to outline the tenets of his campaign proposal: to withdraw all troops overseas and instead spend the military budget to build weapons at home and further scientific and medical research; to continue to protect the environment and look for alternatives to the nation's dependence on foreign sources of oil; and to reinforce America's intelligence abilities and digital communications. "We need to start making America superior to its enemies," Darren said. "But it will come at a price. Our current president has been fortunate to inherit a country that has climbed out of a recession. But as history shows us, we can't just rest on our laurels. We need to make an investment in protecting our country and our land, in shoring up resources and in coming up with new technological and scientific breakthroughs for our people. But I assure you these investments will pay off in many ways, including the creation of more jobs, a stronger government and ultimately a stronger nation.

"We need a new leader to rebuild our government which will, in turn, defend our freedoms, protect our rights, and ensure our prosperity," he concluded. "I have been called to be that leader."

News anchors commented that the event had been one of the most magnificent announcements of a presidential candidacy America had ever witnessed.

Of course the conservative and Republican commentators had a field day with the Senator's speech, saying Darren's programs would not only take the government back into the trillion-dollar debt of years past with all the spending; it would probably plunk America right back into a recession. They said his foreign policy could undermine all of the negotiations the current administration had started in the Middle East, possibly provoke the terrorist regime, and maybe even start another war.

Chessa didn't really like the limelight that had been thrust upon her. But, she had to admit to herself, the thought of becoming First Lady was starting to grow on her.

Ever since she was a young girl, really, she had wanted to "make a difference" in the world by helping those less fortunate. *If Darren wins I'll be able to do that,* she knew. *If I can just put up with him and his ego – or perhaps, ignore him as much as possible. I'll probably be traveling a lot to needy countries anyway while he's back home here in the US. That'll work.*

Chessa was secretly disappointed that her gender still chose to focus on what she had been wearing at the ceremony instead of interviewing her about her views and her goals.

The fashion world bloggers and entertainment reporters were all agog that day saying Chessa Richards made a very elegant, trendy first appearance, looking stylish in a new Donna Karan cream-colored silk dress with a slight ruffle at the bottom and matching jacket with pearl buttons.

"Chic but not afraid to show her femininity," one *Entertainment Tonight* emcee gushed. "Chessa Richards will make a fabulous First Lady if she continues to show up dressed like this."

If it had been up to Chessa, she would have worn something out of her closet. A tomboy growing up and the daughter of a woman who liked shopping at flea markets and bargain basement sales, Chessa had never considered herself a fashionista. Her husband knew her frugality, her disregard for stylish clothing and her aversion to shopping, so he surprised her one night a week prior to the announcement ceremony by coming home and giving her a small gift. Inside a prettily wrapped small box was an American Express card. He told her to use it to buy herself a new wardrobe; she would be needing it. "And because I know you might need some help, I've arranged for my mother to go with you. She's got all kinds of connections at the best shops in New York, not to mention great fashion sense."

Before Chessa had a chance to protest, the phone rang. It was Dorothy Richards, asking her when she would be available to go shopping. "Darren explained how you don't especially like this sort of thing and you may need help, dear, so I promise it will be quick and painless, and maybe even fun!"

Like going to get my wisdom teeth pulled, Chessa thought, swallowing down her misgivings and picking a date. *Let's just get it over with.*

Dorothy must have warned the women at Bergdorf Goodman's, because their shopping spree there really was, if not quick, fairly painless. The experience was a far cry from the shopping trips she had taken with her own mother, rummaging through racks and stacks of mismatched, wrong-sized clearance items to find the best bargains.

Chessa hardly had to lift a finger as stunning outfits; dresses, coats, and even swimwear were brought to her one by one for her approval. Once Chessa, with her mother-in-law's expert guidance, weeded the selection down to about a dozen items, she tried them on in the huge fitting room, assisted as needed by ladies–in-waiting.

I feel like Cinderella again, she secretly admitted to herself, as she twirled around in a gorgeous tea-length dress that whirled around her in soft layers of pale apricot chiffon. "Like a princess," she said softly out loud.

"Like a First Lady," her mother-in-law corrected.

Once they were finished, a waiting limousine picked them up outside the store to take them to the Café du Suisse for lunch. Their bags would be delivered.

Chessa was famished but completely lost her appetite once she saw her next surprise waiting for her in the restaurant. Darren's sister, Deborah, sat at one of the tables, waving and smiling at them as they entered.

Well, the trip had been relatively painless up until now. Chessa did her best to smile as they sat down across from her.

"I called Deborah to join us. I thought it would be another nice surprise," Dorothy said in all seriousness.

"So how did you do? I would have been there, but I couldn't get out of work earlier." Deborah directed her question and comment to her mother, as if Chessa was just a child who was meant to be seen but not heard.

Chessa marveled at how the two of them were so alike. Deborah looked like a younger version of her mother; both of them were blonde (although probably not natural, Chessa would guess) with the same piercing blue eyes as her husband's, and had pale, perfect skin (they abhorred getting too much sun). Both were almost anorexic they were so thin.

In their presence, Chessa felt like a plump teenager. She only felt worse when it came time to order. The waitress took her order first; after she asked for the restaurant's daily special, a filet mignon sandwich with sautéed onions on a baguette, she felt immediately humiliated when both of the other women ordered Cobb salads with light dressing.

"We found some fabulous outfits and dresses that fit perfectly," Dorothy said, pausing to gaze at Chessa as she took a bite of her sandwich.

"Better start watching those calories; television adds about ten pounds," Deborah said directly to Chessa this time, making her feel like Cinderella *before* she was visited by the fairy godmother and had to put up with her evil stepmother and stepsisters. "I'm so jealous. I wish I could find someone like Darren. Never a bride *or* a bridesmaid."

Chessa realized it was a direct dig aimed at her for not selecting her sister-in-law to be in the wedding. "About the wedding, Deborah, I'm sorry—"

"I'm just joking; all is forgiven," Deborah said magnanimously. "I'm sure you'll make it up to me one day. Besides, at least I'll get to buy a new wardrobe to come to all those White House parties and balls. And really, I don't envy you after all. I wouldn't want to have to put up with all the stress that comes along with your position, although I'm sure you'll do fine with it."

Dorothy had ordered three glasses of champagne and raised her glass to toast her son's presidential candidacy. Not a bottle, just a glass each, which they all sipped during lunch. *No alcoholics among the women*, Chessa thought.

Her mother-in-law did ask if she wanted a refill, but Chessa declined.

"It's okay, dear, you're not driving," Dorothy said with a little laugh.

"I know, I'm just not much for the taste," Chessa replied.

"So your family, they aren't big drinkers?" Dorothy asked, although it came out more like a statement than a question.

Time to color the truth a little bit, Chessa decided. If they had known her father, they would have known he drank. *A lot.*

When she was young, Chessa recalled her mother trying to keep up with him, then giving up in disgust. It was part of the reason they had divorced. But Chessa remembered her dad as a happy drunk. She hadn't experienced, like her mom, the complete irresponsibility and selfishness that went along with his drunken gaiety.

Now, a little bit older and wiser, Chessa was beginning to realize that her mother had been forced to pick up the pieces time and again, barely paying the bills to keep a roof over their heads every time Stephen got fired from another job, or spent his paycheck at the bar, or had to get bailed out of jail.

She had always just known her dad as the 'fun guy,' and as a young girl would become angry when her mother would berate or nag him. Only now, through her own experience, was Chessa finally starting to see how difficult it must have been for Theresa Reynolds to live with an alcoholic.

"They like to drink once in a while," Chessa conceded.

"Hmmm. That's funny. I heard you went to one of those alcoholic basher meetings," Deborah said. "I thought you must be religiously against drinking or something, being Methodist and all."

"They're called Al-Anon, and my being Methodist has nothing to do with any of it." *Me thinks me doth protest too much*, Chessa scolded herself.

"I just think you need to be cautious that it may give off, shall we say, the wrong meaning." Dorothy cleared her throat for emphasis. "From what Stephanie has said, those people in Al-Anon don't seem to mean any harm, but I'm sure you can't trust them. And now that you're in the public eye, I would say it's a good idea not to join any such controversial groups that may attract negative attention. Moderation is a virtue."

Tell that to your son, Chessa wanted to shout, but remained silent. *It won't do any good to argue with her anyway. You can't talk to a drunk – or a control freak who's in denial for that matter.*

"From what I've heard, they just seem like a bunch of meddlers and complainers anyway, wanting other people to share their misery. Please tell me you won't be going back there," Dorothy said, sounding more like she was making a demand rather than a request.

"Okay," Chessa said lamely, trying to force down the last of her sandwich without gagging.

Dorothy softened her tone. "Like Deborah said, you and Darren will probably both be under a lot of stress for the next several months. I'm sure he'll be working lots of late hours with the campaign . . ."

He already does, Chessa thought. *This won't be any different.*

"And I know my son only drinks some to alleviate the pressure he's under. Like his father, I'm sure he'll also be wanting you to help take his mind off it all in the bedroom, if you know what I mean." Dorothy winked. "The Richards men have always had big goals, big desires, and big needs. Darren must have seen in you that you could fulfill those needs."

Along with a few other women maybe, Chessa felt like saying, but kept silent. *And this is none of your business,* she felt like adding.

"Well, I say who cares if your husband wants you to help relieve his stress once in a while, so long as you get to buy all these new clothes, go to fabulous dinner parties and are the center of attention. You may even get to see the world!" Deborah sighed with envy. "And it's not like Darren's not good-looking. I think you should consider yourself the luckiest girl alive."

Chessa didn't feel very grateful, but she forced another smile.

Dorothy must have seen right through it. "If you ever need anyone to talk to, you can always call me."

"Or me," Deborah offered cheerfully.

Yeah, right. You two will be the last women I call. Then Chessa immediately felt guilty for her mean-spirited thoughts. "Thank you both," she said aloud.

Ever since she was a toddler, Chessa had always wanted a sister. But her intuition told her she couldn't trust Deborah. *She's not even my friend, much less a sister.*

And in that moment, as Deborah and Dorothy chatted merrily with the waiter who came to deliver their bill, Chessa felt like the loneliest person in the world.

Feeling too uncomfortable to drag Stephanie into her problems anymore under threat by her husband, not to mention her "agreement" to abide by the wishes of her mother-in-law, Chessa went home and called Amy.

She told her everything that had transpired, from Darren's drinking and late nights away from home to her lunch with her "evil" mother-in-law and sister-in-law. She did, however, withhold the fact that her husband had hit her. Amy worked at the Chicago *Tribune* now, but Chessa knew if she told Amy about the incident her friend would show up in New York or Washington DC—wherever Darren happened to be—and start a brawl with him. *And Amy would probably win,* Chessa smiled to herself. *Of course, we would all lose in the long run.* She was learning little by little that some things were better left unsaid.

"Wow, you really are like Cinderella," Amy said, trying to lighten her friend's mood. "I'm afraid I don't have any fairy godmother magic powers, though, girlfriend."

"Go ahead. I know you're dying to tell me 'I told you so.' "

"Nah, you don't need that right now. I'm just giving you a hug through the phone."

Chessa started to cry. "Thank you. You're the only person I can talk to. I just feel trapped. I should have never married Darren in the first place, and now that I did, I don't see a way out."

"Have you thought about seeing a counselor?"

"No, Darren blew a fuse when he caught wind that I went to one Al-Anon meeting. He would kill me if he found out I was talking to someone else about all of this. And since all of our money is in joint accounts, he'll see the checks going out to a therapist. Or an attorney, for that matter. Besides, I still—"

"You still love him?" Chessa didn't miss the incredulity in her friend's voice.

"Yes. No. I don't know. I still want to be his wife. And not just because I'm a senator's wife or because I might become the First Lady. I fell in love with who he is, or who I thought he was, not for what he might become. I just don't know who he is anymore. I swore when my parents got divorced that I would never get married unless I planned to stay in that marriage forever, no matter what."

"Yeah, yeah, for better or worse, sickness and health and all that."

"Well, according to the Twelve-Step program he is sick. They say hate the disease, not the person. I just need a way to cope with all of this."

"Well, you know I'm not super religious or anything but I guess there's always prayer. And you can talk to me whenever you want. I'll always listen. Maybe I can be your fairy god-sister."

Chessa laughed through fresh tears. "That's a deal. And you're right—one of the things I heard at the Al-Anon meeting was the three Cs: You didn't cause the disease, you can't cure it, and you can't control it. I just need to lean on a Higher Power. I feel like I lost God somewhere along the way and I need to reconnect."

"I'll pray for you too. 'Cause you know I got connections girl!"

"Thank you, Sister!" Chessa laughed, appreciative of her friend's humor.

"Amen, Sister!"

She always knows how to make me feel better.

But once again Chessa's hopes that her husband would change and things would get better were quickly dashed.

Darren was tipsy but not full-blown drunk when he arrived home a little after seven the night after his big announcement. He had gone to celebrate with his campaign staff and a few political cronies.

Chessa got up to give him a hug and kiss, telling him she had a casserole warming in the oven.

"I'm not hungry for anything but you," he said with a slight slur. His breath smelled of mint and just a hint of bourbon. He held her tighter and started kissing her neck, and then her mouth.

Chessa was caught off guard and tried to catch her breath, trying to push him away for a moment.

"What's a matter, baby, aren't you hungry too?" Not giving her a chance to respond, he pulled her close and clutched her hair in his hand, drawing her face to his, kissing her hard. Before she knew it, he was scooping her up and laying her down on the living room couch and unzipping his pants.

Caught completely off-guard, Chessa's mind reeled. *This is not what I want,* she realized. *I'm not ready.* But it didn't matter.

"Darren, I'm not…" The protest formed in her head and got stuck in her throat and those were the only words that escaped as Darren ignored her, silencing her with his mouth, his body holding her down. *I'm not in the mood.* A battle played out in her mind.

He's your husband.

Yes, and you're his wife, not his plaything.

You should please him.

Yes, but what about me?

It was over in a matter of minutes. Chessa had just succumbed, silencing her thoughts, stuffing down her feelings. Now she felt used and ashamed. And angry at Darren and especially at herself. *He should have stopped. He should have noticed what I wanted and what I didn't want. But he didn't care. All he cared about was himself and what he wanted. Still, this is all my fault. I should have stopped him.*

She lay there and drew up a blanket to cover herself. But no amount of blankets could take away the chill nor cover up how naked she felt.

Darren merely stood up and wordlessly zipped his pants, straightened his shirt and smoothed his hair. "Now I could go for that casserole," he said, and turned to walk into the kitchen.

Chessa tried hard not to think about what happened as she made follow-up phone calls the next day at work to the women who had called into Safe Horizon to get an appointment with a counselor or join a support group.

These women have real problems, she kept telling herself, focusing on each caller as if she were a personal friend or relative asking for help.

Every once in a while she would think of the poor women and young girls in Africa or in the Middle East. Some of them were being traded as slaves, held hostage, married off way too young, gang-raped by soldiers, brutally beaten, maimed, or mutilated. It didn't make Chessa feel any better about her own situation; it just took her mind off of it. And it helped keep her focused on why she wanted—needed—to become First Lady. She could make a real difference that way. *It's my calling. No one said it would be easy.*

One of the calls that came in surprised her. It was Stephanie, calling to see how she was doing.

Chessa explained to her cousin-in-law that she wouldn't be attending any more meetings. "I'll be super busy helping Darren with his campaign, on top of my work here," she told her.

"But you need to take care of you," Stephanie argued. "This is because Darren found out and asked you not to come anymore, right?"

Chessa was silent.

"Well, you tell that egomaniac that you're an adult and he's not your boss. Or better yet, don't tell him anything at all. They have noon meetings just down the road from where you work. We could go on your lunch break. He'll never know."

"Yeah, but Dorothy or Deborah might find out."

"Oh, so those two are on your case about it too, huh? I should have known. They need the program more than you, but they'll never admit that. Chessa, please don't let them drag you down into their sickness. I promise you none of them will ever find out, even if I have to kill somebody."

Chessa didn't laugh.

"That's a joke. Seriously, though, we've all been in your shoes; we all understand. That's why it's called an 'anonymous' program. You never need to mention any names. You can come in disguise if you want and just sit and listen."

"But everyone knows who I am now that my husband is running for president. Eventually, even if I wore a bag over my head, people would find out."

"Okay, at the very least, please keep talking to me. I know what you're dealing with. If you keep it all bottled up, you're going to explode, and what good will that do anyone? We can work the steps together over the phone."

Chessa realized she was right. *I can trust her. She's on my side.*

"Okay, I'll call you on my lunch break tomorrow," Chessa agreed. "We have a few rooms there where we can talk confidentially. Domestic violence victims often meet with therapists in them because they're afraid their husbands might find out and come after them."

The irony of what she just said struck her like a lead pipe between the eyes.

"Don't worry. You'll find peace and happiness again whether you stay with him or not. Just remember, keep detaching with love. And don't let him cross your boundaries."

I don't even have any boundaries, Chessa realized. *I never had any to begin with. That wasn't something they taught you in school. Or something I learned at home.*

"Okay, I'm throwing too much at you all at once," Stephanie said softly in response to Chessa's silence. "We'll get there. Just remember, one day at a time, and easy does it. I love you."

Chessa said good-bye and hung up before the tears of guilt and grief that stung her eyes started to fall.

CHAPTER EIGHT

LEIF

Leif Mitchell had become a frequent flier to Washington DC, visiting President Greene and his daughter Wendy usually once every two or three weeks after their Christmas get-together.

He had felt guilty for weeks after their illicit tryst in his White House bedroom. So to make it up to her, and since he was old-fashioned, he courted Wendy, bringing her flowers and gifts and asking her on "dates" even if it was just to see a movie or go bowling in the White House.

He had tried to talk to Wendy about the night they had been intimate. He wanted to tell her he felt guilty that he had given in to his base desires when he wasn't sure how deeply he felt about her yet. But each time he broached the subject, she cut him off and said she didn't want to talk about it, that she was fine with what happened and where they were in their relationship.

The couple soon started staying indoors, as it didn't take long for the media—especially the tabloids and entertainment magazines—

to pick up on the fact that the president's daughter and the governor of Kentucky were an item.

The two of them had to literally hide themselves away on Valentine's Day, which they planned to celebrate with an intimate dinner in the president's private dining room.

Leif had met earlier that day with Martin Greene to speak to him about the progress of the Governors' Task Force on the Middle East, which had convened and was in the early stages of writing a report.

He arrived a few minutes early in the private dining room for his appointed date with Wendy and stood waiting by the table, which was already set by the White House staff with linens, fine china and silverware, stemmed crystal goblets, and a fresh bouquet of red roses.

Leif whistled appreciatively when Wendy walked in the room. She was wearing a deep-red sweater dress that hugged her curves and set off her blond tresses, which fell in waves onto her shoulders.

Always the gentleman, Leif pulled out her chair and bowed, holding his cowboy hat in his hand.

Wendy's eyes lit up when Leif presented her with a card and a small gift box. In it was a pair of garnet and diamond earrings.

"So does this mean it's serious?" Wendy asked with a faint tease, although her question sounded sincere for a girl who was rarely serious.

Leif hesitated, unsure of what she meant. "I believe it does," he answered.

The waiter brought them a bottle of cabernet, but when Leif went to pour the wine into their glasses, Wendy held up her hand. "None for me, thanks. I'm on a special diet."

Leif stared at her curiously, setting down the bottle. "Why? You look beautiful just the way you are. But, okay, I won't have any either." He took a sip of his water.

After their meals arrived and they began eating, the formality between them that seemed to emanate from their surroundings began to wear off and their usual comfortable banter filled the room, although Wendy remained a bit more reserved than usual.

"You know, I'd really love for you to come to Lexington and see the farm, and, of course, meet my family." Leif pushed his finished plate aside and reached out his right hand across the table to hold her left one.

"I would like that." Wendy smiled.

"And I could teach you to ride."

"I'm not sure about that."

"Why not? I bet you'd love it. There's nothing like galloping through the open fields, the wind whipping through your hair, your heart racing. It's such a rush."

"I don't know if it would be safe . . ."

Leif looked at her perplexed.

". . . for the baby."

Although she had only eaten half of what was on her plate, Wendy put down her fork and looked expectantly at Leif, waiting for his response, her brown eyes sparkling.

Leif swallowed hard. "Are you saying what I think you're saying? Are you..."

"Pregnant. Uh-huh." Wendy gave him a small, mischievous smile. "Obviously it happened the one night we were together in your room. I guess you have, um, strong swimmers."

Leif sat for what seemed like minutes, looking down at his hands in his lap, not saying a word. His forehead creased with concern.

Wendy's exuberant expression was dampened with guilt. "I'm sorry, Leif, I didn't realize it was that time. This wasn't on purpose; I swear I didn't plan this." Her voice started to rise with fear. "Please say something."

Leif didn't know what to say, his face belying the thoughts and emotions whirling about in his head like a twister. "We're going to have a baby." He stared ahead as one would upon seeing an apparition before him. It was as if saying the words would force his shocked brain to accept the reality of the situation. "A baby." He sat silently again, frowning in consternation.

Wendy started to cry, which snapped Leif into action. He got up and went over to her, kneeling on the carpeted floor before her. He took a cloth napkin and gently wiped away her tears. "I'm sorry; I'm just surprised, that's all. Are you sure? How far along?"

"Yes, I'm sure." Wendy sniffed back any remaining tears. Her tone became flat and a little defensive. "About eight weeks... I took a test when I missed my time of the month. This is a surprise to me too. If you want me to do something about it, you know, get an abortion . . ."

Leif reacted to the word as if he had just seen a huge, poisonous snake. "No! I would never ask you to do that. It's against my faith and everything I believe. I just need time to process this. Come up with a plan." Leif stood and started pacing around the table.

"But you're not happy about it, are you?" Wendy's tone bordered on anger now.

Leif stopped and looked blankly at her. "Are you?"

"I don't know. I thought I could be, but now I'm not so sure, since you obviously aren't. I bet you think this is all my fault." She stood, slapped her linen napkin onto the table, took the small gift box and threw it in his direction, just missing him. "You can have the earrings back. I'm going to my room."

Leif stared at her with a helpless look. "I'm sorry. I'm not blaming you. Let's sit back down and talk rationally about this. I'm sure we can come up with something."

But Wendy was already headed toward the door.. "I'm sorry my Valentine's Day 'gift' wasn't exactly what you wanted," she shot back at him, her voice dripping with sarcasm. "Good night, Leif. We can talk 'rationally' over the phone about this. Call me when you get back to Kentucky." And with that, she walked out.

Leif called her cell phone every morning and every night for the next three weeks, but Wendy refused to answer. Meanwhile, he still had a state to run, a staff to manage, constituents to cater to and lobbyists to deal with if he wanted to get anything done, so he couldn't just fly out to see her and make things right.

He had always believed in God's omnipotence, but he had to try really hard not to question God's plan and His wisdom this time. Still, he got down on his knees every morning and every night to pray for His pardon and guidance.

Leif realized he had sinned and believed he was now suffering — if not God's wrath — than certainly at least the consequences of his actions. Any way Leif looked at it, the situation wasn't good.

One day in prayer, Leif believed he heard God answer him. He suddenly knew there was only one thing to do. As soon as his schedule cleared for a day and he could get on Martin Greene's calendar, Leif was on another plane to Washington.

He had asked to meet with the president, since his daughter wouldn't answer her phone. He also asked Martin to keep their meeting confidential, not giving him any hint of why he wanted to meet but saying it was imperative.

Fortunately the media had backed off of Leif's visits to see President Greene or Wendy, since they had become a common occurrence and were no longer big news.

The two men met alone behind closed doors in the Oval Office. Leif broke the news of the pregnancy and his plan to the president as gently as possible. It was extremely difficult, since Wendy had obviously not told her father anything. When they were finished, Martin summoned his daughter.

Her faced turned pale and her expression showed sheer surprise as she stepped into her father's office and saw that Leif was there.

"Close the door behind you." Martin didn't leave room for his daughter to object, and in that instant, she saw that her father knew everything. The president stood up from where he was sitting behind his desk and quietly walked toward the door, his face not registering any emotion. "I believe you two should talk in private." And with that, he left them alone, warily facing one another.

"You told him?" Wendy's eyes glittered with angry accusation. "You shouldn't have told him. You should have let me tell him."

"I needed to ask his permission."

"For what?"

And from ten feet away from where she was defiantly standing with her arms crossed, Leif knelt down on one knee in the center of the carpet's presidential seal and pulled out the same small box he had given her when he last saw her at their Valentine's Day dinner.

"I told you I don't want those earrings." Wendy didn't budge.

"They're not earrings." Leif opened the box revealing a small gold band with a large white diamond. "Wendy Greene, I've come to ask you to be my wife. Will you marry me?"

Wendy put her hands up to her face in unabashed glee. "Now I don't know what to say."

"Say yes." Leif stood and crossed the distance between them, took the ring out of the box, and slipped it onto her left ring finger.

"Yes!" Wendy threw her arms around his neck, hugging him tight.

When she finally released him to marvel at the diamond on her hand, she became more subdued. "Did Daddy say yes? I'm assuming you asked him for his blessing?"

"He was taken by surprise, that's for sure. And he wasn't all too pleased with me. But somehow, after he mulled over the news and my request, he calmed down and seemed to accept it all. He said he'd worry about the press and how to handle presenting it to the rest of the world. And that he'd tell your mother."

As if on cue, they heard a knock on the door. "Come in," they said in unison, and Martin and Carol spilled into the room, offering hugs and congratulations.

Leif didn't tell his wife-to-be that her father had cut a deal in return for his blessing of their marriage.

The president had seemed truly shocked at the news of the baby, and then his surprise turned to anger, which he unsuccessfully tried to hide. But after much contemplation, Martin told Leif he would offer his blessing of the marriage and the baby if Leif provided his unwavering support for his future father-in-law's presidency and any of his current or future objectives.

Although he had been taken aback by Martin's request, Leif agreed, glad to be a political ally of the most powerful man in the world, even if he wasn't presently the most popular.

They all decided together to announce the engagement right away, to try to keep the wedding small and unobtrusive, and to keep the baby a secret as long as possible.

President Greene's press secretary called a reliable yet well-known reporter with the *Washington Post* to publish the White House statement on the engagement, which was in turn the main topic on the next evening's network news and was, of course, featured on the cover of every newspaper and magazine, on every talk show and on every social media site known to man in weeks to come.

The wedding details weren't revealed yet since they hadn't been decided upon, so the phones rang constantly in the White House, at the governor's mansion, at Little River farm, and even in Logan Reese's office stationed at Leif's old campaign headquarters.

Wendy asked her parents if they could have a small wedding in the Rose Garden.

"Are you sure you don't want something unique?" Her mother proceeded to tell her youngest daughter about Tricia Nixon's wedding there in 1971, the only wedding that had ever taken place in the Rose Garden besides that of Hillary Rodham Clinton's brother and the only White House wedding of a president's daughter. Tricia Nixon's marriage ceremony had gone down in the history books as a huge, glorious event. "I don't know how we can live up to that," Carol Greene said.

"I'm sure we can," Wendy said confidently. "Besides, who will remember what happened here over fifty years ago?"

Wendy had asked her older sister Victoria to be her maid of honor. Since Leif had three brothers and didn't know which one to choose lest he show partiality and cause a family squabble, he decided to ask Wendy's brother, Jordan. The two of them had bonded in the past several months after they had gone out for drinks one night during one of Leif's visits when Wendy had had other plans.

Jordan was a big fan of Leif's music, and the two of them became fast friends. At first Leif had been skeptical that Jordan could become a friend, thinking that he would either be too much like his dad, always the politician, or might be resentful that his father seemingly spent more time with Leif than he did with his own son.

Yet Jordan was completely unlike his father. He was equally as handsome as his father, with his tall, athletic good looks, and he was just as intelligent to be sure, having graduated cum laude from Cornell University. But he was different in personality and character. Jordan was unassuming, down-to-earth, laid back, more refined and had a kinder, gentler side.

And he told Leif he wanted nothing to do with politics. Jordan was content being the undersecretary for history, art, and culture of the Smithsonian museums. It wasn't as significant as being a governor, nor what his father apparently had planned for him, but it wasn't a small job by any means. Jordan told Leif his hope was to become the secretary, or chief of administration, of the Smithsonian, but he needed a few more years of experience.

Leif began to think God's plan really was working; through the baby they had created he would be gaining a beautiful wife, a brother who had become his best friend, and parents who happened to be the president and First Lady of the United States. He was starting to like the added attention and favor he was getting, which he knew would be sure to continue when the baby was born.

But God's plan changed.

Three weeks after the engagement announcement, Wendy started experiencing cramping and bleeding and had a miscarriage in her twelfth week.

Wendy and her family were devastated. Leif was also disappointed, not realizing how much he had been looking forward to being a father. While technically he was no longer obligated to marry Wendy and the invitations had not gone out yet, Leif still felt it was the right thing to do. He did love her, even though he wasn't sure if he had when they first started dating.

Leif tried to comfort her and help her through the next few weeks of grief she experienced. He flew between Kentucky and Washington DC two or three times a week, staying at the White House for a day or two, or as long as he could before needing to return to work.

Sometimes they would just sit in the family parlor and he would hold her while they watched TV or a movie, not talking much but quietly sharing each other's sorrow. Wendy would often fall asleep in his arms and he would carry her to her bedroom and then retire himself in a guest room.

She recuperated after just a few days physically, but it took her weeks to recover emotionally. She had become dangerously thin, her hair was dull and there were constant gray circles under her eyes. Martin and Carole Greene arranged to have their daughter see a counselor, which seemed to help.

Still, while she gained her weight back and started sleeping through the night, Wendy seemed to become a different girl afterward. Gone was her frivolous, fun-loving, flirtatious manner. Wendy emerged more mature, although also more serious and cynical than she had been before.

The only thing that really helped lift her out of her depression was planning the wedding. She became driven to get on with it, and within the month, she was standing with Leif in front of the minister before their immediate family and a hundred close friends in the Rose Garden, professing their marriage vows.

Fortunately, they all fit under the tent that had been erected when the weather forecast called for April rain showers. Unlike Tricia Nixon, who had been lucky to have the rain stop and the clouds part just in time for her ceremony, Wendy walked down the runner without much fanfare to the sound of raindrops splashing on the tent above and could only see some of the gorgeous landscaping from under the tent.

The rain also served to completely obstruct the media's coverage of the event. While the president's Secret Service had blocked the press from getting onto the White House grounds, they couldn't prevent aerial coverage. But all the television public saw was the top of the huge white tent. They would have to be content with photos provided by the president's press secretary. Of course all attendees had been made to leave their cell phones, cameras and any other recording devices at the entrance to the event for later return by security.

A private reception followed in the East Room with dinner and dancing to a string quartet. Most of the plans had been arranged by Carol Greene. Leif had offered to play at the reception, but Carol graciously declined, advising he should relax and enjoy himself instead.

One photo taken at the reception by someone in attendance who had apparently snuck in their cell phone past security was immediately texted to the media and became the most depicted picture of the wedding to adorn newspaper front pages, magazine covers, computer and television screens; it showed the happy groom and his bride smiling at the camera during their first dance, with the president and the First Lady standing in the background looking on. Leif looked dashing in a black tux and his signature black cowboy hat. His arms encircled the waist of his bride in her strapless, flowing white satin gown.

But the camera also caught Martin Greene's expression; he had a stern look on his face, almost a grimace or frown, and his arms were crossed in front of him, while Carol Greene smiled benignly, her hands clasped in front of her. One bold headline above the photo on a blog read "Son-in-Law a Threat to the Throne?" The clip went viral and was later played up in comedy acts and on late-night talk shows.

It also started a buzz for the next several weeks about the possibility that Leif Mitchell might be next in line for the presidency, perhaps before Martin was ready to give it up. After all, the president was only finishing up his first term, and Leif was already vastly more popular than his incumbent father-in-law.

Saturday Night Live even did a spoof featuring actors playing the president and his son, in which Martin unsuccessfully tried to talk Jordan into running for the presidency before Leif did, then conspired with him to poison the Kentucky governor by lacing his mint julep with cyanide.

President Greene was livid at the license these shows took at his expense, but knew he should do nothing but ignore it. After much experience he realized that if he tried to debate the media he would draw even more attention to their folly and their jabs at him would simply become all the more blatant. But he was sorely tempted. His press secretary told him it was normal and would pass. "Bush had it way worse," his secretary said, trying to comfort his boss.

The newlyweds spent their wedding night in the White House and Wendy moved into the governor's mansion the next day.

There wasn't time for a honeymoon, Leif told his new wife. The end of the state's legislative session was looming and he was behind in signing bills and meeting with legislators, lobbyists, officials, and constituents. On top of that, the Kentucky Derby was only two weeks away, and he not only needed to be there to represent the state but had also been asked to sing "My Old Kentucky Home," the famous official state song. In addition, one of the Derby horses was owned by Emir Ali bin Al Thani of Qatar, who would be visiting the United States to watch his Arabian stallion and meet with Governor Mitchell as part of the governors' task force project.

As the town car pulled up to the private entrance of the governor's mansion, Wendy looked at her new home in awe. "I'll feel right at home," she remarked happily. "It's like a mini White House!"

Indeed, the architecture was similar. Both houses dated back to the early twentieth century, and like the White House, the huge mansion served both as a private residence and a public building that was open for tours.

"It still feels too formal to me," Leif said as they walked into the foyer. "Why don't we just drop our bags off and I'll take you somewhere really special. I want you to come meet all the folks at Little River."

"But, darling, this is going to be our new home," Wendy protested. "I at least want to look around."

"There isn't much to see, since I haven't even been here that long and it's just me living here. It really does need a woman's touch." Leif put his arms around his new bride, smiling down at her. "Since we have the rest of our lives together, and since my parents actually invited us for dinner, why don't we go to Little River for the evening, then tomorrow you can get started redecorating?"

"Well, now I'm nervous. Is your whole family going to be there?"

"I was going to surprise you, but yes, they want to properly welcome you to Kentucky. And I have something else special to show you."

Leif stood next to Wendy gazing into the stall of Phillip's Pride, the colt that Little Sally had carried to term over four years ago and that Henry Mitchell had named after his son since Leif had saved its life. The farmhands and trainers called him "Phil" for short.

"He's beautiful, isn't he?" Leif admired the stallion's red chestnut coat, stroking the white streak on his nose. "He didn't win last year in the Derby, but he didn't do too badly either. He's won a few purse races and I'm sure he's got a few more in him before we put him out to stud."

They heard a whinny at the end of the stalls. "That's Little Sally," Leif said with a grin. "Come on, I'll introduce you." Wendy gingerly walked along the hay-strewn stables. She hadn't dressed for Leif's special surprise and had worn her high-heeled pumps. Leif proudly walked his wife up to his favorite horse's stall.

The mare stood warily eyeing the strange woman who accompanied her friend.

"She's a beauty too, huh?"

Wendy didn't seem impressed. "What? Oh yes, she is." She shivered in the night air. They had come from dinner with Leif's family over to the barn before it got too late and the horses were asleep. "I should have changed first. Ugh!" Wendy took a step to get closer to Leif so he could warm her up, and the heel of her pump squished into a pile of manure. "This is disgusting! Can we leave now?"

Leif laughed, putting his arm around her and helping her out of the muck. "I guess this isn't your thing, is it?"

"Not exactly."

"Just give me a minute to say good-bye and we'll go." Leif took off his dinner jacket and put it around Wendy's shoulders. He turned just in time to miss his wife rolling her eyes impatiently. She stood waiting with her arms crossed and a scowl on her face as he entered the stall. Leif stroked Little Phil's mane for a minute and the horse looked at him curiously with big, liquid-brown eyes.

"Your mom did good." Leif spoke softly, fondly to him. "And I bet you're going to sire a winner one day."

Derby Day arrived and Leif had so much on his plate that he was secretly glad Little River didn't have a Derby horse to race that year. He needed to remain impartial and he had to play host to the emir, the royal monarch from Qatar, bearing in mind the independent Arabian country was one of the largest producers of oil and gas in the world, not to mention one of the Middle East countries that fell under Leif's special "project" as head of the governors' task force.

After a breakfast with the emir and his entourage, Leif addressed the media assembled in the pressroom at Churchill Downs with the normal speech about how much the Derby meant to Kentucky, and how privileged he was to be the governor of such a fine state.

Then it was time to take the microphone on the platform in the infield, and address the crowd and the news media from around the world.

Although she didn't like horses, Wendy did revel in the international attention she received as the First Lady of Kentucky that fine Derby Day. Some of her pride and spunk even returned.

She stood flashing the adoring public her gorgeous smile as she stood dutifully at Leif's side, dressed glamorously in a wide-brimmed white hat with red roses that matched her red-and-white polka-dotted dress cinched at her slim waist with a red leather belt. She had been tanning, which set off her blond hair and brown eyes, and the cameras seemed to linger as much on Wendy Mitchell as they did on the four-legged Derby contestants. Wendy seemed in her element, cheerfully sipping Mint Juleps and chatting with the media.

Logan Reese was close by on the platform and handed Leif his guitar when it came time for him to sing. Leif approached the mike to thunderous applause, smiled and waved, looking dashing in his black suit, red tie, and white cowboy hat. He wore a single red rose in his lapel.

When he started strumming the tune and the first words of the lyrics, "The sun shines bright in my old Kentucky home," Leif forgot that he was the governor, the host to Arab royalty, or the president's son-in-law. It was as if he was transported back in time to when he was just a country-rock singer playing for small audiences at taverns or at gatherings on the horse ranch. He went back in his heart to when life was simple and he was just a farmhand tending to the horses. The melancholy in his voice was overpowered, however, by the accompaniment of the University of Louisville marching band which traditionally still played the song at the Derby as it had for nearly the past century, and by the sellout crowd, which sang along as the horses, mounted by their jockeys, strode by in the post parade.

"The one-hundred-and-forty-second Run for the Roses is about to get underway after a brilliant performance of "My Old Kentucky Home" by Governor Leif Mitchell . . ." The NBC sports announcer's voice faded as President Greene turned down the volume on the big-screen TV in the president's quarters living room, where he had been watching the Derby coverage.

He had watched with growing envy as Governor Mitchell triumphantly held hands in the air with Emir Ali bin Al Thani, walked to the infield with a radiant Wendy, melodiously crooned the state anthem with the Louisville band, and was lauded and applauded by over a hundred and fifty thousand attendees and millions more who watched, just as he, the president, did, on their television sets or electronic devices around the globe.

"Wendy adores him, doesn't she?" Carol Greene walked into the room and made her statement before noticing the deep frown lines across her husband's forehead as he stared at the screen.

"Everyone adores him." Martin Greene clicked off the set from a remote in his hand and turned around to face his wife, anger and frustration clouding his eyes. "It's almost as if he's got some kind of Midas touch, or he's God's chosen one. I just don't get it. It's just not fair. Our daughter loves him more than she does me, our son is closer to him than he is to his own father, the media idolize him, and he's more popular now with his music being on the hit charts than I am as the president of the United States of America. In fact, I'd say if he were to run against me one day, he'd probably win, even though the amount of political experience he has could fit on the tip of my little finger." Martin was pacing now, and held up his pinky finger for effect.

"Well, that will never happen, so don't go fretting over it." Carol Greene tried to soothe her husband's ruffled pride. "And he can never take your place as Wendy's and Jordan's father. As for your popularity, you are in the most powerful position in the world, and you know with that comes a lot of people who want to take you down. No president has ever had much more than a fifty percent popularity rating. Americans, even those who vote for you, are fair-weather friends. When they become even slightly irritated with the economy, or anything else for that matter, they go out of their way to support the next guy who comes along. I think you're doing a fine job. You're a great father, a great leader, and one heck of a husband." She slid her arm around her husband's waist, but he stood stiffly in her embrace, his chin in his hand, mulling over the situation.

"Yes, but there's more to it than that. I have put Leif Mitchell where he is today and no one knows it. Not only that, he is totally ungrateful. So I get no credit whatsoever and he gets all the glory. It's almost like the higher he rises, the lower I seem to fall. He's like my albatross." Martin shrugged off his wife's arms and stood with his hands resolutely on his hips. "I need to get rid of him."

Carol looked at him with concern. "What do you mean?"

Martin smiled at his wife with the knowing look of a parent talking to a child. "Well, if you were thinking I was going to off him, that's not what I meant. No, I mean send him away, get him away from me so he's not constantly making me look bad by his looking so good."

"Don't you think that's being a little paranoid? Are you really that jealous if him? That doesn't sound like the confident man I married."

Martin frowned again, angry at the one person who unconditionally stood by his side. "No, I don't think it's paranoid, and I'm offended you'd say such a thing. I think you're the one who's paranoid. What harm will it do if I, say, send him over to a foreign country for a first-hand observation of how his work on the governor's task force might benefit the US?" An idea struck Martin, and a righteous grin lit up his face. "Not just any foreign country, though. I'm going to send him to Israel on a peace mission."

"Why Israel?" Carol was working hard to keep the worry out of her voice.

"Because it's such a battle zone right now that there's no way he can come out of there unscathed, much less successful as a hero this time. The Israelis won't welcome him because they're not happy with us right now, and the Palestinians will think he's being a traitor. He'll be lucky if he gets out of there alive. But don't worry, I'm sure with his luck he'll be fine."

"Martin, what about our daughter?" Now Carol's tone was tinged with panic.

"She'll be fine too. Like you said, she's got me . . . us to rely on. She can even move back in if she wants to."

"I don't like it." Carol was pleading now, but the stern look her husband gave her told her that her attempts to sway him were futile. Still, she had to try. "Please don't do this, Martin. Maybe you can send him somewhere else, or maybe things will settle down and Leif and Wendy will have a baby. That will divert his attention."

"No, that would bring him even more attention. A baby would make things even worse."

"That baby would be our grandchild!" She touched his shirtsleeve but he sloughed off her hand like it was a pesky mosquito.

"Carol, this time you're wrong, and you're not going to change my mind. I'm finished discussing it. It's been a long day, and I have a lot of thinking to do. I'm going to the kitchen for a snack and then to bed early. Tomorrow's a new day, and I have a lot to consider. I am the president of the United States, after all."

Carol watched with a dumbfounded look as Martin strutted out of the room.

CHAPTER NINE

CHESSA

With the deregulation of most of the limits on campaign fundraising and the increases in media advertising and other expenses to make a successful run, the cost of a presidential candidacy had risen to an estimated one billion dollars.

As in the past, it would usually take someone who was very rich or someone extremely popular to vie for president. But with the controversial and sweeping deregulation of the Supreme Court's 2010 Citizens United decision lifting limits on corporate contributions, a successful candidate could also be someone who had the financial backing from a very wealthy company. In the Citizens v. United case, The Supreme Court had ruled that candidates, through SuperPACS, could raise unlimited funding through wealthy corporations.

Thus, Senator Darren Richards was among the elite who had everything going for him. He had curried enough favor among his colleagues in Congress to get a popular backing in almost all fifty states. He had his own trust fund his parents had set up, making him a multimillionaire in his own right. And he had the financial backing of his daddy's company, RA Technologies—the biggest biopharmaceutical corporation in the world.

Chessa had heard the family joke that her husband came out of the womb with a political agenda in his tiny hands. His mother would fondly recall that when he was just five, little Darren would stand on an upside-down milk crate, pretending it was a political soapbox. He would address his "audience," which would consist of family members who would indulge him, or stuffed animals that he would line up the way a little girl might for a pretend tea party.

Dorothy Richards often said she believed he got his activist nature from his grandfather, her daddy, who would sit Darren on his knee and tell him stories about how the Yankees defeated the Confederates, about Abraham Lincoln, and about his own membership in the American Legion.

"His granddaddy would say, 'Darren, you're going to be somebody important, like good old Abraham Lincoln, one day; I just know it'," Dorothy often regaled. "And sure enough, he was right."

Darren had run for class president in his freshman year of high school and had come home nearly in tears after losing to a girl. His grandfather had chastised him that day when he came to visit for dinner. "Maybe I was wrong about you, boy," he had said gruffly. "No grandson of mine would lose to a girl, and then come home blubbering about it."

Humiliated, Darren turned his anger over that loss into a fierce determination to win at all costs. He went on to defeat the same girl in his sophomore year for the top position of student council president, a position he kept until he graduated. He never told his mother, nor his grandfather, that he had publicly humiliated the girl to win by posting a photo a buddy had secretly taken of her sitting on the toilet in the girls' restroom.

Darren called his father to arrange an early meeting one morning in his stunning glass-ensconced office in RA's high-rise corporate headquarters on Manhattan's Third Avenue.

With his status as both heir-apparent and US Senator, Darren easily slipped through the lobby's security force with a smile and a nod, rode the elevator to the fifty-first floor, and stepped out into familiar territory: the highly modern gray granite walls and floors that made up the upper echelon offices of the president, CEO, CFO, and staff.

He was greeted warmly by the middle-aged yet attractive receptionist who led him back to his father's domain, which never failed to impress Darren with its floor-to-ceiling windows that provided a spectacular panorama of Manhattan's East Side.

Donald Richards was on the phone, apparently with a very important client, and motioned for his son to have a seat in one of the leather chairs that surrounded his behemoth mahogany desk.

". . . and I'm telling you let us worry about the negative press. We've dealt with a lot worse and come out better than ever. You just worry about all the profits you'll make once this new drug is put on the market. And say hello to the wife for me. We'll have to get together for dinner soon. Listen, I have to run, the future president of the United States just came into my office." Donald looked at Darren and winked but didn't smile. The crease between his eyebrows that lingered even after he hung up the phone belied that he was obviously concerned about something.

Darren and his father both remained seated, not bothering with an embrace or even a handshake. It wasn't their style to waste time with pleasantries when it came to family, unless they needed to put on a show.

"So what brings you here this morning, Darren? My secretary said you didn't want to say ahead of time what this meeting's about, but I think I can guess. You need some money for the campaign, I bet." The king of the RA empire reached into his desk drawer and withdrew his checkbook. "How much?"

Darren shifted uncomfortably in his chair. "Dad, you could at least let me ask. But I guess a hundred million would be enough to get me started."

Donald Richards's eyes narrowed and the crease deepened. "Maybe you haven't been following the news about our industry, son. Not only are we coming out of this recession, but that little blue pill called Viagra that makes millions of men and women happy and that has made us billions of dollars is now being made generically by our competition. We're losing millions as we speak."

Darren had half expected the lecture from his father. One always came with every request, even throughout his childhood. When he asked to borrow twenty dollars at the age of eleven to put toward a model train set, he was told "neither a borrower nor a lender be" and had to work it off washing his dad's Buick and raking leaves. When he borrowed two hundred dollars at the age of sixteen to put toward a car, he had to sit through what seemed like an hour's lecture on car maintenance. And when he was given money to go to college, his dad never let up on asking about his grades and telling him of his expectations.

So he was ready to engage in the ensuing discussion. "Surely you're looking at other venues to combat the loss and be even more profitable?"

"Well, son, in fact we are, and we have discussed funding your campaign, although not to the tune of a hundred mil. I can't make these decisions alone, you know. But I'm sure I can swing it past the powers that be on the Board, if you can help us in return." His father, looking every bit the corporate president with his tanned good looks, graying hair, and expensive Italian suit, stood and stretched his tall and husky frame. He was still in good shape for a 67-year-old, although too many cocktail parties had given him a small gut. "I'll tell you what. I can cover half of that today and talk them into the rest after you make some strides to help us on our newest frontier."

"What's that?"

"You've heard of egg harvesting?"

"You mean human egg harvesting?"

"I'm not talking about chickens, son." Donald chuckled at his own comment, shaking his head. "We do need a sense of humor in this business. Anyway, let me show you what we've been working on lately."

Minutes later, Donald Richards led his son down a sterile hallway, past a limited-access heavy metal door, and down another hall. Eventually they came to a large plate-glass window overlooking a recessed lab, where three men and two women in white lab coats and facemasks were bent over microscopes and looking at large computer screens.

"As you know, RA is a leader right now in biotechnology and in particular, stem cell research. We are trying to find the latest treatments and possible cures for a myriad of diseases. But what you don't know is that we are really close to achieving a breakthrough with a cure for Type 1 diabetes."

"Wow." Darren looked with awe at his father.

"Wow is right. This could save hundreds of thousands of lives. We've got scientists working in our labs all over the globe right now on this very same project. We only have one problem, and that's where I need your help. In order to continue on, we need more material to conduct our research. We've found the best way to develop a cure is to test stem cells because, by their nature, they have the capacity to develop into many different types of cells and can be manipulated to give rise to potential treatments. But, as you already know, we've taken a lot of heat by religious factions about our massive use of embryonic stem cells, and embryos are getting harder to come by. So we're now using stem cells from zygotes, or newly fertilized eggs, before they become embryos. First of all, they're, in effect, even better to use than embryos because they are brand-new and not yet differentiated, which means they have the capacity to turn into any type of cell at all. And second, the 'heat' we're getting from egg harvest protestors isn't nearly as great as that from anti-abortion and right-to-life groups. Yet." Don paused before his last word, stressing the importance of it.

"So I can help how?" Darren loosened his tie.

"As you know, egg harvesting is legal in most of the fifty United States since federal regulations were passed in 2009. Women are paid for donating their eggs for in-vitro reproduction for couples that can't have babies. A handful of states have recently passed laws, though, banning egg harvesting for research, and some have gone against federal regulations, saying it's illegal for any reason. I'm afraid more states might jump on board if the crazy yahoos still screaming about it have their way. They just don't know that they're interfering with scientific progress and real cures.

"Of course, New York, being the only state to pass legislation legalizing human egg donations for research, has always been a leader, which is why we remain incorporated here. I just need you to lead our country to follow suit by passing federal legislation that's similar to the laws we have here in New York that legalize human egg harvesting for scientific research."

"Dad, just like you, I can't just make decisions and rules on my own, even if I do become president," Darren said warily. "And if the public finds out I'm pushing for stem cell research by my father's company, which just so happens to fund my campaign, it won't sit too well, I'm sure."

"Which is why no one else has to know, son. I'm not saying make it part of your platform. I'm saying get one trusted congressman or senator—maybe one who wants to ride your coattails and wouldn't mind doing you a favor—to introduce a piece of legislation. I'm sure there will be plenty more up there on the Hill to vote it in just to be in your camp. You've got more power than anyone else in the world right now. You can make a difference." Don grasped Darren's arm. "I'm proud of you, son. I know I don't tell you that often, and I know I was disappointed when you didn't join my company and follow in my footsteps, but now I know you have an even greater calling."

Darren knew his father's gestures and words were pure theatrics, and that his motives were entirely self-centered. But, then again, so were his. Still, he had to be careful.

"I have one question Dad. Forgive me if I've been a little busy and haven't been following this issue too closely. I get the anti-abortion stem-cell research protestors. That's been going on for years, and of course part of my platform is my party's stance that a woman has a 'right to choose.' In fact, I'm going to start campaigning on the fact that President Greene has set us back to the Stone Age by making it so hard for young women to voluntarily get abortions. But why is the protest against egg harvesting getting fired up? Surely women still donate their eggs voluntarily and get paid for them, right? In fact, don't they sell them for lots of money? Is there some problem with all of this I don't know about?"

"No one is forcing women to donate their eggs, if that's what you're asking. At least we're not. We can't control what they do over in some backward Third World country. And yes, as far as I know, these women still get paid for their donations. It's just that the need for harvested eggs has risen dramatically since there's more competition than ever before to be the company with breakthrough cures and drugs. RA isn't the only research firm working on this project. So instead of thousands of donor eggs, we need millions. Which means we're encouraging more women to donate, particularly in poor countries where they need the money."

Darren looked at his father still perplexed. "Okay, I still don't see the problem."

"Just like with anything, occasionally a girl has gotten the procedure done at some cheap clinic, by some unlicensed guy who calls himself a doctor, and has become ill or wounded. Then some bleeding-heart woman found out and started spreading the word, forming a protest group, and they called the media, which put it out there on the Internet, and the word started to spread. Now they want to call what we're doing "human egg trafficking." We've got to stop their nonsense before it's too late and millions of people suffer in the long run with diseases that can be cured with our scientific and technological breakthroughs."

Donald's eyes shone with passion now, and he gripped Darren's arm tighter. "You've got to help us. We need to get you in office so we can find a cure. And when we come out with it, none of this other stuff will even matter in the grand scheme of things anymore."

As if on cue, one of the lab technicians looked up through the window and waved at his boss and son, then the rest followed suit.

Donald had a big smile on his face as he waved back, talking through clenched teeth. "Are you with me?"

Darren smiled and waved too. "Yep."

With one last wave, Donald put his arm around his son's shoulders and walked him back down the hall.

They went to lunch at the Ambassador Grill and Lounge in the UN building a few blocks away, and over martinis and overstuffed sandwiches, Donald turned his attention to the subject of Darren's wife, lowering his voice even though they had gotten, upon request, a remote window table. "I understand she was attending Al-Anon meetings?"

Darren turned red with embarrassment. "She stopped once I asked her to."

"Well, she better stay stopped. That whole thing sounds like some women's cult that likes to bash us men just for having a couple of drinks once in a while. It's definitely not good for your image. I think she needs to turn her attention to more, uh, productive things to do with her time."

"What do you have in mind?"

"Darren, you need to use your imagination. Start romancing her again. Take her out to dinner or to a play. Everywhere you turn here in New York there's something to do. Encourage her to visit friends. She does have friends, doesn't she?"

"I only know of Amy, her old roommate who was her maid of honor in our wedding."

"The black girl?"

"Yes, Dad." Darren turned red again as their waitress deposited another round of martinis at their table, embarrassed but not surprised at his father's strong prejudice.

Donald waited until she left before commenting further.

"That one's trouble. Isn't she a reporter now with the *Times*?"

"Uh-huh." Darren gulped down his drink, loosening his tie and wiping a bead of sweat from his brow. "She just moved from Chicago, where she was working for the *Tribune*, back to New York. Chessa said she got some type of great offer. Personally I wish she had just stayed in Chicago. She's another busybody just like Stephanie. I would have taken care of making sure she stayed put if I didn't have a thousand other more important matters to handle." Darren's voice was filled with scorn. He shared his parents' disdain for anyone who they considered lower class, which pretty much included most people of other races and socio-economic status.

"You should have her over for dinner."

"Are you kidding me? You just said she was trouble!"

"Just listen. You could do a little 'information dropping,' give her some tidbits that may fuel a story in your favor, or like they do in hunting, send the dog off the trail with another scent. Feed her some story that takes her time up, but makes her feel like you're helping her out. You'll win your wife over and get her nosy black friend off your tail at the same time. Speaking of tail..." Donald watched as their young blond waitress bent over to retrieve some cash he had 'accidentally' dropped on the floor, and then stared at her backside as she walked away.

Darren stared too. She had smiled at him with a gleam in her eye, recognizing him instantly and fawning over him the entire meal. He clinked glasses with his father and drank down his third martini.

"Romancing my wife, eh? Shouldn't be too hard with that image in my mind." He shared a rare laugh with his dad.

When Chessa returned home after work she was bone tired. It seemed like the phone had rung nonstop that day with calls from young girls who had run away or turned to the streets and needed help. Some of the calls were from young single mothers who had been beaten or were pregnant again and broke, and other calls were from older married women who were stuck in abusive marriages with seemingly no way out. They all needed treatment and counseling, and many needed food and shelter.

During the past year that she had worked at Safe Horizon, Chessa's heart had been broken so many times over these cases that she wondered if it was permanently damaged. Sometimes it seemed that her heart had hardened to the point that she just went through the motions now of listening to the call, giving advice, making the right connection, and finding help from the right resources.

And yet . . . today it somehow broke again over one young rape victim who called. "I know this sounds crazy, but my husband raped me." The tear-choked words still rang in Chessa's ears. "He's been rough before, but this time I said no and he wouldn't stop. He hurt me. And he wasn't sorry. He said this is how it would be from now on. And he threatened that if I ever left him, he would hunt me down and kill me. I know he was drunk, but . . ."

Chessa had to wipe the tears that fell uncontrollably in order to see as she drove. When she pulled into her driveway and opened the garage door, she saw Darren's Porsche gleaming inside. Even though it was Friday and she had been expecting him to come home for the weekend, she still felt the bile of fear rise in her throat, and the nausea of despair claw at her stomach. She found herself saying a silent prayer to a God she felt she hardly knew anymore but still somehow believed in out of sheer desperation. *God, please don't let him be drunk or angry tonight.*

She sighed and walked through the garage door into their spacious kitchen, and her breath was taken away.

Candles were lit on the kitchen dinette where they usually ate together, and everywhere around the room as far as she could see. In the adjacent living room a fire glowed in the fireplace. There was a bouquet of fresh flowers on the kitchen island, and the room smelled of roasted chicken and apple pie, two of her favorites.

Darren had his back to her at the oven, and upon hearing her enter he turned and smiled. "Welcome home, honey. I thought you might have had a hard day, so I figured I'd cook you dinner for a change." He crossed the room, and put his arms around her. Chessa tried not to instinctively recoil and instead let him envelope her. She didn't smell vodka or whiskey or beer. Just a faint smell of aftershave and peppermint.

She wanted with all of her heart to believe this was for real. *Just go with it,* she told herself. *Maybe God actually listened this time.*

After a delicious meal, during which the two of them stuck to pleasant small talk about the highlights of their day, Darren surprised her further. "I know you've been stressed with work and my campaign lately, so I was thinking—why don't you invite your best friend Amy to come over next weekend for dinner or even overnight, however long she can stay. I'll stay out of your way and give you some girl time."

Chessa's mouth gaped open.

"I know I've been a jerk lately and I'm sorry. I want to make it up to you. Get our marriage back on the right footing. Everything's been all about me, and I want to make it more about you."

Amy came for dinner and an overnight stay the following weekend. She sported a new short haircut and had lost weight. With her makeup and navy pants suit, Chessa thought she looked fabulous.

"You're a sight for sore eyes," Chessa said, grinning as she welcomed her best friend through the front door and took her suitcase. "You look fantastic."

"I figured I'd surprise you with my new look." She whistled as she peered around the front foyer and adjoining living room and dining room. "Nice digs. So, is Darren home?"

"No, he's making an alumni appearance at Columbia." Even though he remained in office as a US Senator, now that he had decided to run for president, Darren didn't work as much in DC that summer as he had in the past, keeping busy garnering support for his campaign.

"Hmmm, kind of takes you back, huh? So what came over him to suggest that I come for a visit? I thought he never liked me much."

"He seems to have changed a little lately. He's been the perfect husband. I figured I wouldn't question it." Amy's eyes narrowed with doubt. "Anyway, he'll be home for dinner, so let's not waste time talking about him. Come on out to the sunroom. We have a lot of catching up to do."

The hours passed quickly as the two old friends talked, laughed, looked at old photo albums, and reminisced.

"You look tired," Amy said as they sipped a cup of coffee after lunch.

"Gee, thanks, Amy."

"I don't mean to put you down. I'm just concerned about you."

"I guess I have a lot on my plate that's stressing me out."

"So tell me about it."

Chessa had tried to forego telling Amy again how miserable she had become in her marriage, not wanting to get any looks of pity or hear "I told you so." But the truly compassionate look in her friend's eyes as they sat on the soft leather couch watching the summer sun descend among the trees, painting the sky in soft pinks and blues, drew her emotions out of her, and suddenly she was weeping. Chessa told Amy all about her husband's drinking, her in-laws' contempt and her conflicting emotions. "And yet he really does seem to be changing lately."

Amy just listened, nodding.

The two women were still on the couch talking when Darren walked in the door carrying a bag of groceries and a bouquet of flowers. He'd told Chessa he would fix dinner again, that she didn't have to worry about a thing. Darren bent over and kissed his wife, then gave Amy a hug. "Welcome to our humble abode."

"Humble, my—"

"Amy!" Chessa cut her off, but Darren laughed.

"I know, but wait until you visit us in our next house." Darren winked and went to the kitchen to prepare dinner.

Over chicken marsala and red wine, of which Chessa noticed her husband only had two glasses, Darren asked Amy how she liked her new job at the *Times* and about the stories she was working on.

"Well, we're keeping an eye on you, you know," she said, looking squarely at Darren with a wary smile. "But I'm not covering politics. Right now I'm relegated to some boring stuff about the economy and the environment. Nothing too glamorous, I'm afraid."

"I may have a lead for you," Darren said nonchalantly. Chessa looked at her husband curiously, not noticing her friend's knowing glance. "I'm scheduled tomorrow morning to visit this really cool place called Safe Horizon. Channel Two News wants to do a piece on the work they do there, the fact that they're celebrating their twenty-five-year anniversary of serving our fair city, all the good work they do there, etcetera. Oh, and something about potential First Lady Chessa Richards being one of the staff members there."

"Darren!" Chessa stared at her husband in disbelief. "Why am I just hearing about this now?"

"Because I knew you'd try to get out of it. But I didn't want you to be blindsided either. It's part of the reason I called Amy down."

Chessa turned to Amy. "You *knew* about this and didn't say anything?"

Amy looked at her sheepishly. "Sorry, but I was sworn to secrecy. Don't worry—the story is mainly about the place, not you."

"Oh, well that makes me feel better," Chessa said sarcastically.

"Seriously, Safe Horizon deserves a story for all the people they help, so just be glad you're part of that," Amy said.

"Exactly," Darren agreed, and high-fived Amy across the table.

"You two are actually teaming up against me!" Chessa feigned indignation, but inside she felt confused. She wasn't sure if this strange alliance was a good thing or a bad thing.

"Surprise!" they both yelled in unison.

"You got me."

Chessa did her best to put on a show of humility and delight that her husband and best friend had successfully schemed to surprise her and laud her at work on the news. But she was still suspicious. *Something's not quite right*, she thought. *I just can't put my finger on it.*

CHAPTER TEN

LEIF

Leif was finishing packing his suitcase to take with him when he heard a knock on the front door of the governor's mansion.

Jordan Greene stood on the porch grinning. Leif opened the door and welcomed his brother-in-law into his home, punching him on the shoulder, then giving him a bear hug.

Everything had been arranged. Leif was scheduled to fly to Israel the next day on the US peace mission the president himself had ordained, while Jordan would bring his sister Wendy back to DC to live in the White House while her husband was away.

Jordan had flown down to Capital City Airport in Frankfort in one of the White House's private jets. He planned to spend the night at the governor's mansion and then fly back the next day with his sister.

But Leif noticed Jordan's smile quickly fade into a frown.

"Where's my sister? Is she home?" Jordan looked a bit nervous, standing uncomfortably in the large foyer, his hands jammed into the pockets of his jeans.

"She's upstairs in bed, actually."

"That's odd. It's only seven o'clock. I figured you'd just be finishing dinner."

"She wasn't feeling well today, some kind of stomach bug or something. She might be sleeping, but I can go wake her—"

"No!" Jordan whispered emphatically. "No, I need to talk to you alone."

"All right, we can go to the study."

Jordan followed Leif through the elaborate dining room and hallway into the more conservative but still lavish study. He let out a soft whistle. "Well, it certainly pays to be governor, huh? Maybe I decided prematurely against going into politics."

Leif turned around, his brows raised quizzically.

"I'm just kidding." Jordan smiled his boyish grin.

"Trust me—it doesn't pay, and if I had my way, we'd get rid of half this stuff and donate it to the poor, but you know your sister— she loves it all." Leif motioned for Jordan to have a seat. They sat in two overstuffed chairs, their heads bent forward across the coffee table so they didn't have to raise their voices and risk waking Wendy. "So what's up? Better make it quick, I have a long flight tomorrow, you know."

"You probably won't want to go to Israel after all when I tell you what I know."

"I thought you looked troubled by something. But it can't be big enough for me to cancel my trip."

"That's what you think." Jordan proceeded to tell Leif that he had talked to his father shortly before flying down to Frankfort.

"I was headed over to talk to dad about getting the private jet when I overheard him talking to one of his advisors about lining up the trip for you." Jordan proceeded to tell Leif that as he listened through the partially opened doorway to the Oval Office, he heard his father request the man's confidence, then say that making a big effort to try to strike a peace accord was worth the risk that his son-in-law might get caught in crossfire between Israeli nationalists and Islamic extremists. His father then told the advisor that he hoped his "egotistical son-in-law" would fail so he, the president, could step in and save the day. "In fact," he'd heard his father say in a hushed tone, "I hope he doesn't come back at all, because I'm already tired of that show-off know-it-all stealing my glory all of the time."

Jordan told Leif how he had angrily walked into his father's office and confronted him. With equal ire, Martin Greene lashed out at his son for speaking to him disrespectfully in front of an underling about personal affairs. Once the aide was out of earshot, Jordan pleaded with his father to reconsider sending Leif on the mission.

Martin listened impatiently as Jordan recounted how Leif had carried out the Republican Party's wishes, beating the prizefighter to become governor and then pledging his support to the administration. Martin argued that they were not his wishes so much as those of Ray Silas, and that Leif had embarrassed him more than supported him by showing him up time and again.

Jordan switched tactics and begged his father not to put Leif in harm's way—for the family's sake, for his sister's sake. After about an hour of listening to his begging and pleading, Martin explained to his son that to cancel the trip would bring public humiliation not only to himself and Leif but to the United States, since the Israeli Prime Minister was expecting him. But, Martin assured his son, he would at least make sure his son-in-law was surrounded by extra military guards to ensure his safety.

Although it greatly pained him to do so, Jordan relayed the whole conversation to his friend, who intently listened to him from across the ornate cherry coffee table.

"I'm sure he was just placating me with the safety assurance pledge. He really wants you off his radar screen. I just don't understand why my father is so insanely jealous of you. I'm sorry it's reduced him to being so mean-spirited as to plan something this awful. He is so worried about the upcoming election and his low popularity ratings that he blames you for everything and has made you his scapegoat. Personally, I think he's totally lost his mind. I'm certain once he finds out I've warned you, he'll probably disinherit me or send me off too, probably to Siberia. He does have more power than people think. But I figured it was worth the risk to keep you out of harm's way. I care too much about you to see anything bad happen to you."

"Thank you," Leif said. He cast his eyes down at his hands for several moments, lost in thought, and then looked back up at Jordan. "But I'm still going."

"Didn't you hear what I just said? My father is setting you up. You might get hurt, or worse yet, killed, over there!"

"It's a chance I'll have to take. While I don't approve of your father's means, I believe in the end result we're after, which is to help bring peace between Israel and the Middle East. I have prayed about this every day since your father asked me to go, and I believe God is calling me to do this."

Jordan just sat and looked at Leif wordlessly as seconds and then minutes ticked by on the big grandfather clock in the corner of the room. "Well, I guess you better get packing then." The two men stood and embraced. "Please be careful and come back home." Jordan mustered a brave smile.

"Don't worry, I will. And keep an eye on my wife for me."

"That's a tough assignment, but I'll try." The two laughed and bid each other good night. Leif made sure Jordan was comfortable in a spare room, then headed upstairs to be with his wife. The morning would come soon.

Although there were just as many servants tending to her every need at the governor's mansion as there had been at the White House, Wendy was still happy to be back home with her parents, who seemed to dote on her and pamper her even more than before she had left.

Still, she had come down with a nasty stomach flu that kept her in bed for a few days immediately after she arrived. After two weeks of constant morning sickness, however, she knew it wasn't the flu she had contracted.

Wendy entered her father's study, where her parents were both seated, awaiting her arrival. She had asked ahead of time to have a talk with them, so they sat expectantly watching as she stood before them. She got right to the point.

"Mom, Dad, I'm pregnant again."

Her mother immediately sprang up and gave her daughter a hug. "Oh, Wendy, that's wonderful news! You hear that, Martin, we're going to be grandparents!" She suddenly faced Wendy with concern. "Are you all right? Have you seen a doctor?"

"I've been a little sick, as you know, but haven't seen a doctor yet. I just took the home pregnancy test a few days ago. I was hoping you could go to the doctor with me since Leif is overseas."

"Of course I will."

"I'm sad I won't be able to tell him the news in person," Wendy said hesitantly, glancing at her father. "And I'm a little nervous, I guess. I waited more or less the time period the doctor said to wait to get pregnant again. We actually weren't trying; it just happened, I guess. I'm not really sure how Leif will take it."

"I'm sure Leif will be happy," her mother said, smiling. "We'll have to bring him home soon, right, Martin?"

Martin sat through the entire discussion just staring beyond his wife and daughter, as if not seeing or hearing either one of them.

"Martin?"

Martin Greene spoke to his wife in a low, even voice that seethed with an underlying rage. "If that man really cared about our daughter, he wouldn't have let this happen. He would have taken precautions."

"But I want a baby, Daddy!" Wendy's voice rose an octave.

"I'm sure they both want to start a family," Carol said to Martin as she soothed her daughter with a hug. "Come on, Wendy, you should go rest. I'll fix you some chamomile tea." She looked back at her husband, still seated at his desk, as she was walking out of the study behind Wendy. "Martin, you're being irrational. Everything will be fine. Wendy needs to stay calm, so please try to stay positive about this."

Martin didn't answer but continued to stare, his face a stone mask.

Wendy's announcement couldn't have come at a worse time. Leif received the call from his wife about her pregnancy in the middle of a celebration dinner with Israeli Prime Minister Abel

Rozen, his wife, and his daughter. As politely as he could, he excused himself and took the call from Wendy on his cell phone. He tried to reflect joy and excitement in his voice although it came out strained. After all, he was under an extreme amount of pressure to smooth American-Israeli relations, which meant constantly having his charm and diplomacy on cue. And it was rude to leave his guests in the middle of a meal, especially according to their customs.

He returned to the table and was faced with concerned looks from the women and a frown of annoyance from his host. "Everything is okay." Leif didn't want to lie, but also didn't feel it appropriate to tell virtual strangers about the pregnancy, especially so early on when the last one had ended badly. "It was my wife, who isn't feeling well and just wanted to hear my voice. I'm sorry for the interruption, but I haven't spoken with her in days. I do hope you understand."

They all nodded their understanding and the conversation resumed.

Leif was asked to escort Leah Rozen, the prime minister's daughter, back to her hotel in Tel Aviv that evening. She had been visiting her parents on a break from England's Cambridge University. Leah had stayed with them at home for several days, but needed to fly out early from Ben Gurion International to return to school, and thus had decided to stay close to the airport the night before.

"Would you like me to get a limousine or taxi?" Leif held the door of the restaurant open for his pretty young ward.

"Oh, can we walk? It's such a beautiful night!" Leah looked up at him with childlike anticipation.

"I think it's about two miles. Are you sure you don't mind walking that far?"

"Not at all since I've got you for a bodyguard." She flirtatiously batted her long eyelashes at Leif, gazing at him with big almond-shaped honey-brown eyes.

Leif grinned. "Okay, let's go." Always the gentleman, Leif offered her his arm and they were off. There was a full moon that lit up the night and they walked along the busy streets of Tel Aviv, which had quieted some with the nightfall.

"So tell me about your wife, is she going to be okay?" Leah was youthfully inquisitive and guilelessly outgoing.

"She's pregnant."

Leah slowed her pace a bit, a frown on her face. "Oh, I see." She looked up at him with her big brown eyes. "Well I hope then that the baby is alright and you both will be happy."

Now it was Leif's turn to frown. "I hope so too. My wife Wendy had a miscarriage last time. I don't know if she could handle another one."

Leah stopped walking and stood still so Leif stopped too. She reached up, putting her arms around his neck, and gave him a big hug then a kiss on his cheek. "I'm so sorry. I will pray everything goes well for you this time. I just know you are a special man, Leif Mitchell. Your wife is a lucky woman."

Upon Leah's suggestion, the two had after dinner drinks in the hotel bar where they talked about Leif's "Peace" concert he had given two days earlier to a crowd of Americans, Israelis, and even some Muslims who had gathered in an ancient outdoor stadium, leaving their battles behind for a few hours to hear the popular country-rock star play.

Leif had written a song just for the event, which would play on airwaves around the world. When he sang the refrain, the whole crowd sang out that cool, clear night:

"If you believe that one God created us all,
and we're His children under one sky,
then lay down your arms and open them wide—
come on, live, you don't want to die,
let them live, they don't want to die."

News stations had covered the concert globally and in less than twenty-four hours the concert went viral on the Internet. There was widespread talk that the success of the concert symbolized an anticipated positive outcome of Leif's mission. Some predicted that it could be the start of peace in the Middle East if everyone could carry the goodwill generated that night forward and rally behind their kings, presidents, and prime ministers.

No details were released but the media reported that talks of a prospective peace conference were being hinted at once again thanks to the concert and Leif's successful meetings with Prime Minister Rozen and several other Palestinian and Muslim leaders. At the core of any potential peace would be an agreement in which the borders between Israel and its neighboring countries would become permanent, and these borders would be supported and secured by both sides, allowing peaceful crossings by all citizens like those between the US and Canada or Mexico. Leif had purportedly engaged the respective leaders to at least consider such a possibility.

Martin sat across his desk from his daughter Wendy in the Oval Office. He had summoned her alone while Carol was out visiting her sister, who had just discovered she had cancer.

"How did Leif react to the news?" Martin got right to the point, his voice was terse like that of an interrogator. "What did he say when he found out you're pregnant again already?"

Wendy's voice was tinged with annoyance. "Well, he didn't say much. I guess he was busy entertaining this dignitary and his family over there and he was impatient to get back to his dinner. To be honest, I was really disappointed in his reaction. I know he's busy with all of these political maneuverings and world peace and such, but still, this is his child, Dad."

"Which is why it's so hard to tell you what I'm about to tell you." Martin's expression was grim. He held up a manila envelope in his right hand and got right to the point. "I didn't want to show you these, but you need to know the truth about this man you call your husband and now the father of your child." His last few words dripped with sardonic contempt. "This is the man who claims to love you. It sickens me because I love you and never want to see you hurt. But you need to know the truth. I am so angry I can't see straight. If Leif were here, I'd strangle him to death. How dare he get you pregnant, then go off and . . ." He let his words trail off for effect.

"Off and what, Dad? You're scaring me. What?" Her voice was shrill, panicked with fear.

"I'm sorry, Wendy. Here, look for yourself." The president slid the envelope across the desk toward his daughter. "I don't know how to tell you this other than to come right out and say it. Your husband has been caught cheating."

He waited for the last word to land on his daughter's ears as she opened the envelope and sat staring at the top photo amid the stack. He watched her expression change the way a storm gathers and grows into a hurricane, from wonder to shock to anger to rage. She started flipping through the photos—slowly at first, then faster in her fury.

In the first photo, Leif was walking at night along a city street, arm and arm with a gorgeous young Israeli woman. The camera lens had captured her face. She was smiling, perfect white teeth in an unlined olive face, with large, kohl-rimmed, almond-shaped eyes that twinkled with amusement, as if Leif apparently had said something quite entertaining.

The photos were apparently arranged in progression as if the photographer had snapped away, unfolding the affair before her eyes.

In the second photo, Leif and the woman were sitting at a bar laughing over drinks. In the third, the woman was kissing Leif on the cheek. The fourth depicted her embracing him with her arms wrapped around his neck. It was hard to tell where his hands were since it was a shot from the shoulders up. Wendy could only imagine. The next showed the two stepping into the David InterContinental Hotel, Leif's arm around her waist.

She had long flowing jet-black hair and was probably in her early twenties. She had a perfect face and the figure of a model, which was accentuated with a form-fitting long dress made of sheer material that was cinched with a belt around her tiny waist.

"Unfortunately, I have men over there that have confirmed that Leif is, in fact, having an affair. Her name is—"

"I don't want to know." Wendy's voice was frighteningly deadpan.

"What do you want to do?" Martin stood, came around the desk, and hugged his daughter. It was only then that she broke down in hysterics.

"Daddy, what do I do?" she wailed.

"I'll take care of everything, princess." He held her, stroking her hair as the tears fell on his shoulder. "Leave everything to me. It will be okay."

If jealousy had taken an already fragile Wendy to the edge of stability and rationality, the abortion sent her over it. Since the news of her husband's alleged "affair" had come from her father, whom she completely trusted, and was coupled with photographic evidence, Wendy believed the lie and was thereafter a fearful ball of putty in her father's hands. Martin could now advise her to do his bidding as if she were a child again.

He had waited to take care of his daughter's unfortunate pregnancy until his wife was away again on another trip to visit her sister. Carol was expected to be gone about two weeks.

When the First Lady returned to the White House, the deed was done. Martin gently broke the news to his wife that their daughter was in a psychiatric facility, that she had lost her baby again and was so distraught that she had become suicidal.

Then he told her about Leif's "affair" leading to the "miscarriage," how his men had reported to him about his son-in-law's indiscretions, and how he had asked them to get proof. "Wendy was beside herself when I showed her the photos. She totally lost it. I'm sure it's what caused her to lose the baby," he said, consoling her.

Martin had told Wendy that they needed to hide the whole truth from her mom since Carol was already stressed and would get too upset. He also warned her that if anyone found out she had gotten an abortion they would tell the media, who would question her relentlessly and drive her completely mad, and then she would never get well and get out of the psych ward.

"I just can't believe it!" Carol nearly shouted with indignation. "If I ever see Leif Mitchell again I . . . I don't know what I'll do. How could he do this to our little girl? Does he even know the baby is . . . gone?"

"No, I don't think we should tell him until he gets back home. He's probably wrapping up the peace talks as we speak and should be home in a few days. Meanwhile, I had an attorney friend draw up divorce papers, which I had Wendy sign while she was having a good day. They're pretty clear-cut. There's no way Leif will be able to fight the claims of abandonment and adultery since we have proof of both. I hope you can see now why I've always had misgivings about him. But on your encouragement I gave him the benefit of the doubt. It makes me sick to think he's representing me in the Middle East right now, while I'm picking up the pieces of the mess he's made. But I'm glad I'm here for Wendy. And I'm glad the truth came out and we can finally get rid of him once and for all."

Carol insisted she immediately accompany him to visit their daughter, who was staying temporarily at Washington Hospital Center's Behavioral Health Services until she got well again.

Martin had taken Wendy to the hospital for the abortion procedure, then recommended she sign herself into the behavioral health wing. It was known as one of the best facilities of its kind in DC. Plus, the president had strong connections to the hospital's board of directors, and had facilitated several hefty research grants on their behalf. He knew they would keep his secret.

Martin briefed his wife on the drive to the hospital about Wendy's condition, but Carol was still unprepared to see her daughter so thin and frail. Wendy had lost about ten pounds and lay thin and gaunt in the hospital bed, her stringy blond hair tucked behind her against her pillow. Her face was pale, and she had gray circles under her lifeless eyes.

Carol cried as she hugged her daughter, then pulled herself together.

Martin had warned her that although Wendy was mildly sedated, she still could get upset easily which could cause her to have a panic attack. In turn her blood pressure might rise dangerously, which would mean that she would need more medication.

Carol tried to smile brightly, and made small talk, telling Wendy about her trip.

"So how are you, sweetheart?" Carol gently asked, sitting next to her daughter's hospital bed.

"I lost the baby," Wendy said emotionlessly.

"I know, honey, and I'm sorry," Carol said, smoothing Wendy's hair.

"It's all Leif's fault," Wendy said as a tear trickled down her face.

"I know that too. I know everything that happened, honey. But maybe it was meant to be, sweetheart. Maybe God was looking out for you." She wiped her daughter's tears away and held her tightly. "It will all be okay. We'll make sure of it."

If Martin Greene thought Leif had been a threat to him when he became a sensation by defeating giant opponent Leon Slater and winning the Kentucky governorship, the president realized now he had greatly underestimated the power of his son-in-law.

Leif came home to the United States a national hero.

For the first time in history, someone had achieved a real start to peace in the Middle East that had heretofore only been given lip service by the various leaders involved to pacify the public over and over again through the conduit of the news media.

There was much work left to do to draw up a treaty involving the proposed new border controls, including garnering the backing of the United Nations' countries as well as many of the Middle Eastern nations. But there was no doubt a start had been made and Leif Mitchell was to be credited for it.

But Leif's pride and joy over his triumphs overseas were short-lived and quickly overshadowed with grief over his personal tragedies back home.

Leif received a phone call immediately after his plane touched down at Dulles International Airport that Wendy had lost the baby and was staying at the home of Doctor Terrence Brand, the chief psychiatrist from Washington Hospital, and his wife in their posh DC suburbs.

Martin had arranged with his good friend Terry, whom he trusted implicitly, to have his daughter brought out of the sterile, impersonal hospital to live under the doctor's direct care in a wing in his secluded mansion. That way, Martin had told Wendy, she would feel more at home in her surroundings, and more importantly, wouldn't be disturbed by those pesky reporters.

The voice on the other end was unfamiliar, terse and cold. "This is Doctor Brand of Washington Hospital calling for Governor Mitchell regarding your wife, Wendy Greene."

"This is he. What about my wife?"

"I'm calling to inform you that your wife had another miscarriage and is recuperating at my estate at the direction of her father. She has had a postnatal psychiatric breakdown of some significance. I am the hospital's chief psychiatrist, as well as a good friend of the president. Therefore…"

"Whoa, back up. What do you mean my wife had another miscarriage?!" Leif shouted into the phone, oblivious to the airport passersby staring at him. He had been talking as he briskly walked down the airport corridor, rolling his suitcase in one hand, phone to his ear in the other. A couple strolling behind him nearly banged into him and had to walk around, bumping into other strangers, causing a domino effect. Leif ignored them, listening intently.

"I'm sorry Governor, but Wendy lost the baby she was carrying. She has physically recuperated but had to be treated at the hospital for severe anxiety and depression. She was released into my care for further treatment…"

"I want to see her. Tell me where you live."

"I'm afraid I'll need to get her permission first…"

"Tell me where you live or I'll find it myself!" Leif yelled, exhausted and irritable from the international flight.

"Hold just a minute."

Leif paced in the middle of the busy airport, wildly distraught. A security guard who had been informed by someone witnessing the spectacle walked up to him, but was stopped in his tracks by Leif's glare. "Governor, is everything alright?"

Leif nodded, finally realizing he was causing a scene, and forced himself to calm down.

Doctor Brand returned on the line.

"She said she is feeling up to seeing you. Here are the directions…"

When Leif arrived at the gabled stone mansion, he was informed by the on call visiting nurse at the house that Doctor Brand had been summoned into the hospital for an emergency.

On Wendy's request, the nurse left the room to give the husband and wife privacy, but not before instructing Leif not to "disturb" her patient unnecessarily, warning him she was under strict orders to maintain an atmosphere of calm.

When the nurse was out of earshot, Wendy broke down and told Leif everything that had transpired while he was away.

"How could you cheat on me with that . . . that Arab woman over there?" Wendy raised her voice. "I was pregnant with your baby!"

They heard a knock on the door. "Is everything okay Mrs. Greene?" The nurse's sharp voice crackled.

"Yes, we're fine." Wendy took a deep breath, calming herself. She then put her hands to her belly, cradling it as if her womb wasn't really barren as she rocked back and forth in a big wooden rocking chair.

Leif looked around the room, noticing Wendy's surroundings. Doctor Brand had tried to make her living quarters cheerfully feminine. But in her current frail state, the room made Wendy look like a little girl. She started to cry quietly as she rocked back and forth. Her shoulders shook as she wept.

Leif immediately went to her and knelt down beside her, reaching out his hand to her shoulder to comfort her, but she looked up at him with her miserable, mascara-streaked face and shoved his hand away.

"Wendy, none of that is true. Whoever told you I had an affair was lying." He stood up, looking helpless and confused.

"Are you calling my father a liar?"

"Your father told you I was cheating?"

Both Leif and Wendy knew if they raised their voices they would lose their privacy, so they struggled to keep their voices to a strained whisper.

"He *showed* me."

"What do you mean?"

"I mean he gave me photos that showed you and your lover hugging, kissing, going into the hotel together . . .".

"I don't know what you saw, but it wasn't what you think. I was just her escort. She—"

"Stop." Wendy's tone was flat with resignation and exhaustion. "I don't want to hear any more of your lies. I did what I had to do."

Understanding dawned on Leif's face and his voice came out a cracked whisper. "Please don't tell me…did you get rid of our baby because of what your father told you? Did you have an abortion?"

Wendy sadly nodded.

Leif balled his hands into fists of silent rage. "How could you? I don't know why your father made up these lies, but so help me I'll—"

"He wants to kill you, you know." Wendy's tone changed from grief to anger.

"We'll see about that. I'm going to get to the bottom of all of this." He walked toward her and knelt next to her again. "Look, even though I'm upset about this, I know it's not all your fault. And it's not mine either. None of what your father said is true. .."

"Just get out. We're done. My father made sure you could never hurt me again. I signed the divorce papers his attorney friend drew up, so all you have to do is sign them and you can get on with your life. My father took care of me, Leif. He's not the liar and the cheat. You are. So just go."

Leif stood up and hesitated, unsure what to do.

"Go! Get out!" Wendy shrieked and the nurse burst through the door.

"Mr. Mitchell, I'm afraid you'll have to go…"

"That's okay, I'm leaving." Leif quietly turned away from Wendy, who rocked back and forth, her head turned from him now as she stared out the window. The nurse comforted her patient. Leif left the room, softly closing the door behind him. And then he leaned against the wall and wept, his shoulders heaving, grieving for the second child he had never gotten to hold.

Leif finally sniffed and choked down his tears, willing himself to think. He tried to put it all together: Jordan's warning about the mission overseas, and now the abortion and the divorce. It all made sense to him now. Martin Greene really did despise him for some insane reason and wanted to get rid of him.

Leif sought out Ray Silas to confide everything Wendy had told him.

"How do you know she's not crazy and what she's saying is true?" Ray sipped lemonade from his wicker rocker on the old-fashioned porch that wrapped around his Southern plantation-style home in Alexandria, Virginia. He was wrapped in blankets despite the warm summer dusk that fell around them.

Leif noticed Ray's health had deteriorated rapidly since the last time he had seen his mentor and friend several months ago. A mini-stroke had turned Ray's graying hair white, and had slowed down the eighty-three-year-old Republican Party leader to the point where he wasn't making any public appearances. He was still sought out for his sage advice, however, by dozens of politicians and government officials, which he meted out from the confines of his home.

He had always had a special place in his heart for Leif Mitchell. Leif was like a son to Ray, especially since he and his own sons had never been close. But more than that, he believed Leif was truly destined to be a great leader. That he was a man after God's own heart. Ray suppressed a knowing smile. Right now Leif just didn't know it. But give him time...

"I asked for hospital records, which confirmed it all." Leif paced back and forth across the wooden slats, his voice raised. "Can you believe that Martin actually had his own daughter have an abortion just to get at me? He killed our baby! His own grandchild! And then he had divorce papers drawn up. And to top it all off, the man is so crazy he committed Wendy to a psychiatric institution. Now he's got her housed with her psychiatrist, like he can lock her away so she won't tell anyone."

"But she told you." Ray continued to rock slowly back and forth, sipping his lemonade.

"Yes, because I think she still loves me despite her father's lies about me having an affair. Like I'd have an affair!"

"Did you?"

"Of course not! Ray, please, let's focus on what's important here. The point is, the man is off the charts with jealousy and rage, and I truly believe he wants to get rid of me. As in permanently."

"You think he wants to kill you?"

"Don't you?"

"Hmmm." Ray sat his empty glass down on a small wooden coffee table and drew his blanket up around his shoulders. "Sit down, Leif." Leif did as he was instructed. "I think you need to take a deep breath, calm down, and think about this rationally."

"It's kind of hard to think rationally about someone who is so obviously irrational."

"Exactly. You're probably right that he wants to kill you."

"Great, that's really comforting, Ray." Leif couldn't hide the sarcasm in his tone.

"But if he's acting out of fear, which I'm sure he is, and he's not thinking rationally, which I'm sure he's not, then I would say you have the upper hand in the matter."

"It doesn't feel like it. So what do you think I should do?"

"The right thing, of course."

"And what's that?"

"You tell me."

Leif frowned. He should have known Ray Silas would say that. The very wise old man had an unnerving way of guiding people without telling them what to do, letting them make their own decisions.

"I guess the best thing I could do is nothing at all. I'm a firm believer in 'what goes around comes around.' I guess I just have to have faith that God has a plan, and that Martin will probably have to face the consequences of his own undoing."

"Sounds like the right thing to me." Ray yawned. "I really should be getting up to bed pretty soon. Can you lend me a hand?" Leif helped Ray in the door and through the living room to a first-floor master bedroom he now inhabited alone since his wife had passed away a few years prior.

Ray shuffled slowly and unsteadily, using a cane and the support of Leif's strong arms. He sat on the edge of his bed. "Thanks, Leif. I'll be fine from here."

"Thank you, Ray, for everything. You always know what to say."

"I didn't say much of anything. I think you're hearing a Power much greater than me. Keep listening to Him, Leif." Ray lay down on the bed, his eyelids drooping closed.

Leif turned to go but was stopped by Ray's last words.

"You're a great leader, Leif. God chose well. You'll make a fine president."

Leif began to question his mentor about his last comment but was left in puzzled silence, noticing the wise old politician had already fallen asleep.

Still unsettled by his visit with Wendy and reeling from feelings of grief, anger, and fear, Leif decided to turn to his best friend for support, despite the fact that the same man was also his worst enemy's son.

He showed up unannounced in Jordan's office at the Smithsonian an hour later.

Jordan was bent over the paperwork that blanketed his desk in "The Castle," the historic red brick building that used to be the sole Smithsonian museum when it was founded in 1846 but now served as headquarters to the world's largest museum complex. Leif walked into his office after clearing his way through security and two secretaries.

"This is a nice surprise!" Jordan threw down a sheaf of papers, stood, and came around his desk to hug his best friend.

Despite all of the bad news and grief he had just been dealt, Leif smiled. "Thanks. I missed you."

"Congratulations on all of your hard work over in the Middle East. Thanks to you I can sleep a little better at night. Sit down." Jordan motioned for Leif to have a seat in the sitting room that was adjacent to his spacious office while he poured some coffee for them both.

"I was just doing what your father asked me to do." Leif watched Jordan's face to see his reaction to his words. A quick frown etched the president's son's features, but Jordan remained quiet as he brought over two mugs and sat them down on an immense coffee table littered with magazines and newspapers. "I just came from seeing your sister. My wife. Or should I say soon-to-be ex-wife and mother of my child who never had a chance to be born." Leif couldn't help the bitterness from seeping into his voice.

"Leif, I'm so sorry." Jordan was sincere, his voice cracking.

"You know I didn't have an affair, don't you?" Jordan nodded and Leif continued. "So what have I done that's so awful that your father not only had our baby killed but wants to kill me as well?"

"Whoa, back up a minute. What do you mean 'had your baby killed'? I thought Wendy had a miscarriage."

"Then you don't know about the abortion?"

"Wendy had an abortion?" Jordan sounded truly incredulous.

"Not only did she have an abortion, her own father—your father—talked her into having it after showing her pictures he had his hired hands take while I was in Israel; photos that made it look like I was having an affair. But it was all a setup. He actually encouraged her to kill our baby and then sign divorce papers. No wonder she ended up in that mental hospital. I thought you knew…"

"I knew about Wendy losing the baby. And I knew she wanted the divorce because she thought you were cheating on her. I didn't really believe mom and dad when they told me you had an affair. I've been meaning to call and ask you all about it but they asked me not to contact you out of loyalty to my sister. But I had no idea that my father…"

His words trailed off. Leif assured Jordan that he had confirmed everything but that the news had not gone beyond their immediate family since the doctors were sworn to secrecy at the risk of losing their careers.

After hearing his friend out, Jordan stood up in a daze. It took him a few moments to find his voice. "This is just horrible!" He shook his head, still trying to comprehend what Leif had just told him. "I know he's always been jealous of you, but this is really crazy.

Even if what Wendy says is true, I can't believe that he wants to actually kill you."

"Will you help me find out?"

"Obviously my father doesn't tell me anything anymore, now that he knows you and I are friends. But I'll help you any way I can."

"Okay, I think I have a plan . . ."

Leif had already been scheduled many months ago as one of the entertainers invited once again to perform that night at "A Capitol Fourth," the annual Fourth of July celebration in Washington DC televised on PBS.

Despite all that occurred, the president had not rescinded the invitation, nor had Leif declined, and the country rock star's photo had already been plastered over all of the online promotional sites and marketing materials.

A small, private dinner was planned before the concert and fireworks to be held in the Family Dining Room off the State Dining Room just for the Greene family, a few close friends and dignitaries.

The evening arrived, plans intact.

The White House butler made an announcement that dinner was to be served and everyone took their seats. It wasn't until then that Martin Greene noticed an empty chair across from him between Jordan and Victoria.

He glared at his son but kept his voice to a casual whisper. "Where is Leif?"

"Oh, I'm sorry, Dad, he can't make it tonight. He's with his family in Kentucky for an emergency on the horse farm. He asked me to tell you he's very sorry and he hopes you'll understand."

"And why am I just finding out about this now?" Martin hissed the words through a forced smile, his eyes gleaming with anger.

"It was last-minute; he just told me where he was headed a few hours ago from the plane. I didn't get a chance to tell you before now."

"Son, as soon as dinner is finished, you will meet me in the Green Room to discuss this." The president smiled and stood to make an announcement, cutting off the chatter around him.

"Jordan just informed me that, unfortunately, my son-in-law Leif Mitchell won't be able to join us tonight for dinner or the concert due to a family emergency back in Kentucky." A series of disappointed gasps and grumblings ensued. "But not to worry, we have many great performers lined up, not to mention our wonderful fireworks display, and I know you will all have a fabulous evening. Enjoy."

As soon as dinner was finished and the Greene family had bid farewell to their guests, Martin met Jordan, who was waiting for him in the White House Green Room.

The president ominously closed the main door behind him, and the two men faced each other in the middle of the small, dimly lit parlor.

Martin's words came out low, seething with rage. "I know you're lying, son. Where is Leif?"

"I told you, Dad. He's with his family. He said something about one of their best horses being in trouble. You know how he feels about those horses."

Martin started to slowly, menacingly walk toward his son, who stood about ten feet away, closing the gap between them. His voice was still low and filled with scorn. "How could you stay friends with him, Jordan, knowing how he's betrayed our family?"

"What has he done wrong, Dad?"

Martin's voice began to rise with contempt. "What has he done wrong? He got your sister pregnant and then when he was in Israel he had an affair!"

"I don't believe he had an affair. I think you set him up. What I don't get is why you hate him so much. You're the one who brought him to DC and into the family in the first place."

"Why you little ungrateful brat. You don't know how conniving he is. How he's out to take away my presidency. I know things you don't know. My sources have told me that Leif Mitchell is going to try to sabotage my candidacy and then run in my place. I trusted him, and now he's out to stab me in the back and ruin this country. He swore he'd be loyal to me and he lied. He's a traitor and has no loyalty to this family, to me or to you. I'm sure one day he might threaten your chance at the presidency too. Your allegiance is to the wrong side, son. Leif Mitchell has got to be stopped. It's the only way to keep him from committing treason. Of course, now he's ruined everything tonight."

Jordan looked at his father warily. "Why are you so angry he isn't here tonight? I know it's a little embarrassing, but you've had worse happen. It's not like you don't have enough entertainers, plus the fireworks, right? And everyone still believes he and Wendy are together but that she's still recuperating from an illness, right?"

"You don't understand."

"You're right, I don't. What do you mean he has to be stopped?"

Martin wandered over to the window facing the South Lawn, which had a good view of the fireworks and the National Mall, where thousands were already starting to gather for the concert at the Capitol. There was a telescope set up in the window, and Martin looked into the viewfinder for a moment and then waved Jordan over.

"Come here. There's something I want you to see."

Jordan walked over and looked into the telescope. Through the powerful magnification of the instrument he saw the concert stage, which was lit up and now had a crew of engineers and sound-check people scurrying back and forth checking band equipment, microphones, lights, and wiring. It was about an hour until show time.

He lifted his head and turned toward his father, confused. "So?"

"Let's just say I had something special planned for Leif before he would have even walked onto that stage. And I had a ringside seat through this baby." Martin patted the telescope, smiling wickedly.

"What do you mean?"

"If I didn't know better I'd swear you weren't my son." Martin growled, turning to face the window again and lowering his voice, a quiet menace in his tone. "You can't see them, but there are special agents out there who were ready to take care of my pesky ex-son-in-law."

Jordan listened with his mouth open, speechless.

"Now you see why I'm so disappointed your friend Leif couldn't join us tonight." Martin was actually half smiling. "No one would have heard a thing with the fireworks. With this crowd and all that's going on out there, it would have looked at first like he was passing out. And then with all the chaos . . . it was the perfect plan. But I'll find another way."

"Not if I report you."

"It will be your word against mine, son. I don't think you want to go there."

Jordan's eyes widened with fear for his friend. "Are you crazy? You have really gone off the deep end, Dad! Leif has done nothing to deserve this. He told me everything—including the fact that Wendy didn't have a miscarriage but an abortion—which you talked her into getting!"

"Why, you little punk!" Martin landed his fist into his son's face. Jordan reeled backward into the telescope and both crashed to the floor. Martin looked down on his son. "You are a no-good, worthless mama's boy who never amounted to anything. That you would choose this greedy, back-stabbing, evil cowboy singer over me...this selfish nobody who pretends to be a politician but is really out to get all of us . . . you disgust me. You are not my son."

Martin turned and walked out of the room, leaving Jordan lying there, his mouth bleeding and tears running down his cheeks.

Jordan sniffed and tried to get a hold of himself. He grabbed onto the desk and got to his feet, still rubbing his jaw and wiping the blood from his mouth. He went to stand at the window, which looked like it was on fire, glowing red from the fireworks that burst in the sky just yards away. He picked up the phone and dialed.

Leif was still at Little River when Jordan's call came.

"I hate to say it but your plan worked. I got the truth. Dad got really angry when he found out you weren't going to be at dinner. You were right. He was planning to have you . . . killed." Jordan rubbed his bruised jaw. "I just had no idea my father was this consumed with jealousy and hatred, this insane. I'm really sorry. What are you going to do?"

"I don't know. It's not like I can hide from him. I do have a state to run."

Jordan was silent for a minute before an idea struck him and he thought it out loud. "I think you should run against him."

"For president? Now I think you've gone a little crazy."

"Well, you know I've never had the desire to follow in his footsteps. And he can't win a second term. Not with all we know that he's done. Even if it would never get out, which is next to impossible, we know how sick and crazy he's become. He can't run his household much less the country."

Now Leif was quiet for a minute before responding. "I'll think about it on one condition."

"What?"

"If I decide to run, and get far enough that I get on the ballot, you'll be my running mate and run for vice president."

"I'm honored that you would even ask, Leif, but I don't know...I have no experience, no track record..."

"True...plus it would completely push your father over the edge I guess. As much as he's hurt me, I don't want to be responsible for that."

"I think he's standing right at the edge now. I don't think it matters what we do at this point. It's like he's lost all sense of morality or reason, all touch with reality, and lost touch with God. I almost believe that Satan has taken over his soul. I believe this country needs someone who has faith in God, who has a spiritual vision as well as a political one. America needs you as its next president."

Jordan heard footsteps approaching. "Look, I've got to go. Call me tomorrow and let me know what you're going to do."

Leif spent the night at Little River in his old bedroom. Before he went to bed, he took a stroll through the stalls to spend time with the horses stabled there. After he gave them all treats of carrot and apple pieces and talked to each one, rubbing their soft muzzles, he sat down to strum on his old acoustic guitar, which he had left behind at the ranch.

He sat on a bale of hay at the end of the barn and mindlessly strummed a few chords. It was his favorite way to meditate and think about what was ailing him that day. He almost always found a solution by listening to the still, small voice within, which he believed was God talking.

It usually helped if he did some praying first. And singing was his favorite form of prayer. He softly sang to the horses:

"Lead me, God, lead me on, down the path of truth,
I can't seem to find my own way,
Life is hard, and I feel that I can't go on,
Please lead me, God, today."

Leif sat back, listening to the horses pawing and neighing, and the silence of the night. One horse whinnied louder and more distinctively than the rest. Leif smiled and walked down the long line of stalls until he reached Little Sally's.

"I didn't forget you girl," he said, stroking her white streaked forehead. "It's just that I have a lot on my mind." He talked to her like he would an old friend. "I'm not sure what I should do. I made a deal with Martin Greene that I would remain loyal to him if he gave me his blessing to marry Wendy. But now it all seems to have fallen apart anyway. Still, how will it look if I run for president against my own father-in-law – or even ex-father-in-law? Of course, when the people find out all he's done...but no one will probably believe even half of this crazy mess. I just don't know..." He looked into the mare's wise, big brown eyes and could almost swear he could see compassion – perhaps even an answer there.

"Thanks Sal." Leif realized — not for the first time — that God even spoke through horses sometimes.

PART TWO

CHAPTER ELEVEN

Ray Silas died in his sleep of a massive stroke on a mild, mid-October evening in his home in Alexandria. Although he died peacefully and without fanfare, his funeral would be one to be remembered.

Not only was the former US congressman, Speaker of the House, senator, and current Republican National Committee chairman going to lie in state in the rotunda of the Capitol in DC—a rare honor granted over time to less than three dozen federal officeholders, including eleven presidents, the last being President Ronald Reagan—Raymond Silas was going to have a state funeral at the Washington National Cathedral, where he would be serenaded with an elegy by national recording star Leif Mitchell and eulogized by none other than President of the United States Martin Greene.

The church, of course, would be overflowing, and anyone who didn't want to get stuck in hours of traffic was warned by news stations to stay off the roads in downtown Washington DC until late in the afternoon. Ray Silas had been a man long revered and loved, and in addition to his family and friends, his political "family" and followers numbered in the thousands.

In attendance would be Ray's two brothers and sister and their families. His parents had died many years ago, having conceived him in their forties. His mother had prayed to God for many years and had finally had her prayers answered beyond her wildest dreams when Raymond was born.

No one knew whether his two sons would show up or not. Ray Silas had had such high hopes for them when they had each passed the bar and become judges, one in Maryland's district court and one in the same state's circuit court. He had almost used his political power to help his oldest son become appointed to the US Supreme Court. But an investigation showed Silas's oldest son had been involved in accepting bribes, and he was subsequently disbarred. Son number two was suspected of some shady dealings as well, although they had never been proven, and ended up leaving the bar quietly for a job on Wall Street.

Neither would ever become half the man their father had been even if they lived to be twice his age. It had caused Ray a lot of anguish over the years, but he had finally given up on the thought of his sons following in his footsteps. He had turned his attention to mentoring and helping more godly men who were more worthy of his support.

Ray had, of course, never sought out Martin Greene as the candidate for president since he had been naturally in line for the job as the current vice president. He had always had misgivings that Martin might not be the best man for the job. But since fate was already in play, Ray had had little choice but to give Martin Greene his full endorsement and support.

He had chosen Leif, on the other hand, both to run for governor and to be a part of his funeral. And unlike Martin, who was expected to speak as president, Ray had asked Leif a long time ago, before he had even known he was dying, to participate in his funeral service by singing.

Leif had written a song to sing acoustically as his elegy titled "Wise Old Man." The lyrics ended on a particularly poignant verse sung to God:

"You created him, then called his name to lead a nation strong,
He did his best to know Your will, discerning right and wrong.
He heard Your voice and bravely lived to stay true to Your plan.
He died a courageous, kind and just, faithful wise old man."

Martin Greene was getting dressed in his best black suit in his private quarters when he heard a knock on the door. He couldn't imagine who it could be since his wife had long since left with their daughters for hair appointments and no one else was supposed to be on the second floor of the White House. Jordan had told his mother the night before he would meet them at the church.

So the president frowned with puzzlement as he opened the door to his dressing room.

Upon seeing who had knocked, Martin's annoyed expression turned to shock, as if Satan himself stood before him.

"Mornin' Martin, may I come in?" Leif was dressed from head to toe in black formal wear, except for the black cowboy boots and black cowboy hat he wore.

"H-h-how, how d-did you get in here?" Martin stammered out the words.

"Oh, it was easy, in fact. The help downstairs must still be fond of me. Even though I know you're not. Are you, Martin?" Leif suddenly seemed to tower over Martin by several inches.

Martin cowered before him as if Leif were going to strike him at any moment.

"Answer me!" Leif grabbed Martin by his expensive pressed shirt, causing him to visibly tremble.

Martin yanked himself out of Leif's grasp so hard that his shirt ripped. Leif was left standing with a handful of torn white linen while Martin furtively searched the drawers of a nearby bureau.

"Are you looking for this?" Leif took a .38 Special revolver from his coat pocket and lifted it up, dangling it by the butt with the fingers of his left hand, and letting the torn cloth drop from his right.

Martin stopped searching and turned to face Leif, staring at the gun with wide-eyed incredulity and fear, speechless. He fell back a step, leaning against the bureau.

"I was in here earlier looking for you and found it in the top left drawer." Leif's voice was calm, emotionless. "I was actually coming in to ask you for an extra tie to wear since I forgot to pack one. I thought I'd look in your bureau since you weren't here. Imagine my surprise when I found this." Leif held the gun up and out, still dangling, closer to Martin's face. "So I guess you were planning to use it, since its chamber is full." Leif's words came out as more a statement than a question. "And I can only imagine that it was intended for me."

Martin remained silent. He was sweating now.

"I'll take your silence as confirmation." Leif gingerly laid the gun down behind him on a rolltop desk, without taking his eyes off the president. "Jordan told me about your plan to kill me during the Fourth celebration, Martin. But why? All I've ever done is respect you, serve you. Even love you. Not just as the leader of my country but as my father-in-law."

Leif noticed Martin hadn't moved, and his former father-in-law's eyes remained focused on the gun the entire time he was talking. "You were afraid I was going to turn your own gun on you, weren't you? You know, for a second it actually crossed my mind. Not out of defense, to save myself, but because of all you've done to betray me, and especially all you've done to Wendy, your own daughter. But you know, I'm not like you. I heard a small voice inside me say that if I shot you, even if it was justified, it would make me as evil and as sick as you. Sure, I could cover it up; make it look like self-defense or an accident or even suicide. But God would know. Just as He sees and knows all you've done. I believe that God will keep me safe from you, because He knows the truth. He knows who should lead this country."

Martin suddenly went all limp and slumped forward, sliding down the bureau into a sitting position on the carpet. He covered his face with his hands and wept aloud, his shoulders shaking with sobs.

After a few long minutes he finally looked up at the ceiling, closed his eyes and moved his lips in silent prayer, then looked at Leif. His voice was choked with emotion but his eyes were lucid with clarity. It was as if something – or someone – had suddenly struck him, almost like an electric shock, and his whole persona had changed. He looked and sounded utterly changed – into someone defeated, meek, humble. "I'm sorry." Martin sighed with resignation, still sitting slumped on the floor. "You're right. I thought you were going to kill me. And you would have had every right. I've let my jealousy toward you fester into a cancer that has eaten away at me until I've become literally sick with rage. My obsession with getting rid of you has taken over my life and I've lost everything, everyone, because of it." Martin put his face in his hands and started quietly crying again.

"Martin, look at me." Leif spoke with firm authority, commanding the commander in chief of the United States. Martin looked up again obediently. "You can make this right. Step down from the presidency once your term is up before it's too late. Spend time with your wife and daughters. Let me run instead."

Martin nodded with a sigh. "Will you promise to protect them? My secrets can't get out. If they do, I will probably be impeached . . . and they shouldn't have to bear that shame when none of this is their fault."

Just then a knock at the door startled the two men. "Who is it?" Martin shouted through the closed door.

"Secret Service. Mr. President, Governor Mitchell. It's time to go to the funeral."

Leif reached out and helped Martin stand up. The two quietly shook hands. It was a deal.

The funeral procession and church service were televised throughout the world.

Following Leif's beautiful solo elegy, President Martin Greene stepped up to a podium on the magnificent altar to deliver the eulogy.

". . . and for all of this and more, Ray Silas was one of the greatest men of our times." Martin had pulled himself together and eloquently spoke of Ray's life as a son, brother, husband, father, grandfather, war veteran, congressman, senator, and party leader. He then thanked him for his service to his country. "He was someone who I always wanted to make proud. I'm afraid I didn't do such a good job at it." Martin looked up to the vaulted ceiling of the church. "Forgive me, Ray." He looked back out at the congregation. "Ray Silas was truly a man of God. I thought I was, but . . ." Martin hesitated, a sob catching in his throat. He struggled to regain his composure, and looked up at the ceiling again. "Maybe since you're up there now and you've got a better connection, you can ask God to forgive me, and tell Him I'll try to do better from here on out."

Several people in the pews laughed at Martin's last comment, but most uneasily murmured and shifted uncomfortably in their seats—especially his staff members, who were flabbergasted that their boss was admitting his failures in front of millions of voters.

The president's agents shielded him from the onslaught of cameras and microphones outside the church. His press agent, who had been instructed ahead of time, stopped and addressed the media, announcing the president would hold a brief press conference later that day following the funeral procession and burial.

It was time.

Martin Greene arrived at the White House Press Room and stood at the podium. The media would later report he looked somewhat haggard, with more gray in his hair and lines on his face than anyone remembered seeing before, but with a look of peaceful resignation replacing the constant worried frown that had been etched there for many months.

A murmur swelled among the reporters, who were in suspense as to why the press conference had been called. The buzz was that it had something to do with the president's comments during the funeral.

Martin held up his hands and waited until everyone quieted again before he spoke. "I realize this might come as a shock to most of you, who don't know that in the past few months my family has suffered a good deal of pain through the loss of my two unborn grandchildren." The media gathered started to mutter amongst themselves. It was the first time they were hearing the revelation that Wendy Greene had lost another baby. "After much consideration, I have come to the conclusion that I can no longer be divided between my family and my country. If I cannot be a good husband and father, then what good can I be as your president? I had actually talked to Ray Silas about all that has been transpiring, and it was his recommendation that I consider not running again for a second term in office—thereby allowing someone more fit to serve to step forward as the Republican Party candidate in next year's presidential election."

A collective gasp was now heard among the reporters, who scribbled furiously in their notepads. "I know Ray highly favored the man who I am about to introduce as that candidate, and I know he'd be honored that I am announcing right now, following this morning's celebration of his life, the candidacy of Leif Mitchell."

The reporters had no time to ask questions. Leif suddenly entered the room and joined Martin at the podium, and the two shook hands amidst a flurry of flashes. All of the press gathered rose to their feet and started clapping.

Martin stepped to the side of the podium and motioned for Leif to make a statement.

Darren Richards watched the televised conference from his family room on his huge flat-screen TV, his mouth agape.

Chessa was making an early dinner in the adjoining kitchen. She had caught glimpses of the three-hour funeral coverage and subsequent press conference as she cooked and cleaned.

She heard her husband's moan, put down the mixing bowl of chicken salad on the counter and rushed in to see what was causing his reaction.

"Unbelievable!" Darren was standing, staring at the screen just two feet away, his hands clenched in fists. Chessa thought for a minute that he might just smash his hand through the screen. His face was red with fury.

"What happened?" She looked on and saw the president and the governor of Kentucky holding up their hands together at the White House podium to the sound of applause.

"Shhhh." Darren ignored her and turned up the volume with the remote in his hand. She watched, standing a step behind her husband, afraid he might turn his fury on her if she got too close.

"Thank you, Mr. President." Leif cleared his throat, smiling. "I am deeply honored to accept your gracious offer for me to take your place as a Republican candidate for the presidency, and thank you for your support. Ray Silas came to me five years ago to ask me to run for governor of Kentucky. And then he told me just the other night as I visited him at his home in Alexandria—the last night he was alive—that he thought I would make a good president one day. I just didn't think it would be this soon."

Nervous laughter erupted in the room. "But God works in mysterious ways I guess," he continued. "I too, have always wanted to make Ray Silas proud. I too hope and believe he is up in heaven looking down smiling on all of us gathered today, and that he is happy and at peace with all that is transpiring here and now. I am both humbled and honored to be following his guidance; you can all consider this my public announcement that I will be running in the primaries next year. After hopefully winning the backing of the Republican Party, I look forward to being on the ballot next November, winning your vote, and becoming the next president of the United States of America."

Darren clicked the television off and threw the remote onto the couch behind them. He pushed past his wife, grabbed a coat from the closet, and headed out the front door of their home without a word of explanation or good-bye.

Chessa sat down on the couch and watched with interest as Leif Mitchell eloquently fielded the questions fired at him by the press assembled. The chicken salad sat uneaten on the counter, congealing.

Leif Mitchell is engaging, she thought as she watched the conference end and the network coverage switch to the news pundits pontificating about both the president's surprise announcement and that of Leif's candidacy. *Charming and handsome too.*

Chessa caught herself, feeling guilty for a moment about her assessment of the man who had now instantly become her husband's chief enemy.

CHAPTER TWELVE

For the next week the Internet, news stations, talk shows, and even comedians had plenty of fodder again now that Leif Mitchell had thrown the proverbial hat in the ring for the presidential election set for the following November.

Leif didn't waste time and officially filed October twentieth among a relatively small gathering of about a hundred friends, family, and supporters at Little River. His parents and brothers had rallied to host the affair, held in a heated outdoor pavilion with an old-fashioned barbeque.

He asked his former gubernatorial campaign manager, Logan Reese, to manage his presidential campaign. Logan enthusiastically accepted Leif's offer, and immediately gathered a hardworking staff to begin fundraising and marketing efforts.

Although governors usually fared well historically in presidential elections, it would be a grueling uphill climb since Leif didn't come from money like Darren Richards and would most likely face tough primaries in just a few months.

While no candidates had announced they would run against the incumbent Martin Greene, who had been considered a shoo-in despite his falling popularity, once Leif announced his candidacy, three more Republican candidates had come forward. They said that they were considering running now that the election would be "up for grabs" against a newcomer, even though that newcomer had gained widespread notoriety with his achievements in the Middle East.

They had plenty of targets to shoot at to try to bring him down. There was Leif's lack of experience, having only served five years in political office; there was his age; at 36-years-old he would become the youngest president, younger than Theodore Roosevelt who had been 42, and John F. Kennedy who was 43; there was Leif's Tea Party leanings; and there was the fact, now publicly known, that he was divorced from the president's daughter. Most damaging were the allegations by the press that suggested perhaps Leif had conned his father-in-law somehow into refusing to run again to pave his own way. Martin had stayed mute on these issues, as had Leif, both sticking to a no-comment response each time they were barraged with questions.

With no real opposition, Leif handily won his gubernatorial seat once again that November and thankfully had a strong lieutenant governor, cabinet and staff in place to run much of the state's affairs while he was campaigning.

He managed to spend a relatively quiet, albeit busy, holiday season at his family horse ranch that Christmas. At the ranch, Leif, his family, Jordan, Logan, and his campaign staff set up an informal headquarters and spent countless hours on the phone on all but Christmas Day calling supporters to turn out to the first major contest of the upcoming election year, the Iowa caucus, scheduled for the first Tuesday in January.

With the help of Logan, a brilliant speech writer, Leif had drafted a platform speech for his caucus meeting leaders to deliver that included defending Israel and enforcing peace in the Middle East as the only real solution to peace at home and worldwide, a "less-is-more" government approach, a promise to continue to maintain the country's prosperity without raising taxes, and a commitment to protect the "right to life" of all human beings.

Darren keenly followed all the media hype that circled Leif with the help of his highly paid crackerjack campaign staff led by Pete Connor. Even though he was more concerned with the upcoming primaries against his two Democratic foes, Darren still wanted to keep tabs on Governor Mitchell and the other Republican candidates.

Besides sleeping together most nights, Darren and Chessa had literally spent only about an hour or two in each other's presence during the Christmas holidays.

Chessa wasn't jealous, per se, of Darren being with his campaign staff instead of with her. Although Darren had made an effort to be courteous, kind, and even sober most of the time in her presence, she was secretly glad he was gone a lot. The memories of his drunken rages still lingered, lurking in her subconscious and resurfacing from time to time like jumbled dreams from a horror movie.

However, she found herself increasingly jealous that Darren was doing what *he* wanted to do and she hardly ever got to do what *she* wanted to do. She had always valued her alone time and especially guarded it lately since she had so little. But now when Darren would disappear after quick visits to the traditional Richards holiday family functions as the campaign trail called, Chessa was expected to stay and represent them both, which meant listening to her mother-in-law and sister-in-law jabber on about family recipes and what styles were in—or worse, gossip about in-laws on the outs, and how their friends or neighbors were so gauche or rude.

Chessa got to a point where she almost had forgotten what she actually did like to do with her free time because she was always doing what was expected of her: either working, entertaining, or showing up to support her husband. And the little bit of time she had alone made her realize she had no true friends with whom to spend it. The cold, dark winter nights that enveloped her in their huge New York mansion didn't help, making her feel isolated.

She called Stephanie in despair the night before the Iowa caucus.

She and Darren had just returned a few days earlier from a campaign jaunt to the Midwest. During the flights both out and back, Chessa had tried to focus on the magazine in her lap as Darren and Pete strategized and laughed over private political jokes she didn't get, trying hard not to dwell on the thought of stumping for days, pretending to be someone she wasn't. Chessa started to realize she hated her life. The seeds of a deep depression started to grow in her like a weed.

"I don't think I can do this anymore," Chessa told Stephanie, lying in bed in her flannel pajamas. Darren had gone out for drinks with Pete and their campaign staff to discuss "last-minute preparations."

"And it's only just beginning. I don't know if I can make it one more month, let alone another year. And if he wins—"

"Remember—one day at a time." Stephanie responded with her favorite Al-Anon saying, but Chessa was tired of the program jargon.

"That's easy for people who aren't looking ahead to possibly becoming the First Lady of the United States of America, and who want nothing more than to get out of the country and escape to some remote island. Stephanie, I need you as a friend, not a sponsor, right now. I'm supposed to get on a plane to Iowa early tomorrow morning, and I feel sick about it. I can't stand my husband's phoniness, or my own. I hate the thought of stepping foot again in the Midwest in the dead of winter and plastering a smile on my face, then going to the parties that night where everybody has too much to drink. I'm at the point where I really hope my husband makes such a drastic mistake that he loses in the next few weeks. Maybe I should just publicly humiliate him by announcing I'm going to divorce him. But then, of course, that would be completely selfish, and I wouldn't be able to live with myself and the guilt of it all."

"Have you prayed about it? Asked what God's will is?"

"Stephanie! You're not hearing me. This isn't your typical Al-Anon problem, you know."

"There are no typical problems in our program. Chessa, all I know is that our little slogans and sayings are the tools that really work. Remember, with Al-Anon no situation is too difficult to be bettered and no unhappiness is too great to be lessened. Let me ask you this: Do you still love Darren?"

"I don't know." Chessa sighed aloud, tired of asking herself that question and not knowing the answer.

"Okay, what do you think is the next right thing to do?

"You tell me."

"How about suit up and show up?"

"What about 'to thine own self be true'?"

"Are you being true to yourself if you don't show up tomorrow and instead get on a plane headed out of the country? Will you be able to live with that? What will make you feel better about yourself? Whatever that is, it will eventually be what makes you happiest I suppose."

Chessa moaned. She knew Stephanie was right. She should do what would make her feel best about herself. After considering her options, Chessa knew she would feel terrible in the long run if she didn't stand by her husband. Even though she thought about it more and more often as time went by, Chessa believed divorce wasn't the answer. She had seen what that had done to her parents.

She did realize deep at her core that she no longer felt love for her husband. Somewhere inside that feeling had left her when he started being drunk and abusive. Yet, she also knew she could still *choose* to love him.

Ironically, she was proud of her husband lately, for all he had accomplished, for his ambitions and mission. And she knew he was trying, after all, to be a decent husband, even if it was to put on a good show.

She was proud of his platform too, which he had shared with her, practicing reading it aloud in their bedroom to her on the nights she wasn't already asleep when he came home. Darren said he would be working to create jobs to improve the nation's economy, especially those in "green" industries which he said in turn would better the environment. He was planning to pull all troops out of the Mideast, leaving them to their own affairs, and would use the millions of dollars in military savings to focus on building better weapons, technologies and security at home.

He also told her about RA Technologies' plan to use stem cell research to find a cure for diabetes. Darren said he had to defend the research against "misinformed" attackers who said it was promoting the killing of unborn fetuses, human egg harvesting, cloning and genetic selection. And, of course, he was fighting for women's rights, including the right to choose.

Chessa hung up from Stephanie, if not happier, then at least feeling a bit more peaceful. She couldn't help but hear the Serenity Prayer in her head as she busied herself packing her suitcase: *"God, grant me the serenity to accept the things I cannot change, the courage to change the things I can, and the wisdom to know the difference."*

There's nothing I can change, at least not tonight, she thought. *So acceptance must be the answer, at least for now.* She told herself she had to accept that she was married to Darren because she didn't want to end up divorced like her parents. Plus she still did want to become the First Lady of the United States so she could have virtually unlimited resources at her disposal to work for the poor, underprivileged, abused and suffering people of the world. So, as his wife, she decided she needed to accept she was going to Iowa the next day and all that went along with it. She could only change her outlook and her attitude.

Who knows, maybe Iowa won't be so bad after all, Chessa hoped, picking out her fanciest dress for the parties the next night.

For company while she packed, Chessa flipped on the television in their bedroom. She heard the voice of Leif Mitchell and looked over at the screen to see the young presidential candidate talking in the microphone to a reporter about the upcoming Iowa caucus.

The female reporter, Chessa noticed, had sidled up to the country-rock star closely, apparently to hear his answer to her question. ". . . Sure, I'm nervous but I feel confident I can do a good job representing the American people and leading them in the right direction," Leif said.

"You know, Iowa doesn't historically have the best record of picking winners, at least on the Republican side," the reporter said.

"In the last five GOP primaries without an incumbent, the winner of the Iowa caucuses went on to win the nomination just two times—in 1996 and 2000. Still, political analysts agree it's very important to place roughly in the top three in Iowa. The only GOP nominee since 1972 who did not finish in the top three in Iowa was John McCain in 2008. Does that make you feel any added pressure?"

"On the contrary, ma'am," Leif said, his words escaping in his slight Southern drawl. "McCain came out in front in the long run, right? And I only have three people in the ring with me, so I'm bound to at least come in fourth just like good old John did. How bad can that be?" Leif flashed the reporter a big grin. She seemed to become flustered, as if he had cast some type of spell on her.

"Um, uh, okay then, good luck, Governor Mitchell," the reporter finally stammered out. "May the best man win."

"That's all I ask, ma'am." And with that Leif tipped his cowboy hat to the camera, which then cut to the anchors with other news.

Once again Chessa found herself thinking about Leif Mitchell well after she had turned off the television set. *I'll probably end up meeting him eventually,* Chessa thought. *I just hope I'm not like that dumb reporter, all swooning. But I have to admit, there's something about him that's . . . special.* It was more than just his rugged good looks or his cowboy charm, Chessa realized. *Something spiritual. Something good.*

Following the Iowa caucus, Leif was scheduled for his first televised debate. Attending would be his archrival, U.S. Senator Patrick O'Rourke, an outspoken Republican who was second to Leif in the polls and primary elections held thus far, along with the other two trailing candidates – an elderly but very wealthy conservative businessman from New York and a U.S. Congresswoman from Michigan who had climbed the political ladder for nearly thirty years.

O'Rourke was expected to push Leif on the issue of abortion to declare his stance since Leif had been relatively silent on the matter to date, as well as question him as to his divorce and suspiciously quick rise to the top.

Leif was on the defensive during most of the debate, but managed to be truthful without giving too much information away that would damage the Greene family reputation in any way. He had given Martin his word. He admitted that he didn't have political aspirations before Ray Silas had approached him and his brothers, but ever since entering the field of government he enjoyed serving the public and felt it was now his calling. He admitted he didn't have the most experience with American politics or government, but said his trip overseas to Israel had given him a whole new perspective. He said he believed the only way to maintain world peace was to stay involved in the Middle East, protect Israel and maintain the United States as a superpower, no matter what it took.

When questioned on the pro-life versus pro-choice issue, Leif didn't hesitate to give his view. "I'm wholeheartedly against abortion, and not just because my faith is or my party is," he said, his voice choking with genuine emotion. "My former wife and I lost two babies. I would give the world to have them back and can't fathom anyone willingly destroying an innocent life for any reason."

His answer seemed to not only satisfy the audience but stir compassion for him, and his opponent quickly abandoned the topic to discuss the economy.

The polls the next day surprisingly showed Leif out in front of O'Rourke by a two-to-one margin. The other two subsequently dropped out of the race shortly thereafter.

Darren had to debate two other Democratic candidates that had come forward in the race. One was a relatively bland US Congressman from Idaho who was new to the political arena, was not well known, had little funding and didn't really stand much of a chance.

The other candidate would be a bit more challenging. He was a charismatic U.S. Senator from California who had lots of experience and seniority as well as popularity among his constituents, including those in Hollywood. He was also the son of a popular Christian minister and had his own inspirational TV show. Darren was banking on the hope that the guy's extreme left-wing liberalism and ultra-religious persona would actually offend voters rather than attract them.

So Darren focused his money and advertising on the California senator and ran enough television ads prior to the debate—depicting him as a radical extremist and Bible-thumping Holy Roller out to convert everyone to his beliefs without knowing a lick about governing a nation—that he practically beat him before he came out of the starting gate.

The bottom line remained: Darren Richards had the personality, experience, support, agenda, and most of all funding to shut everyone else out and to win, and he was running for office in a time when money meant everything.

The sweeping changes in campaign financing rules set forth in the Supreme Court's 2010 decision in Citizens United versus the Federal Election now allowed corporations like RA Technologies to use their treasury funds to air political ads. The new law also struck down the McCain-Feingold Act that formerly prohibited "electioneering communications," or television commercials that slammed a candidate within sixty days of a general election or thirty days of a primary.

So Darren took full advantage of this no-holds-barred political arena, running commercials against his primary candidates during prime-time network programming, including the AFC and NFC football league championship games and even the Super Bowl.

Darren continued to win the caucuses and primaries in state after state, from Iowa and New Hampshire to the handful of races on Super Tuesday in March to New York and California. Darren Richards kept pummeling his Democratic adversaries until, finally, each had dropped out and he could focus on the one man leading the opposing pack: Leif Mitchell.

Although it was a boon to his campaign, Darren's wealthy upbringing and status could prove to be his greatest challenge, according to critics, who said he might alienate or be unable to identify with the poor, working, and middle classes.

Ironically, in the presidential race that was shaping up, the Democratic candidate was the rich man and the Republican candidate was the one who had come from, if not a poor family, definitely a working-class one.

Compared to Darren, Leif had to work harder with less funding to defeat his Republican foes in the primaries. But his Tea Party stance continued to distinguish him from the rest, his humble upbringing endeared him to the lower and middle classes, and his cowboy, rock-star magnetism kept him in the limelight despite his lack of funds, putting him consistently ahead in popularity polls not only with the conservatives but with many Americans, especially women who found him irresistible.

Although he didn't win them all like Darren, and he had to struggle a bit more with less funding than his Republican adversaries, Leif ended up out front in most of the state caucuses and primaries from east to west leading up to the summer national conventions.

Thus, both Darren and Leif found themselves the primary leaders in their respective political parties and thus, the upcoming stars of the biggest event the Republican and Democratic parties threw every four years.

The winner of the bid for host city of the Republican National Convention, which would take place at the end of August, was New Orleans, with its one-million-square-foot Ernest N. Memorial Convention Center, the sixth largest convention center in the country, situated along the Mississippi River within walking distance of the French Quarter. New Orleans had put a competitive bid out, hoping to further boost its flagging economy, which had finally started growing after the long drought of business following Hurricane Katrina.

With its musical origins and Southern flair, Leif was happy to hear about the venue, knowing he would feel right at home. He even hoped he'd be able to hook up with a jazz band or two to jam with at night once the politicking was over.

Meanwhile, the Democratic convention would be returning in early September to the newly expanded convention center in downtown Baltimore, the city that had first hosted the event in 1832.

With their unyieldingly tight schedules of late, Darren and Chessa were also happy to hear about their destination since it was close to home and meant less travel time. Chessa had also never spent any time in Baltimore and hoped to see the Inner Harbor and savor some Chesapeake Bay seafood.

Both conventions drew about fifty thousand party members each, a record number, and were considered a huge success. Along with the candidates' enigmatic and electrifying personalities, the election was already shaping up to possibly become one of the most enthralling in U.S. history.

Darren had been repeatedly questioned by the media, holding them off like dogs at bay, about who would be his running mate during the conventions.

But his announcement soon after took even the most jaded media by surprise. Darren chose the beautiful, charismatic, well-spoken young actress, political activist, and U.S. Congresswoman Janine Secour as his vice-presidential running mate and let the world know on a sunny Labor Day at a live press conference just outside Rockefeller Plaza following NBC's *Today Show*.

Janine was also a New York City native, a former Miss New York, and had graduated from Saint Mary's College in South Bend, Indiana, where she had majored in political science and minored in theater. While in college, she had served in the Reserve Officers' Training Corps and continued active duty for two years before beginning her acting career on Broadway and then getting married. Discovered on stage, Janine was offered a small part in a movie that became a blockbuster hit, which launched her acting career. She had quickly landed leading parts in two big-name movies, starring as a husband-stealer in a romance-comedy and a young wife dying of cancer in a drama adapted from a *New York Times* best-selling novel.

But she had always kept involved with activist groups, championing veterans' and women's causes, including, respectively, increased welfare, unemployment and veterans benefits and the "right to choose." She had recently run for the U.S. congressional office in her home state and easily won, and was just starting her second term, having put her acting career on temporary hold.

Darren and Janine stood behind a podium bedecked with a dozen microphones, with flashes popping and video cameras whirring. They appeared quite the dashing couple, he in his pinstriped dark-navy suit and red tie, and she in a turquoise suit with a white blouse and winter white overcoat with a just a touch of red in her lipstick and scarf to match Darren's tie.

Janine was a blond bombshell. Many compared her to the late Marilyn Monroe. She had even had her hair and makeup styled to match Marilyn's for the announcement event, causing many to do a double take.

Of course, Chessa was standing at her husband's other side as they made their announcement, with Janine's husband, John, beside her. A quiet, conservative businessman, John dutifully smiled and nodded at the right moments, as did Chessa. But no one was really paying them much attention, given the presence of the handsome U.S. senator from New York and the beauty queen at his side.

Leif had selected none other than Jordan Greene as his running mate following the conventions. His televised announcement on the front lawn of the governor's mansion that early September morning was an even bigger shock to the media and the country than Darren's.

The ruddy, golden-haired presidential candidate and his darker-haired but equally handsome running mate smiled for the cameras amid a gathering of about two hundred supporters, and were dubbed by one clever reporter as the new "Butch Cassidy and the Sundance Kid."

But Darren and Janine—touted by news magazines and fashion columnists alike as the "new Kennedy king and queen" of the times—had plenty of mud to sling at their opponents. Both were U.S. military veterans, while it was pointed out often that neither Leif nor Jordan had served in the military. In fact, Leif's Middle East achievements already started to fade a bit in comparison, according to opinion polls. Second, both Darren and Janine were married, a family value that apparently wasn't important to their opposing team according to critics. Detractors claimed that Jordan, an unmarried yet eligible single man, might become distracted on the campaign trail, and Leif, a divorcée, couldn't even keep his marriage together much less handle an entire country. Third, Darren Richards was ten years older than Leif and had a whole lot more political and government experience. And last, but certainly not least, the Richards campaign and media alike claimed Leif Mitchell's candidacy had already been tarnished by his father-in-law and party predecessor, President Martin Greene, who would forever be branded as a president who was not only a failure but a quitter as well.

So despite Leif's growing popularity as a country-rock singer and the name he'd made for himself—at least among those following the peace proceedings in the Middle East—he was way behind his opponent in experience and campaign funding, and his curious choice for running mate had now rallied even more ammunition for his opponents to use against him. And this time there was no Ray Silas to lead his way.

With his selection of Janine Secour, Darren's star had risen even higher.

And with his selection of Jordan Greene, Leif's had fallen a little.

Still, Leif's poll numbers defied all the naysayers.

Coming out of the first four-day event in the Crescent City, Leif had climbed to within a two percent margin of Darren in the polls. Following the second convention in Charm City, Darren's popularity had inched a little further ahead and he was favored over Leif by ten percent of the popular vote.

"He's still too close for comfort," Darren often grumbled to Pete Connor, his closest aides, his family, his wife—basically whoever was within earshot of late.

After the first presidential debate, about which Darren had originally proclaimed that Leif Mitchell wasn't even worthy of his time and attention, the polls actually tipped temporarily in Leif's favor before seesawing back again.

Chessa grew weary of his constant surly attitude, and late one night after he came home in a particularly bad mood, she couldn't help but offer the suggestion that he do something about it.

She watched as her husband visibly struggled to hold back his temper, grunting instead of yelling a retort and grabbing a bag of chips and a soda instead of reaching for the closest bottle of anything alcoholic.

Sometimes I think I preferred him when he was drinking, she thought, surprising herself. She had heard an Al-Anon member or two say the same thing out loud at a meeting and often thought the person daft. Now she understood. *At least then he wasn't holding it all in, ready to explode. At least then he could take the edge off. Yeah, I never knew what would happen next, but now I feel like all I'm doing is waiting for the next big storm. I see it brewing, gathering force. Hurricane force.*

"Why don't you try to get an interview on the news or with the paper and go over the issues again? That's what voters should care about, not your personalities."

"You don't know what you're talking about," Darren growled at her, smashing the nearly empty potato chip bag between his hands. "I have no control over the polls."

"Well, at least you're still ahead," Chessa offered, attempting to cheer him up, trying to keep things peaceful.

"Not far enough," Darren said, slumping down in an armchair in their living room. "Every time I get a little bit ahead, he does too." And then he sat up straight, his face lit up. *Uh oh, here it comes, another one of his brainstorms,* Chessa realized. She had seen that face before. "Instead of trying to get ahead, I think I just need to bring him down." Darren stood and started pacing the room with agitation. "I need a drink to help me think."

And before Chessa could protest, Darren reached into the liquor cabinet nearby—there was one in nearly every room of the house— and drank a few gulps of bourbon straight out of the bottle, no ice, no glass.

Soon he was smiling mischievously, his brain hatching a plan.

Chessa quietly slipped up the stairs without him even noticing her exit. She instantly knew intuitively that she would be sorry for what she had wished for just minutes ago.

CHAPTER THIRTEEN

The commercials started off somewhat innocently enough that early fall.

The first was a contrast of the two candidates. Clips of Darren in public service showed a young man the day he was going off to serve in the Marines, then in his late twenties giving a speech at his alma mater, next as a U.S. Senator dynamically speaking before Congress, and finally as the man today on the campaign trail. These were interspersed with shots of Leif giving a country-rock concert, singing at the Kentucky Derby, grooming a horse at Little Falls. The commercial ended with shots of Darren and Leif juxtaposed: the former looking very professional in a suit and tie, the latter with a five-o'clock shadow dressed in beat-up jeans, boots, and a cowboy hat. The narrator at the end said, "Who is this guy, Leif Mitchell? And why should Americans trust some backwoods cowboy singer to lead them? We know who Senator Richards is, that he's a legitimate candidate for United States president, and the only real choice for voters."

The commercial played everywhere and often, costing millions, but only had a small impact on Leif's popularity ratings. So Darren's creative campaign staff writers launched an even more negative series of commercials to follow it in just a week's time.

The first to air portrayed a young towheaded boy of about eight running through a cornfield. At first he looked playful, then a look of panic came across his face and he ran faster. A somber male announcer's voice-over said, "If things keep going the way they are, our children will have no place to run from an economy that is dangerously close to collapsing again." The next camera shot showed Leif Mitchell and President Martin Greene standing in the White House shaking hands, smiling. "President Greene couldn't boost the economy, with his focus on Middle East countries instead of ours. And now his former son-in-law, Leif Mitchell, has the same wrong focus." Another shot showed Leif over in Israel, shaking hands with Israeli adults and hugging their children. "If you elect him, we'll have nothing left to give our own children." In the final footage, the blond-haired boy was standing hunched over, as if cold and hungry, and was reaching out his hand, looking up with doleful eyes like Tiny Tim. "Like Charles Dickens said, 'Charity begins at home.' I'm presidential candidate Darren Richards, and unlike my opponent, I plan to stay in the United States and work with those here at home struggling to find jobs, earn a living, get ahead, and live the American dream."

The second commercial showed Leif once again shaking hands with Israeli leaders and citizens. Interspersed with that visual were shots of various negative side effects that, according to the announcer on the commercial, were the direct result of President Greene's tenure in office—problems that would only worsen if people voted for Leif Mitchell. The shots showed a homeless bum, a huge oil spill in the ocean, gas prices rising. The voice said Leif Mitchell's plan to increase military spending in the Middle East would only make the poor in America poorer. The next shot showed a teenager who looked just like the same blonde-haired boy from the prior commercial making a drug deal on a dim street corner. "Protect America . . . vote for Darren Richards. He's a family man. He cares about *our* families."

While this last line was read, the camera showed Darren and Chessa standing together waving to the crowd at the convention. They were smiling, happy.

When Chessa saw it air, she had to admit to herself that she looked pretty good, and she looked happy. She only wished she felt the way she appeared.

Leif, who didn't have a tenth of Darren's coffers, stuck to a more grass-roots campaign, which included minimal television advertising, his commercials remaining positive and sticking to his agenda to keep America safe by keeping peace abroad, creating jobs to boost the economy by supporting big business through incentives and a ban on tax hikes, and a "less is more when it comes to government" motto. He was pro-life and pro-prayer and argued that God had created America as a great nation and that America owed God its gratitude. And he stated that America should show its gratitude accordingly, as the founding forefathers had planned—by going back to saying the Pledge of Allegiance with its "one nation under God" at all public functions and singing songs at all national events like "America the Beautiful," with its ode to the divine Creator, expressed in the words, "God shed His grace on thee."

He also promoted his relatively humble beginnings and faith that God would lead him to victory if it be His will. He spoke at shopping malls, American Legion halls, churches, women's societies, unions, and religious groups—anyone who would have him.

His campaign staff, led by the energetic boy wonder Logan Reese, worked from the same headquarters that Leif had set up when he ran for governor. Leif worked from his home base at the governor's mansion but was rarely there, flying all over the country to get his message out while Logan kept the office humming.

Meanwhile, Darren was increasingly sulky around everyone seeing that the commercials, aired during prime-time shows, the network news, and even NFL games—and costing him tens of millions of dollars—were still not affecting his opponent very much.

"I just don't get it," Darren said one night after he and Chessa had finished dinner. "A year ago no one had ever heard of Leif Mitchell. This guy starts out as a nobody, a horse farmer. Okay, so he wins as governor. Then suddenly he's a leading presidential candidate, and nothing I say or do will defeat him. I thought with Ray Silas dying the guy wouldn't stand a chance. But it's like he's untouchable, being guided or protected by something, someone powerful."

"Maybe you're reading too much into it all," Chessa offered, still trying to be the dutifully supportive wife and cheerleader and pacify him. "You're still in the lead, right?"

"Not by much. The election's only two months away. I've got to come up with something."

"I don't see how your commercials can get much tougher," Chessa said out loud, instantly wishing she hadn't.

"Whose side are you on anyway?"

Chessa saw the gleam of derision in her husband's eyes, then watched as his countenance changed from dour to delighted with himself, again brightening with an apparent idea. "Hmmm. . . you've just hit on something."

"That your commercials can't get any tougher?" Chessa was puzzled.

"No, that they're still not tough enough. We're holding back. We just need to find the nail to drive in the coffin, so to speak."

Chessa willed herself not to frown, trying to hide what she was feeling. *This doesn't sound good*, she thought. *I can't imagine how his commercials could get much nastier.*

Up until lately she had thought her husband was making progress spiritually and emotionally, treating her with more respect and keeping his anger at bay. *But now . . . now he's acting just as sick as ever,* she realized. *Why did I think he would change?*

And that night Chessa got on her knees and said the Serenity Prayer, asking God for the grace and strength to do the next right thing, and to do His will, whatever that might be.

Darren and Pete Connor were having a brainstorming session one crisp autumn afternoon in their Manhattan headquarters office on Ninth and Broadway when a young college intern burst through the front door, out of breath, and claimed he had "the answer."

"You're not going to believe this," the young man said excitedly, out of breath from hurrying past cubicles where staffers talked on phones soliciting contributions, typed up databases for direct mail campaigns, and monitored all of the social media and news.

"Calm down and come into my office." Darren beckoned the student—a scrawny Asian teenager wearing an NYU sweatshirt and baggy jeans—to enter the enclosed private room in the back of the first-floor offices. He sat down behind a large desk, motioning for Pete and the kid to sit across from him. Behind him hung a huge red, white, and blue poster on the wall with his photo that read "Senator Darren Richards for President."

"Have a seat, take a deep breath, and tell us." Darren leaned back in his typical composed state, rolling up the sleeves of his starched white shirt.

Pete crossed his arms, obviously impatient that he and his boss were being interrupted. He too wore a dress shirt and pants. He had kept his well-built physique from his college football days, when he and Darren had met and become instant buddies. Although he was clearly a little leery of the Asian student's excitement and how urgent his message could possibly be, Pete didn't say anything since Darren was in the room and appeared willing to give the kid his attention.

The student sat down breathing heavily and opened a book bag he had been carrying. He pulled out a rumpled piece of paper and pushed it across the desk.

Darren's eyes opened wide in genuine surprise. In his hand he held a copy of a medical release form from Washington Hospital Center signed by Wendy Mitchell. At the top it clearly stated the words "Voluntary Informed Consent for Medical Abortion." He gazed at the paper, his mouth wide open. "Shut the door behind you," he softly commanded the intern, who obeyed him with a small smile of satisfaction.

Darren slid the paper over to Pete, whose mouth dropped open as he read it. "Where did you get this?" Pete's tone was incredulous.

The student proceeded to tell them that he knew someone who worked as a nurse at Washington Hospital and had come across the form, copied it, and given it to him to bring to the campaign office.

"No offense, son, but why should I believe this is legitimate? You need to tell me who this nurse is, how she or he found this paper, and then why in the world that person would give it to you." Darren kept his tone even in an effort to conceal his amazement.

The Asian boy looked down, obviously worried.

"You want to protect this person, huh?" Darren asked. The boy nodded. "Well, I'm sorry, son, but without that information this is useless. But let me tell you what—I give you my word that no one outside of the two of us here in this office will ever know what you tell me."

"It's my mom," the boy said almost inaudibly. "She wants me to do well in America. She wanted me to get some credit here and figured if I help you, you'd remember me when you become president of the United States. My dad died a few years ago, and my mom doesn't speak English very well. She scrapes together all she has for me to attend the university. She wants me to become someone important one day. I'm majoring in political science." The student looked at each of them and smiled with pride.

"Okay, I believe you so far." Pete learned forward, resting his elbows on the desk. "But how did your mom get this in her possession?"

"She was the nurse on duty when Mrs. Mitchell had her abortion."

"Shhhh." Pete held his forefinger up to his pursed lips and then motioned with his hands for the boy to keep his voice down.

"She was instructed to shred the paper immediately, but she had already made a copy, as she usually did, for safekeeping," the boy whispered. "This is the copy."

Darren and Pete exchanged glances and allowed themselves a smile of satisfaction, delighting in the wondrous possibilities this would open up. Darren suddenly rose and shook the young man's hand across the desk. He saw in his bright eyes the hope that he would be rewarded. "Thank you, young man. I can assure you that I will remember you when it comes time to fill my new staff after I'm elected."

The student grinned, thanked him, and sauntered out of the offices. Darren knew he was probably lying to the young fellow. He didn't even like Orientals. But, the consummate politician, he said what he needed to say to accomplish the mission at hand.

Chessa thought perhaps she was imagining things when she heard what sounded like a champagne cork popping. But minutes later she found out her hearing was correct.

Darren entered their master bedroom carrying two stemmed flutes in one hand and a chilled magnum of Dom Perignon in the other.

He was smiling victoriously.

"Did I lose track of time? Did you win the election already?" Chessa tried to be light and witty to mask her feeling of foreboding upon seeing the champagne and her husband's already giddy demeanor. *It looks like he's already drunk down a bottle*, she thought.

"No, silly, although when I tell you what I just found out, you'll see why we have reason to celebrate the fact that I am now a shoo-in. But first—a toast to my wife, the next First Lady of the United States of America." Darren poured the bubbly into the glasses, handed her one, clinked his glass to hers, and downed his contents in one gulp. "Now wait until you hear this."

Darren imparted to Chessa all he had learned that afternoon from the young intern. "Can you believe it? That arrogant country singer has the whole world believing he's pro-life and pro-family when in fact his own wife had an abortion! Wait until we run a commercial about this!"

Chessa must have been frowning outright because Darren stopped smiling and was staring at her. "So once again you're not happy for me?" His smile flipped downward into a menacing grimace. "I'm beginning to think you're not going to vote for your own husband."

Chessa couldn't help but look at the empty glass in Darren's hand as he stood beside the bed where she sat, propped up against some pillows, the book she had been reading overturned in her lap. He had already poured and drank four glasses while telling her his juicy story. She had inadvertently counted.

He saw her eyes turn dark green as she gazed at the empty glass. "Come on, Chessa!" Darren was clearly exasperated. "This is only champagne in a tiny glass. I wanted to celebrate the good news with you. I'm done now." He put the cork back in the bottle and sat it down on an end table.

"It's not just the drinking, Darren." Chessa found the words slipping from her mouth before she could stop them.

"Then what the hell is it?"

She could see anger starting to brew as he began to pace the floor in front of the bed. "You would think my own wife would want to celebrate with me, but instead, here you are, being all negative and worried again."

"Are you sure this is true? And even if it is, do you really want to go down this path?" Chessa startled herself with her outburst. *Why do I care?*

"Of course it's true. Pete Connor wouldn't have even bothered me with it if he hadn't verified it first. And what do you mean, 'down this path'?"

Chessa thought for a moment. *Am I trying to protect my husband? Or is it Leif Mitchell I'm really concerned about?* In asking herself that last question, she realized she might be starting to develop some type of feelings for her husband's archenemy. That bothered her...

Darren was looking at her, waiting for an answer. "You know, exposing this to the public," Chessa said, "...it's really personal. And it might make you out to be some type of monster for putting it out there."

"Well, first of all, I'm only exposing the truth: that Leif Mitchell is a lying, hypocritical imposter who doesn't deserve to even be in this race. And second . . ."

Darren stood still, staring at Chessa, his eyes glazed, not really seeing her. *He's hatching one of his brilliant ideas again,* she realized, then knew it was true when his eyes cleared and refocused and he smiled at her.

"Chessa, congratulations, you've done it again."

"Done what?"

"Made me think of another great idea. You're absolutely right. I can't expose this. Some people might really think I am a monster. But if the press exposes it . . ." Darren sat on the edge of the bed, absentmindedly stroking his wife's arm. "Now, who do we know that's a reporter with a major newspaper?" Darren pretended to concentrate, knitting his brows. "I've got it! Amy Darlington!"

Chessa smiled despite herself. "She would love a story like that, wouldn't she?" Chessa could picture her best friend tackling the story like a shark smelling blood. But her concern for Leif quickly overshadowed her delight for her best friend, and warning bells sounded somewhere in her distant conscience.

Darren continued, excited about his scheme. "Do you think you could talk to her? I don't think it's appropriate if I call and tell her. She'll be skeptical if it comes from me. But you—she'll believe you, and I'm sure she'll appreciate the lead. This could be a big story for her."

Since when did he start caring about Amy? Chessa wondered. *He's right though. Amy will be thankful for a story like this.*

Chessa suddenly felt like she had an angel and devil sitting on her right and left shoulders.

"If it is true, then just like Amy always says, the American people have a right to know, don't they?" The little devil whispered in her ear. *"Besides, you're married to Darren, not Leif. Of course, if you want to give in to your lust . . ."*

"It's not lust but love," the tiny angel whispered back. *"Love for doing what's right. Love for your fellow man. And yes, love for this man who you hardly know but who you believe to be the best candidate to lead this country. Your country. He's a man after God's own heart, unlike your husband . . ."*

"But then you are still married and if your husband wins, you will be First Lady don't forget. Besides, it won't be worth fighting your husband over now, will it?"

The little devil does have a point, Chessa thought, figuratively whisking the pesky characters off her shoulders, deciding to act of her own volition. *And if my husband wins I will be able to do lots of good in the world,* she reminded herself. *So perhaps the end this one time would justify the means . . .*

Chessa trusted that Amy, more than anyone, would get all the facts and would be accurate and fair in her coverage.

"Okay."

"So why don't we celebrate under the covers, my lady?" Darren leaned toward her, kissing her cheek, lips, and neck.

Chessa really wasn't in the mood, but it had been a long time, even months, since she and her husband had been intimate. *He is being awfully sweet and romantic*, she reasoned. *Even though his breath smells like champagne. Better than whiskey or beer though.* Chessa forced all other thoughts out of her head and focused on pleasing him.

Chessa met Amy at a designated time and place in a secluded spot in the middle of Central Park. It was cloudy, cold, and windy for an early October afternoon, and there weren't too many people about since those who weren't in school or at work would usually stay indoors in this weather. Chessa was accompanied by a bodyguard, who was assigned to her by the Secret Service since she was the wife of a presidential candidate and it was getting close to the election. The man in the suit stood casually watching from several yards away, trying not to attract any undue attention as he had been instructed in his training and by Chessa herself.

So anyone who happened to walk or jog by saw only a young white woman—indistinguishable because she was wearing sunglasses and her head was covered by the hood of her jacket—and a nondescript young black woman embrace and then sit on a park bench chatting.

Chessa had briefed Amy by phone. She figured sending an e-mail would be too dangerous, and kept her conversation brief, saying she had a possible lead on a news story that would potentially make very big headlines, and that she had documented proof that she had to show her in person. Besides, Chessa said, it had been way too long since she had seen her old friend anyway. But Chessa also warned her that she had to stay incognito, since it pertained to the election.

When Chessa handed Amy a copy of the same paper the intern had shown Pete Connor, the *New York Times* reporter couldn't stifle her surprise and let out a loud whistle.

Chessa uncomfortably asked her friend to "act natural."

"If this is for real, this is huge," Amy whispered.

"It's definitely real." Chessa suddenly felt a nauseating sickness rise up within her, and for a moment she wanted to snatch the paper back, tear it up, say it was all a mistake. But it was too late.

"Just be careful. And for God's sake, please don't say it came from me. You promise, right?"

"Yes. If . . . when I verify that this is legit, it won't matter who gave it to me. And of course I'll protect you. But now I'm curious. Why wouldn't Darren want to jump on this?"

"Oh, he will all right. He just didn't want to be the one to leak it. He figured it should get objective coverage. And he thought you might want to have the first crack at it—you know, get the scoop."

Amy laughed. "Yeah, maybe I'll be promoted to editor-in-chief. Except I like being a reporter and wouldn't want that job no matter how much they paid me. But you're right, I just love getting the scoop and exposing the truth. And yeah, getting my byline on the front page every once in a while is good for a girl's ego. Maybe I'll even get a raise. Thank you."

The two women stood and hugged again and then parted company, walking in opposite directions. Chessa's bodyguard stayed a safe distance behind so as not to draw attention to her.

The same nauseating feeling hit Chessa in the gut as she sat in her living room watching the news two nights later.

". . . abortion paper signed by his wife." The television reporter was live outside the governor's mansion in Kentucky and was almost breathless with excitement in her delivery. "Prior to the revelation of the document, Governor Mitchell has claimed his wife, Wendy, lost their baby and has since vehemently spoken out against abortion as part of his platform.

"Governor Mitchell had no comment when we tried to question him on the matter. But we do have his opponent, presidential candidate Senator Darren Richards, who is live in our New York studio to comment on this latest breaking news." Chessa suddenly saw her husband sitting next to the female news anchor at the network news station. "Senator?"

"Well, I think the facts speak for themselves," Darren said with earnestness. "It will be preposterous now if the American people can vote for a man who deceived them, who is clearly hypocritical, who doesn't practice what he preaches. It makes me wonder if his whole candidacy has just been a sham from the start . . ."

Reporters in the field came on next with spokespeople from both parties to give their viewpoints. Then the female anchor came back on. "With the election only weeks away, I don't see how Leif Mitchell can possibly recover from this," she said conclusively.

CHAPTER FOURTEEN

Leif was going over some financial statements at his desk in his private office in the governor's mansion when Logan Reese stormed through the door without knocking.

Logan slammed the *New York Times* down on the desk in front of Leif, who looked up, startled. Leif had never seen Logan angry before, so he was shocked to see his loyal campaign manager visibly enraged at him.

"How could you let this happen?" Logan barked in a shrill voice. "You have betrayed us."

Leif stood up, stunned. "I don't know what you're talking about." While he was Logan's boss, in effect, he had always treated Logan as an equal. In turn, Logan had stood by Leif as his chief supporter and friend for many years, just as he had when they were kids. Still, Leif was the governor, and Logan had never raised his voice to him before.

"Just read the headline."

Leif looked down at the front page of the *New York Times* and saw the big black letters, taking a few moments to comprehend them. "Leif Mitchell's Wife Had Abortion."

"It's all over the Internet too. Why didn't you tell us?" Logan's tone changed from angry to disappointed, sad, resigned, and he stood staring at Leif from behind his horn-rimmed glasses, the servant looking to his master for an answer that would save them all. "Is it true?"

"Yes, I'm afraid so. And I didn't tell you because it was personal. I had nothing to do with Wendy's decision. In fact—and you must keep this to yourself—Martin Greene talked her into it when he wanted me out of the picture. He basically framed me."

Logan's boyish face reddened. "That son of a—"

"He told her I was fooling around in Israel, then talked her into the divorce and the abortion," Leif continued. "She came unglued. I wasn't even in the country when she had it, and we can prove that by the dates on the documents. But I guess none of that really matters now." Leif bowed his head in silence for a moment. *What matters is the damage this is going to cause—to Wendy, to Jordan, even to Martin and Carol. I gave them all my word I'd protect them.*

"I'm sorry for what you've gone through." Logan's voice was sincerely compassionate but then his resentment returned. "But Leif, what about us? Are you going to just give up? You have thousands—no, millions—of people who have supported you, who are counting on you."

Leif looked up from his reverie. Like Logan, Leif had never been prone to showing his emotions, but now a righteous fury started to fill the reservoir of sadness and regret within him. He picked up the front page of the paper and tore it in two.

"Of course I'm not going to give up."

He picked up his cell phone and called Jordan, who had been campaigning in his home state of Georgia. "I just saw it too," Leif said, hearing that Jordan had just received news of the story and had been blindsided by reporters right after his campaign appearance. "I'm sorry. We will fix this. How is Wendy?"

Jordan had informed Leif that he had quickly called his mother, who had told him she gently broke the news to Wendy, and that his sister was going to be staying at home with them at the White House for a few days until the media storm passed.

"Good, thank you; she will need to be watched. Right now we need to get together and come up with a plan. How soon can you get here?"

Jordan said he would get on the next plane to Kentucky.

"Great, I'll see you then." Leif looked at Logan, who was standing in front of his desk looking confused but hopeful.

"Don't just stand there," Leif ordered. "I need you to rally every single campaign staffer and bring them here as soon as possible. We'll have more room here than at the headquarters. We're going to fight this, and we're going to win. I'm sure Darren Richards was behind this, and by God, I will make him pay."

Leif was inspiring to many youths with his music, and as a result was able to recruit many passionate young people from college campuses. Many were students who were going after their political science degrees and wanting to intern to gain experience. Most were not only eager to help but extremely intelligent. So he had his own batch of bright interns.

The Committee to Elect Leif Mitchell leaders, headed up by Logan Reese, channeled the students' energy into investigating anything and everything about Darren Richards—his childhood, background, family, friends, work, military and political endeavors—including anything that might unlock a potential scandal for Leif to use if needed.

And from this band of college campaign warriors soon came the key to his revenge.

One of the most exceptional interns, who was double-majoring in science and government at Columbia, had been on the team investigating RA Technologies.

There were just three weeks left before the election on the day Logan called Leif and Jordan into the new campaign headquarters conference room in a wing of the governor's mansion and shut the door behind them. The student, known only as Charlie, sat at the end of the long conference table to tell them his findings.

"We've discovered something important." Charlie, a tall, gangly young man wearing a Columbia sweatshirt and jeans, sipped on a can of energy drink. He looked disheveled and haggard for his young age, as if he had been up all night, but his eyes glittered with excitement. He pulled a sheaf of papers from his worn backpack. "It's all right here, but I'll cut to the chase. We've found out that there's been an increase—a huge increase—in the shipments of oocytes, or human eggs, coming into the labs at RA over the past year."

"And why is this important?" Leif asked. "Excuse me, but you'll have to fill us in."

Leif, Logan and Jordan were all aware of the debate over the ethics of stem cell research. The Mitchell for President campaign had included rhetoric that called for resurrecting stricter regulations on providing federal funding for it under laws that had been passed in 2001 but were abolished eight years later.

But Leif was largely unaware, as were Jordan and Logan, of the proliferation of human egg harvesting in the U.S., and of the growing outcry against it.

Charlie was a fountain of knowledge on the subject, however, as he had written his dissertation for his doctorate on it. He told the men gathered that he had become engaged in the topic when he noticed flyers on campus enticing female students to "help a good cause and make money" to help fund their education at the same time. Upon further research, Charlie found out college campuses were ripe with female students engaging in the process of donating their eggs not only for in vitro fertilization to help infertile couples get pregnant, but for scientific research involving cloning. In fact, sometimes the young women donors didn't know or care why or to whom they were donating—just so they got paid, which often amounted to about five thousand dollars per donation.

"It's all over the Internet." Charlie said. Then he added he had discovered that a friend who had talked to him for his paper about going through the process ended up having some serious side effects. And he found out she wasn't alone.

Charlie outlined the process, apologizing ahead of time for using so much scientific jargon. "The average woman only produces one egg a month. In order to build up her egg supply for maximum collection, a donor goes through a process called hyper-ovarian stimulation, a procedure in which she takes large doses of hormones that over-stimulate her ovaries into producing approximately a dozen eggs.

"The eggs are then extracted by a long suctioning needle, which is guided into each ovary using a tube attached to an ultrasound probe inserted into the vagina. Donors are given anesthesia, and usually stay in the clinic for one or two hours following the surgery."

Jordan spoke up in a soft voice. "So, I'm afraid to ask—what are the side effects?"

"Most girls experience fluid buildup, cramps – the same symptoms as a bad period. But some—usually about one in ten—suffer from what they call ovarian hyper-stimulation syndrome or OHSS."

"And what happens to them?" Logan asked.

"The drugs they use to stimulate the ovaries can sometimes cause permanent damage," Charlie said quietly. "Some have to have their ovaries removed and can no longer have children of their own. What's more, since egg retrieval involves surgery, these girls can suffer damage to other organs like their kidneys, bladder, bowel or uterus. There have been many women who end up with serious infections, and even some who have died."

"It sounds like the money's not worth it. Why would these girls possibly take those kinds of risks?" Logan spoke up, baffled.

"A lot of times they're not told the truth about the side effects." Charlie sadly shook his head. "My friend was only told to sign the papers, and that there would be only mild discomfort and minimal risk involved at the clinic she went to."

"So what happened?" Leif and Logan asked at the same time.

"She donated her eggs several times over the course of two years. She also wasn't informed that the risks increase the more you donate. She was saving to finish college since her parents had divorced and couldn't afford to send her any longer. Her ovaries developed cysts and had to be removed, and now she's no longer able to have children of her own one day." Charlie sighed. "She was devastated."

"And all of this is legal." Leif made the statement with disgust. "And these women apparently still volunteer. So how is that going to help us bring down RA Technologies and Darren Richards?"

"Egg donations made by US women aren't nearly enough to conduct the research being done at RA," Charlie responded. "It's all about the numbers. There are only sixty million childbearing females in the US, and of course only a fraction will donate their eggs. Average estimates suggest that at least one hundred human eggs are needed to create just one stem cell line. The number of eggs necessary for stem cell research is astronomical.

"So research companies like RA are turning to poorer countries, where young women are happy to make a few hundred dollars for their eggs. And if their country forbids egg harvesting, they go to countries like Cypress, where the practice is booming. Eastern European women are actually being recruited for their eggs. Sometimes the ovaries of these women are hyper stimulated so that they produce thirty or forty eggs at a time, which greatly increases the risks they face. But the money to them is huge—even if it's just a hundred bucks, which is more than they can make in months working in slave labor camps, in the fields or factories, or as prostitutes.

"Which is why what we found at RA is important," Charlie said, draining his energy drink. "The huge increase in egg shipments points to one thing."

"Human egg trafficking?" Leif asked astutely.

Charlie nodded with a tired smile. "These young women overseas are obviously being recruited, or more accurately, exploited, for their eggs. Most are being lured by the money and aren't told of the long-term effects. But we found through our research—and this is really sad—that some young girls are actually being forced into it. In fact, in some of the poorer, war-torn countries, their own families or governments make these girls undergo the procedure as soon as they become of child-bearing age—as early as twelve or thirteen-years-old. By the time they reach their twenties, these girls are used up and usually wind up handicapped or dead.

It's ironic: they give up a part of themselves so that new human lives can be created or people can be healed, and then their own lives are crippled or destroyed—all in the name of research."

Leif, Logan and Jordan sat quietly, taking in all of Charlie's grim information.

"And you think that RA is practicing human egg trafficking?" Leif asked somberly.

Charlie rubbed his eyes, weary from his presentation. "I would say it's more than possible. These documents are a good start, but proving it is another story."

"Ah, don't worry about that; we'll prove it, all right." Leif stood and resolutely crossed his arms. "Leave that one to me. Thank you, Charlie. You deserve an A on that paper of yours."

"I just want justice for other women," Charlie responded.

After the gentlemen left one by one, Leif retired to his private office. He looked through the file on his desk that held newspaper clippings of the articles that had subsequently gone viral on the Internet stating his ex-wife had had an abortion, destroying the baby that was his.

He felt sick to this stomach all over again, but took a deep breath, held down his breakfast, and looked for the article that had broken the story. It was in the *New York Times* with a byline by a reporter named Amy Darlington.

Leif wanted this Amy Darlington to have the same opportunity to write a piece about Darren Richards.

He picked up the phone, trying to keep his rage at bay.

Amy called Chessa early that Sunday morning as she was getting ready to go to the local corner market for a few groceries. Luckily she had left her cell phone on vibrate so Darren, who was sleeping, kept right on snoring.

"You won't believe it, but I got a call yesterday from Governor Mitchell! He sounds as sexy on the phone as he looks on TV. And he wants me to investigate a big story. I almost fainted!"

Chessa went downstairs to the kitchen, cell phone to her ear, and listened as Amy confided that the story involved RA Technologies.

"What about RA?" Chessa immediately came to attention, her senses on high alert now.

"Well, he didn't elaborate; he just said that the methods they're using on one of their current research projects may be immoral and unethical, and I might want to check it out. Since I'm your best friend, I thought you should know about it before you read it in the headlines." Amy's tone changed from schoolgirl excitement to real contriteness. "I'm sorry. I know it's your family's company. But I hope you understand. I'm a news reporter. I've got to do my job. And if I don't do it, somebody else will. It sounds like a big deal."

Chessa knew what her father-in-law's company was working on, and she knew how they were accomplishing the task. Darren had told her about it proudly one night when he had been drinking and loose-tongued. He had said that he was hoping they could reveal the cure right before the election, and then swore her to secrecy. The only people who knew about the top-secret diabetes cure research were Donald Richards, his CEO and CFO, a handful of scientists directly involved, Darren, and now Chessa.

She had done her own little investigation online about stem cell research and egg harvesting and didn't like what she had seen. After all, she worked at a job where she was constantly defending women's rights.

But she also believed that the cure for diabetes was a noble one, and if they were really close to finding a cure like her husband said they were, perhaps the effort and the donations of all those young girls would not be in vain.

Alarms went off in her head now as she listened to Amy, and a fire burned inside urging her to stop her friend before it was too late, or at least delay her until she could have a chance to think this through.

"Amy, I need you to do me the biggest favor you've ever done for me," Chessa chose her words carefully. "You know that Leif Mitchell is just trying to get even for the abortion story Darren capitalized on. No offense, but why else would he have singled you out?"

"Because I'm a great reporter." Amy sounded defensive.

"And we both know you are. Still—how many reporters work at the *Times?* Don't you think he singled you out to use you?"

"Okay, you're probably right that he picked me for a reason. But I still have an obligation to look into this."

"I know you do. So here's the favor. I'm going to ask you to just hold off for twenty-four hours and embargo the story so I can find out more information myself. I do know the company is getting close to making a huge scientific breakthrough that will make whatever story Leif Mitchell is trying to dig up look like it belongs buried on the back page in comparison. If I find out they're close, I promise to share the news with you so you can break the story. And if they're not, then I will give you all the inside information you'll need to really do a good job on it. But if I don't get in there while they're unaware there's a story brewing, then chances are they'll be on red alert and nothing will get out. And then all you'll have is a bunch of conjecture by a bitter candidate who's trailing in the polls."

"Well, it is Sunday and there's no one I can reach anyway." Amy reluctantly agreed to embargo the story and give Chessa a twenty-four-hour reprieve based on her trust that her friend would never deceive her.

As soon as she turned off her phone, Chessa began pacing the kitchen floor, trying to think her way through this. She had just bought herself some time to take a look at this latest development and hopefully do something about it. She just wasn't sure what that should be. She walked back and forth, pondering her options.

On one hand, she thought, *if I just do nothing and let Amy go ahead and cover the story, maybe that will truly lead to Darren's downfall and he'll lose the race. Then, once the pressure of all of this is off, maybe I can quietly divorce him and be free. On the other hand, if I find a way to stop Amy from investigating this and Darren wins, at least I will have hopefully saved a whole bunch of people from suffering and dying from diabetes and I'll become First Lady.*

And I will be stuck in this marriage forever.

Chessa realized she had been thinking on and off about divorcing Darren for quite some time. Always it came down to a mixture of wanting to do the right thing, which in her mind meant staying married no matter what, and lacking the courage to go for it.

She had come to realize through Al-Anon that she was 'co-dependent' and a 'people pleaser'—both considered potential 'defects of character' among people in the program. Chessa knew she had always justified her actions—whether it be as a child trying to step between her parents and keep them from fighting, or as an adult trying to please and support her husband no matter what—as "keeping the peace."

But looking back, she realized there was a fine line between being a peacemaker and a people pleaser—maybe she was a bit of both—and that it had come at a great cost.

I've lost myself along the way, she thought sadly, standing in her kitchen, immobilized now by regret, resentment, remorse.

Chessa felt her head was so full right now it might just explode, then it struck her that she needed to ask for help. For the first time in a very long time—since she was a little girl, in fact—she folded her hands in prayer and closed her eyes. "Dear God, please help me do the right thing. Please help me to know what that is." She desperately wanted out of the marriage and was beginning to realize she didn't even care if her husband became president of the United States and she became First Lady. It just wasn't worth it anymore.

Suddenly the answer came with an intuitive thought that she realized must have been from God. *Go to church and pray about it.*

Chessa hadn't been in a church since she had gotten married. She quickly pulled out her smart phone and looked up the service schedule at Christ Church. If she hurried, she could just make the nine-o'clock service. Her bodyguard had already been waiting to follow her to the grocery store. He would just have to tag along.

She arrived a few minutes after the Methodist service started and sat in the last pew. A woman cantor was just finishing singing a beautiful song about God's call.

Chessa's mind drifted between her own thoughts and the minister's words of welcome.

She snapped back to attention when he read the gospel.

"...you know the way to where I am going." The minister read from the Gospel of John Chapter 14. "Thomas said to him, 'Lord, we do not know where you are going. How can we know the way?' Jesus said to him, 'I am the way, and the truth, and the life. No one comes to the Father except through me. If you had known me, you would have known my Father also. From now on you do know him and have seen him.'

I do not know Him, Chessa thought as a tear rolled down her cheek. *Why have I stayed away so long?*

'...whatever you ask in my name, this I will do, that the Father may be glorified in the Son. If you ask me anything in my name, I will do it.'

Can I really believe that? Chessa wordlessly asked the God of her limited understanding.

'...If you love me, you will keep my commandments...' the minister continued.

Chessa's mind reeled on that part. *Do not commit adultery. I know that's one of them.* She remembered being taught the Ten Commandments as a child in Bible school. *And I know that the Bible teaches that divorce is wrong and remarriage after divorce is a sin because it's considered adultery...*

'...Peace I leave with you; my peace I give to you. Not as the world gives do I give to you. Let not your hearts be troubled, neither let them be afraid.'

My heart is troubled and afraid. Chessa knew she had to give up any outcomes or expectations and pray only for God's will, for His peace, which He alone could give. So she prayed the only prayer that came to mind. *God grant me the serenity to accept the things I cannot change, the courage to change the things I can and the wisdom to know the difference.*

And suddenly Chessa heard a possible solution: that she seek out Leif Mitchell and warn him not to give Amy the story, and then hope beyond hope that his goodness in refraining from stooping to Darren's level may curry the favor of the people—and of God—and he would win the election.

The thought of that outcome sent an immediate icy fear through her being. For suddenly she knew that if she somehow kept Amy from reporting the story and Leif won—and Darren found out, which he would inevitably do—he would be so furious he would come after her in all his rage, seeking revenge. *He will want to kill me.*

Her fear, she knew, was real. So now she had a choice. She heard the words from someone she had heard in the rooms of Al-Anon talking in her head. *"We can choose to act out of faith or act out of fear."*

There's only one solution, she realized as the minister finished delivering his sermon and the congregation was being called on to stand and pray. *I have to go to Kentucky to see Governor Mitchell.*

Suddenly Chessa felt a wave of peace and clarity flow through her whole being. *The wisdom to know the difference.* She wiped her tears and smiled. *All I know is that I can no longer just sit by and accept the way things are. I need to have the courage to change things. To make a gesture of peace that might just make a difference.*

Who knows where it will lead? Chessa didn't care. All she knew in that moment in time was that it would all be okay.

The choir broke into the hymn, "Be Not Afraid," and Chessa sang along through her tears.

CHAPTER FIFTEEN

Chessa left two hours later that Sunday bound for La Guardia International Airport and the next flight she could get out of New York.

Darren was still asleep when she quietly slipped back into the house after the church service, packed a few items of clothing in a carry-on bag, and went back out the front door into a waiting taxi, which was followed by a car carrying two Secret Service agents.

She left him a note on her pillow.

"Dear Darren,

I'm sorry I had to leave so early this morning without saying good-bye. I have a friend who's in trouble and I had to go help out. That's all I can say for now, as the friend's information needs to stay anonymous. I will tell you all about it when I return. I should be home by tomorrow.

Love, Chessa."

She knew he would be upset when he read it, but she couldn't possibly tell him the truth. *And besides, this is for his own good*, she justified to herself. Plus, she knew Darren had a tremendously hectic two days that lay before him campaigning in Pennsylvania.

But inside she knew she wasn't taking off at noon on a Sunday to fly down to try to see Leif Mitchell in order to save her husband's campaign or even his dignity. She was doing it because she believed in her heart it was the right thing to do. She couldn't let thousands of people suffer and possibly die of diabetes, not to mention stand by while thousands more lost their jobs at RA Technologies. The ripple effect of the repercussions of both could affect tens of thousands of innocent people.

Most importantly, she had to stop Leif from doing the wrong thing—from doing something so underhanded that it would cause him to lose the election and cost him the presidency. *And he is by far the best candidate – the only candidate fit for the job*, she knew. *He is God's choice.*

Chessa didn't consciously admit it to herself, but deep down she also wanted to meet this country-rock singer her husband had claimed as his archenemy. Her old reporter's curiosity was still very much a part of her. She wanted to see for herself, live and in person, if this man was as great as she believed him to be.

After a two-hour flight, Chessa's plane landed at two p.m. on October fourteenth in Lexington. There were just twenty-two days left until the election.

She had traveled with a scarf wrapped around her head and with big sunglasses on so that no one would recognize her. A bodyguard accompanied her on the flight.

Still, she was almost stopped by a flight attendant who looked at her long and curiously as she walked toward the end of the plane's aisle. Luckily, the attendant's attention was diverted when a couple behind her, dressed in somewhat outrageous drag queen attire (Chessa wasn't sure if they were both "girls," "guys," or one of each) started singing "Killer Queen" rather loudly, obviously having drunk too many Bloody Marys.

Chessa took advantage of the performance to slip out of the plane's exit door unnoticed, her bodyguard in tow.

She arrived by taxi a little before three at the quaint yet elegant bed and breakfast on the outskirts of Lexington. She had decided to stay in the six-bedroom B&B so as not to be noticed. She had an old newspaper friend from college who lived in Lexington help her book the room.

And since this same friend had made a lot of connections through his position as editor-in-chief at the Lexington paper, he was the perfect person to keep tabs on Leif Mitchell and inform her of where the governor would be the night of her arrival.

It turned out Governor Mitchell had made plans to fly in from a campaign stint in the northeast that morning, meet with staffers for a briefing at his headquarters, give a speech at Churchill Downs, and then have a quiet dinner with his parents at Little River, where he might stay or return home to the mansion before flying out again the next morning for a trip out west.

So Chessa would have a limited window of opportunity to meet him. Her friend advised her against showing up at the racetrack rally or even his headquarters, where there would still be too many people around, and thus layers of possible interference between them.

Her best shot at actually getting face time would be at Little River, he said.

Chessa had balked at his suggestion at first. How crass, to show up unannounced at his parents' home and barge in on their intimate family dinner, she had argued.

And yet, much to her chagrin, that was the very scheme she had cooked up, and now sat worrying about in the large soaking tub in the private bathroom that was part of her bedroom suite.

Exhausted, she had tried to take a nap after arriving at the quaint hotel. The owners had allowed her to book the entire bed and breakfast so that no other guests would be around to bother her, and had agreed not to say a word to anyone about her whereabouts.

Chessa had far too much on her mind, however, to sleep, so instead she drew a bath to try to relax before her excursion to Little Falls.

She arrived at the Little Falls homestead in her nondescript rental sedan as the sun started to touch the treetops, which were ablaze with color, taking her breath away. Chessa had instructed the Secret Service agent who had followed her to wait for her in his car and he unhappily acquiesced, making sure she took a two-way radio with her to the house.

The stone farmhouse sat at the highest point of the ranch, with the stables in the distance on the right, and rolling, fenced-in pastures as far as she could see. The American flag flew high on a pole in the front yard.

Growing up in the city, Chessa had never been to a real horse farm, but she had ridden horses on trail rides as a girl with the Scouts. She had always loved animals, especially horses, and had dreamed of growing up on a farm just like Little Falls.

Although she had traveled a lot, especially recently on her cross-country jaunts with her husband, this was by far the most gorgeous place she had ever been.

She took a deep breath, dressed once again in her sunglasses and scarf, and rang the doorbell. *This is absolutely crazy,* she thought. *I am the enemy. What makes me think they'll let me in the door, much less see him?*

But I have to talk to him, she reasoned with herself. *I have to tell him that what he's about to do will harm a lot of people. And knowing what little I know of him, he doesn't want to be known for stooping as low as Darren, with his mean-spiritedness and negative campaigning. He's a good man, and he deserves to be president.*

Her thoughts were interrupted by the front door opening.

A short, stout woman who appeared to be middle-aged and of Spanish descent stood glaring at Chessa, not saying a word. *Must be one of the help,* Chessa thought, since she knew from her research that it wasn't Leif's mother.

"Is Governor Mitchell home?" Chessa tried to sound nonchalant, friendly, but inside her heart was pounding.

"And may I ask who is calling and what is the nature of the call?"

How very primly Southern. Chessa held back her smile, now wanting to giggle at the absurdity of her visit, having the same uncontrollable urge she would often have as a child to laugh in church at precisely the wrong moment. *You're an adult,* she admonished herself, biting the inside of her mouth.

"I'm Mrs. Richards, and I have a delivery for the governor's horses," Chessa said matter-of-factly, praying beyond hope that this woman did not know who she was.

"Well . . ." The woman hesitated for a moment. "Okay, I think he is up at the stables. Drive down that gravel road over there; you can't miss it." She pointed out the door to the left.

Thank you, God. Chessa said a quick prayer of thanks as she started her car and drove, followed by her Secret Service agent, down the hill along the windy path. Obviously the woman had no idea who she was.

Chessa also congratulated herself on her choice of clothing. It was an average day weather-wise for an October evening in Kentucky, with temperatures ranging in the high sixties, so she had worn layers and dressed casual, again, not wanting to give away her identity until the last possible moment. She had on comfortable brown shoes, a cream-colored lightweight sweater top and dark blue jeans, and had brought along a teal green cropped jacket that matched her eyes and scarf.

Arriving in the barn, Chessa was taken off guard immediately as a stable hand—a large, muscular man who looked like a Native American Indian with black hair tied back in a ponytail and a mouth full of chewing tobacco—seemed to appear out of the dark interior of the stalls like an apparition.

He nodded at Chessa, sizing her up with his eyes. She still had not removed the scarf or sunglasses, even though she clearly didn't need the latter, with the sun starting to fade into the dusky orange sky.

"Evening, ma'am. May I help you?" His deep, scratchy voice had a barely detectable yet undeniable tone of wariness.

"Yes, I was sent here to see Governor Mitchell." Chessa kept her distance from the dark towering hulk.

"I'm afraid he's not here right now. He went out riding, and I don't know how long he'll be."

Think. Chessa realized she had to forge ahead. "I have a delivery of apples, carrots, and grain for the governor's horses in my car that I was hoping you could unload for me. And something I must hand him myself," she said, pulling an envelope out of her jacket. "It's urgent."

The big man gave her a wide, tobacco-stained grin. "Well, little lady, the only way you can do that is to ride out there and find him." He crossed his beefy arms in front of his barrel chest, clearly satisfied that he had shut her down.

"Okay." Chessa watched the hulk uncross his arms and open his eyes wide in surprise. "I've ridden before. Could you please saddle up one of the horses for me?"

The stable hand continued to stare at her in disbelief, apparently unsure what to do next.

Come on, I'm wasting daylight. In exasperation, Chessa flung off her scarf and sunglasses and matched the big man's stare. "I'm Chessa Richards, wife of Senator Darren Richards. If I don't go give Governor Mitchell these papers tonight, there will be serious consequences. I realize I will ride at my own risk. Please. . ."

She let a slight helpless female quality seep into her plea and it worked. She saw that while he was obviously dumbstruck by her tenacity, he also now realized that such a slip of a woman, who was also clearly unarmed, could not possibly harm his boss.

He reclaimed his composure and his voice. "Only if I ride with you." He then hurried to saddle and bridle two horses while Chessa went to talk to the Secret Service agent and inform him of her plans.

The Indian-looking man brought out the horses: a stunning Palomino gelding for Chessa and a huge black quarter horse for himself. Introducing himself only as Shiloh, he helped her hoist herself up and then mounted himself. "You're on Sunny." Chessa hoped her horse's name was an indication of his personality. "This here's Nightwatch." He patted his horse's neck affectionately and Chessa did the same with her horse.

Before they took off, Shiloh pulled a cell phone from his pocket. "I need to call and see where he is." Not wasting words, he talked into the phone quickly. "Yes . . . we're coming out there to meet you . . . someone who has an urgent message for Leif . . . on Choctaw Ridge? We'll see you in ten."

Before Chessa had a chance to question him as to where they were headed or with whom he had spoken, Shiloh put his cell phone back in his jacket pocket and started walking his horse around the stables toward the open pastures, giving her little choice but to follow.

Like out of some romance novel, they came out of a clearing in the woods and rode into the sunset, the sky a never-ending canopy of color, with cirrus streaks of scarlet and tangerine cutting across aquamarine and navy.

Chessa took a moment to appreciate the sky God had painted, but then quickly refocused on her horse. *I need to concentrate on staying on top of the ton of warm moving muscle beneath me*, she realized. Their horses walked for what seemed like a mile until they reached the end of a fenced pasture and were out on the open plain. Shiloh glanced back at Chessa, nodded, then gave his horse a quick kick of his heels. It started trotting, then broke into a canter.

Sunny followed her lead and Chessa held on, gripping the horn of the Western saddle with her left hand, holding the reins and some of Sunny's blonde mane in her right, and clamping her thighs tightly to the sides of the horse beneath her. Chessa was exhilarated.

After a quick jaunt the horses slowed to a trot, then a walk, as they crested a narrow grassy hill. As their horses stood still while Shiloh tried his cell phone again, Chessa looked down at the breathtaking scenery before her. A stream wound its way through the forest to their right, and woods bordered their left as far as they could see. A valley stretched down the hill before them, and then another hill sloped up from there into the horizon.

Chessa and Shiloh could see three horses and their riders sitting on the far hill, appearing as tiny silhouettes against nature's magnificent backdrop.

Sunny and Nightwatch pricked up their ears, sensing the other horses and their riders on the far hill. Suddenly they all heard a horse whinny and a human's shrill whistle.

In an instant, Nightwatch took off into a full gallop down the hill and into the valley below. Sunny raced right behind him, and Chessa hunkered down, held her breath, and prayed she stayed on, the wind whipping at her hair and tearing at her eyes.

Their horses pulled up into a trot again once they started up the hill, and then slowed to a walk. Chessa blinked and realized she had been holding her breath and nearly shutting her eyes in her razor-sharp focus on simply not falling. As the horse beneath her stopped, she caught her breath, straightened in her saddle, and looked around her.

Less than ten feet away, Leif Mitchell sat atop a roan mare and was flanked by two other men on their horses. All three were dressed similarly in cowboy hats, boots, jeans, and leather jackets. Chessa was unaware that she held her breath once more as she sat staring at Governor Leif Mitchell.

While the horses approached each other and touched noses in familiarity, Shiloh dismounted and then held up his hand to help Chessa off of Sunny.

Meanwhile, the three men exchanged glances, and then Leif quietly came down from his mount and stood facing her, just two feet away.

Chessa's shoulder-length hair had shaken loose from the scarf, which had fallen off along with her sunglasses during their ride, and was in wild disarray from being tossed in the wind.

She took a moment to get her "land legs" back and then peered into Leif's piercing blue eyes. Her voice caught in her throat for a moment as she gazed at his features. Amy was right. *He is gorgeous.*

Leif had a slight five-o'clock shadow, which Chessa guessed was from not having shaved in a while and which made him look more ruggedly handsome than he did on camera in her opinion.

His look of amusement quickly turned to irritation as he recognized her.

"What are you doing here?" His voice was tinged with disdain, and he put his hands on his hips, standing his ground.

"I'm sorry for not telling you in advance of my visit. I'm Chessa Richards." She extended her hand to shake his, but it was left dangling, so she awkwardly put it back in her pants pocket.

"I know who you are." Leif's tone remained icy. "I asked what you're doing here."

"I came to give you this." Chessa pulled the envelope out of her jacket pocket. "It's a document from RA Technologies stating the purpose of their latest stem cell research. I also brought along a carload of apples, carrots, and horse feed for your horses. I hope you consider it a peace offering. I've come to stop you from making a big mistake—not because I care about my husband, who's the biggest jerk I know, but because I care about what happens to you . . . whether you win."

Leif looked at her now thoroughly confused and still wary, but took the envelope from her outstretched hand and read the document, which stated that RA was doing research on the cure for Type-1 diabetes. Chessa told him she had recently found it in one of her husband's private folders in his home office when he was sleeping off a drinking spree, and had retrieved it right before leaving for her trip to Kentucky.

"Why..."

"Just hear me out." Chessa cut off his question, glancing up at Shiloh, who stood a few feet away looking uncomfortable, and then up at the two men, apparently his Secret Service agents, still seated on their horses, waiting patiently for a sign from Leif on what to do next. She spoke softly so they couldn't hear. "Can I talk to you alone?"

Leif hesitated for a minute, then gave orders to the others to ride back to the stables without him and inform his parents that he would be home a little later than he had thought.

Since it was beginning to get dark, he told them he and Mrs. Richards would talk as they rode back.

After the three men rode off, Leif and Chessa got back on their horses and started to ride at a slow pace back down to the stables. Their horses, familiar with each other, were content to walk side by side.

"First of all, I'm sorry for what my husband did to you, planting the story about your wife's abortion."

"Ex-wife," Leif interjected, then said sarcastically, "Yeah, a real class act, your husband."

"I know. I live with him. He's worse than you know. I should have left him many times. It's my fault the story was leaked to Amy Darlington, so if you're going to blame anyone, blame me." She watched Leif's expression become agitated when he heard Amy's name spoken aloud, but he remained silent. "I know about your call to the *New York Times* reporter," Chessa continued, carefully watching his face register surprise that she knew. "She told me. She's my best friend. And while I can't say that I blame you for wanting to seek revenge on my husband for what he did to you, I believe that it would be a really bad idea for you and for all concerned. So I've asked her to hold off on talking to you for now."

Leif frowned. "Even if she doesn't do the story, I can leak it to someone else, put it on the Internet, bring it out in the next debate or just run commercials about it. You can't stop me. Your husband deserves this for what he did to me. You may have helped him leak the facts, but he took full advantage, twisting it into a nightmare."

"You're right. But if you get revenge you'll just be stooping as low as Darren. And trust me—he has enough money to run ten times the amount of commercials and online ads you run to counter you. He could practically buy the Internet at this point. So he will make whatever you say look like lies anyway."

"Why should I believe any of what you're saying?"

"Because of your strong faith in God, Governor Mitchell…"

"You can call me Leif. And what does my faith in God have to do with any of this?"

Chessa smiled. "Leif, even though I've never met you before, I've kept close tabs on you. Unlike my husband, I know that you are a good man who believes in God. I know in my heart that you're the best man to lead our country as president. If you follow through and give this story to Amy, or try to run commercials about it, a lot of harm could come of it. Many people could lose their jobs."

She could tell by Leif's expression he still was unconvinced. "You're not aware of this, but RA Technologies is coming close to finding the cure for Type 1 diabetes that they outline in that letter. So if you stand in their way, thousands of people—maybe millions—could unnecessarily suffer, and perhaps even die of diabetes. I'm sure RA and the Richards family will release the news about the potential cure if they're attacked, and the shutdown on it that will inevitably occur, which will make you look like the bad guy. There's no way you would win after that."

"Do you even know where RA is getting all of its material to do their stem cell research?" Leif smugly challenged her. "Have you heard about egg harvesting and human egg trafficking?"

"I have."

Leif looked impressed, then perplexed.

"And I'm not saying it's right," Chessa countered. "In fact, I'm against all of it. But I think the best way to combat these issues is for you to get into office and then pass legislation that will work. You need to act on it, not just talk about it in campaign rhetoric that will be forgotten once the election's over. Look, you might ruin my husband's chances if you go forward with this story. But you'll also destroy what's been done so far on this cure. And you might just destroy your own chances in the long run. If the voters see you as a candidate stooping to an all-time low in negative campaigning, you may make Darren look like a hero. And God forbid he win."

"How can you not want your own husband to win?" Leif was still wary. "You would lose becoming the First Lady of the United States, living in the White House."

"None of that matters if it comes at the price of knowing for the rest of my life that my husband is a big fraud."

"But you're not sure what will happen with the electorate, or any of this, one way or the other."

"That's true. But if you win without engaging in this battle, you won't have to live with the burden on your conscience of having harmed innocent victims as a result, or worse yet, having won out of spite and revenge. You do believe in the truth of the Bible verse, 'vengeance is mine sayeth the Lord,' right?"

Leif slowly nodded, still eyeing her warily, not sure where her discourse was headed.

"That's why I said earlier that I believe your faith in God will lead you to realize that what I'm saying is true. If you believe in God's will, in God's justice, in God's plan, than you will leave this all in His hands."

"Let's say I agree not to pursue this, not to call your reporter friend again…if your husband has the temper you say he does, won't you be at risk once he finds out that you've betrayed him by visiting me?"

"I'm afraid of that, yes. But I also have to leave it all up to God." Chessa sighed and looked up to the sky, which had turned indigo, allowing what seemed like a million stars to shine.

"Why didn't you just leave him?"

"I ask myself that every day. Believe me, I've prayed about it over and over, and I just haven't felt it was the right thing to do. I keep praying for God's will, and I guess secretly hoping God will change him. Meanwhile, at least I have friends who help me deal with it all."

They arrived at the stables, which were lit up from within. Leif's men, including Shiloh, had already taken care of their horses for the night and had disappeared.

Even though it was dark now, Chessa could make out the silhouette of a man standing a few yards from the stables. Chessa saw it was her bodyguard, standing with his arms crossed, and waved to him. She watched him nod. It was too dark to make out his expression. *He's probably mad at me*, she thought. *Oh well, he'll get over it.*

Horses neighed and whinnied their hellos to Sunny and Sally as Leif and Chessa dismounted. Chessa watched as Leif lovingly brushed the horses after removing their tack, and then gave them each half a carrot and an apple he had cut up.

Chessa rubbed Sunny's velvety soft, wheat-colored muzzle. "I could do this every day," she said, and then laughed. "It was such a thrill, galloping down that hill like that—although to be honest, I thought I was going to die for a minute there."

Leif started to laugh too. "You should have seen yourself when you got off that horse."

"Hey, I didn't look that bad, did I?"

"You looked like you had just been on the most terrifying thrill ride of your life. And no, you didn't look bad. You looked . . . beautiful."

Chessa blushed and tried to avert her gaze from his, but Leif stepped closer to her. Their eyes locked for a few moments.

Chessa suddenly looked away, feeling desire run hot through her entire body.

"I'm sorry Mrs. Richards…"

"Please, call me Chessa."

"Chessa."

She liked how he said her name. *Don't get sidetracked*, she reminded herself. *You came here on important business, remember.*

"I shouldn't have said that. Forgive me for being so forward."

"That's okay. So, Leif, do we have a deal?"

He backed a step away from her and squinted his eyes, thinking. She watched as conflicting emotions contorted his face. He frowned. "I'm sorry Chessa. I want to believe you but…I can't agree to your request. I need to win this election. I need to bring your husband down."

"But you could still win even if you don't."

"I don't see how. Besides, I'd be condoning your father-in-law's company and human egg trafficking."

"But two wrongs don't make a right. You don't know the whole truth at this point."

"I know enough."

But…I thought you were starting to trust me. I thought you were starting to like me. I thought we just shared something… Her thoughts were left unspoken. Instead she said, "I thought you were a good man. But you're just as bad my husband." Chessa wanted to take back her words, said in desperation, but it was too late.

Leif raised his voice in indignation. "You don't even know me! I don't know why I listened to you this long. Talk about truth…maybe you need to face your own truth. You want to divorce your husband

and yet you're here defending him. You say you're really trying to protect me, but what you really want me to do is in his—and your—best interests. If any sane, rational person looked objectively at what you're asking of me, they'd say I'd lost my marbles if I were to agree to it. None of this makes sense."

"You're right, it doesn't." Chessa was starting to have doubts herself. *Maybe I shouldn't have come here.* "I thought I was trying to do the right thing, look out for the greater good. I guess I was mistaken."

At the same time, Chessa also felt humbled by what Leif had said. Even though his words were harsh, she knew he was right. She felt like she had just had a "light bulb" moment. *I really do need to face my own truth.* "Maybe you're right. Maybe it's time I face reality, win or lose. It's time I look at my own life and make some changes instead of waiting to see what happens. I need to find out who I am. Not who Chessa the wife of Darren Richards, US senator and presidential candidate is. But, of course, you probably think I'm just saying that now to get you to agree with me and drop the story."

Leif remained quiet for a few moments. "It's late. I think you better go."

Chessa looked at her watch and gasped in horror. She had told her husband she'd be flying back later tonight and had booked an eleven p.m. flight.

Maybe if she hurried she might just make it. "I have to run. I'm sorry. Good luck."

"Same to you, Chessa."

Gravel flew as she drove off with the Secret Service agent in the car behind her. *Oh well, I tried,* she thought, attempting to console herself and stop the tears that threatened to cloud her vision.

CHAPTER SIXTEEN

Chessa was dropped off by taxi at her empty house in Manhattan at three a.m., again escaping any media attention, and more importantly avoiding her husband. Darren was already in Pennsylvania. He had told her before she left that he would be arriving home later that evening for dinner after giving speeches at the University of Pennsylvania and Philadelphia City Hall.

She caught a few hours of sleep, then got up, showered, and headed into work at Safe Horizon. Chessa had only been working sporadically at the women's counseling center since she had been going on the various campaign trips with Darren. The staff understood, but Chessa missed her work and wanted to do what she could when she had the opportunity to help.

She met Stephanie for a quick lunch at the local deli, her bodyguard sitting at a table nearby. Knowing she faced a difficult challenge ahead of her in having to tell Darren about her trip, Chessa figured she should seek the comforting advice of her cousin-in-law.

Chessa knew she had to tell her husband about her jaunt to Lexington before he found out from someone else and thought the worst. *God forbid he see it on the news or read about it in the paper,* she thought. *Or worse yet, hear it from the Secret Service.* Even though she hadn't broken any laws that would give her bodyguard reason to talk about the details of her rendezvous in Kentucky, Chessa still didn't know who she could or couldn't trust. *And however he finds out, Darren will think the worst anyway, so better that I be honest and come clean as soon as possible.*

Being honest was usually not easy, especially when so much was at stake, she realized. But she also knew the truth in the Al-Anon saying, "You're only as sick as your secrets." Even if he didn't find out from other sources, until she told him the truth, her secret would fester inside her like a cancer eating away at her insides.

Stephanie recommended sticking to the facts: She had gone to see Leif Mitchell to dissuade him from giving the story to the press, which she had been warned by Amy he was about to do, because she was concerned about the welfare of thousands of innocent lives that could be damaged as a result.

Chessa felt a little better when she arrived at the shelter again after lunch. Then Amy called, sending her mind spinning. She shut the door to her small office so no one at work could hear her conversation.

"So what did you do?" Amy's tone was mildly accusatory.

"What do you mean?" Chessa hadn't told anyone else about her trip.

"You know what I mean. Leif Mitchell called me last night and left me a message that he was mistaken and didn't have a story after all."

Chessa couldn't believe what her friend was saying. *That must mean Leif had changed his mind!* Relief flooded through her. "I went to see him."

"You what?"

"I know it sounds crazy, and if you tell a soul I'll deny it. You and Stephanie are the only two who know.

"Your husband doesn't know?"

"No, I'm planning to tell him when he comes home tonight."

"Are you out of your mind? Darren is going to kill you."

"Let's hope not. Maybe it is good that you know, so you're my witness."

"So back up. Why did you go see Leif Mitchell? Where was he? What did you do? Oh my God, don't tell me—"

"Nothing like that happened." Chessa knew her friend was referring to an affair. "Although he is really handsome close up."

"You lucky bum."

"Amy, lest you forget, I'm married. Anyway, at first he was really mad at me, of course—me being the enemy and all. Then at last he heard me out. I went down there to offer my support to him. I've decided I don't want Darren to win the election. I know Leif is the best candidate. And I don't care anymore if that means not becoming the First Lady."

"But Chessa, all the good work you were planning to do! You can't give up now."

"I know, but living with the truth is more important."

"So what happened to my story?"

"I guess Leif realized there was no story—that he was just digging up dirt to throw in Darren's face because he was mad about your story on the abortion." *Okay, so I don't really know what his thought process actually was but it is some form of the truth.* Chessa was doing her best to kill her friend's interest in the story and keep her from stirring the political pot further as it seemed already about to boil over. She also didn't want to see one more person enter the fray.

But Amy was a tough sell. "And you helped him realize that, huh?" Frustration and wariness crept into her friend's tone.

"Amy, you have to believe me when I tell you there's a much bigger story waiting for you if you just hold off until after the election. It won't be one of these fly-by-night election sour-grapes stories that will be forgotten in a day or two. But if you start snooping around now, you'll only waste your time—and perhaps shoot yourself in the foot, since no one who's legitimate and doesn't have a political axe to grind will want to talk to you."

Amy's tone turned from annoyance to disappointment. "Okay, I'll back off for now. But if I'm not the first one to break this story, I may have to disown you as my friend."

"Deal."

"So tell me about Leif. What's he like?"

Chessa told Amy that Leif was true to the persona people saw on television, only more intelligent, kind, and good-looking. She left out the details of the horseback ride, the way he looked into her eyes, and her feelings toward him. Those she would have to somehow bury, or take to her grave.

Chessa lost track of time once she was back at Safe Horizon. A young woman carrying an infant in her arms had come in with a swollen, bruised face and a bloodied lip she had received from her boyfriend for leaving him. Like so many others in similar situations, she had stayed with him to try to make it work until she could take no more. Unlike so many others, she had finally walked away and sought help before it was too late.

So Chessa was later than she meant to be when she pulled up to their house on the Upper East Side. She had wanted to get home at least an hour before Darren to fix a nice dinner for him. She had planned to dress in something pretty and fix one of his favorite dishes.

But as soon as she entered the house, she knew none of that mattered. There was a long stretch limo parked there, two Secret Service vehicles, and another half-dozen expensive cars parked on the street out front. She could hear music and laughter coming from within before she even opened the door.

Darren had obviously thrown a party for his loyal followers and was apparently inebriated. No one in the crowded room even heard her enter. But Chessa heard her husband before she even saw him. Darren was off in a far corner of the large living room, loudly talking to Janine Secour, who was dressed in a sparkly blue cocktail dress that hugged her curves and glittered when she moved. His running mate started laughing and then abruptly stopped when she noticed Chessa standing close by.

"Hi, honey! You're just in time to join the party!" Darren's face was flush, his tone elevated, and he reeked of whiskey. "Hey, everybody, my wife is home!" He clumsily wrapped his arm around Chessa's waist, and she wanted to gag from the smell of stale alcohol on his breath, but stifled it.

"You didn't tell me we were having a party tonight," Chessa said between clenched teeth. Out of the corner of her eye she caught a glimpse of her father-in-law chatting with Pete Connor.

"Awww, sorry, honey. It was shpur of the moment." Darren's words came out slightly slurred, and Chessa felt her heart drop in dismay. *There's no way I can talk to him tonight now, not in this condition*, she realized. Chessa grabbed a glass of champagne from a waiter's passing tray and gulped its contents. I may as well surrender and catch up with them.

"So where were you, Chessa?" Like a chocolate-covered lemon drop, Janine's voice was sweet on the outside but had an undercurrent of tart suspicion, or even accusation.

I don't have to answer to you, Chessa thought, but realized she had no choice. If she didn't she would probably rouse further suspicion. "I was visiting with a friend who needed to see me in person, but everything is okay now."

Chessa turned to go so Janine wouldn't be able to ask her any more questions. "I have to go upstairs and freshen up a bit, since you all caught me off guard," she told her husband and the beautiful blonde. "I'll be right back."

"Don't be shilly; you look fantashtick," Darren said, holding her tighter.

Chessa knew he was lying. All of the ladies gathered had dressed especially for the occasion in pretty cocktail dresses with expensive shoes and perfect hair and makeup. Chessa hardly had any makeup left on her face after her strenuous day, and was dressed only in slacks and a plain sweater. She felt totally out of sync with the rest of the party.

"You are such a politician." Chessa tried to sound light but realized belatedly her husband took umbrage to her statement. She quickly covered, "in a good way, of course."

"Yes, he certainly is; you should have seen him today," Janine cooed. "He was brilliant. He had them all eating out of his hand."

"That's our Darren." Chessa could barely breathe; she wanted to leave this scene so badly, she blurted out anything that came to mind, sounding sarcastic in her own ears. She was starting to feel lightheaded from not having eaten since lunch and not getting enough sleep the past few nights. "I really need to go to the kitchen and get something to eat," she said firmly. Janine looked at Chessa's waist but didn't say anything.

"I know—television adds ten pounds," Chessa said, a hint of defensiveness creeping into her tone.

"You look fine, dear." Janine shimmied off to work the rest of the room, and Chessa watched her husband's eyes follow her behind. But she didn't care. All she wanted was for these people to leave her house.

Chessa snuck to the kitchen, where a few more guests were standing talking. She fixed a plate from the catered spread but felt like she was interrupting, then had to remind herself this was her kitchen. *I feel like a stranger in my own home*, she realized. *But then, I've felt that way for some time now.*

More than an hour later, the last guests finally left and Chessa and Darren were alone. Darren stumbled up the steps to their master bedroom, lay down on the bed still fully dressed, and before Chessa came out of the bathroom after brushing her teeth, he was snoring. She quietly climbed under the covers on her side of the bed, turned off the lamp, and said a silent prayer that she might find the courage to speak to him in the morning.

The morning, however, brought with it another obstacle.

Darren was suffering from a massive hangover. Her husband finally came downstairs close to noon. Chessa brought him a cold compress for his forehead, a hot cup of coffee; and at his request, a Bloody Mary.

As he sat back in his recliner in the living room, propped against some pillows sipping his drink, Chessa drew a deep breath and began, trying desperately to ignore the fear clutching her insides with its icy claws. "Darren, I need to talk to you about my trip."

Darren looked at her and nodded, chewing on an ice cube.

"I went to see someone you wouldn't approve of me seeing…but I did it for you, for us, for all of us. I believe it was the right thing to do."

"Chessa, can you get to the point? It's been a long day and I have a splitting headache."

Although his eyes were tired and bloodshot, Chessa felt that they were like lasers focused on her now. There was nowhere to hide, and no way to postpone the truth any longer.

"I went to see Leif Mitchell."

Darren sat up on the edge of his chair, knocking his drink over and sending its contents across the cream-colored carpeting. He let out a swear word as he picked up the glass and banged it down on the end table next to him. "Please tell me you're joking."

"No, I'm not." Chessa's words tumbled out in a rush. "I found out from Amy that Leif was going to give her a story on RA Technologies and their use of harvested eggs for stem cell research along with an allegation that what the company was doing constituted human egg trafficking. I knew that if the story broke, not only would it possibly damage your candidacy but could harm a lot of people if it stood in the way of the cure for diabetes. I wanted to catch him off guard, so I went down to see him in Kentucky unannounced. And I was successful. Leif agreed not to talk to Amy about—"

"Leif?!" Darren stood up and screeched the word at her. "You're calling him Leif? Like you're best buds or something? This is my enemy, and you went to see him?" As he hurled questions at her like poisonous darts, he strode toward her slowly, his voice lowering into a snide growl. "You went to talk to Governor Leif Mitchell—let me guess—at his horse ranch, I bet? Did he sing you a song? How could you betray me like this? How could you go behind my back and actually go see him? I bet he got quite a kick out of it. I bet he's still down there laughing at my expense. And you actually believed him, didn't you?"

Chessa stood up, her heart pounding. Her husband continued to walk slowly toward her, until his face was inches away, towering over her. He advanced, his big frame backing her against the living room wall, his red eyes bulging with rage.

She cowered backward until her back was against the wall and there was nowhere left for her to go. "I d-did. He's actually not so bad—"

"Why, you little . . ." Darren reached out and wrapped his beefy hand around Chessa's throat.

He's going to strangle me... Chessa closed her eyes and felt his fingers pressing into her neck—hurting her—and her airway start to constrict. She tried to fight back but flailed helplessly against him. She couldn't breathe and she started to gag. *I'm going to die,* she thought, starting to lose consciousness.

Then suddenly she felt him loosen his grip. She opened her eyes in time to see him stumble backward, clutching his hands to his chest. She doubled over, heaving, then slowly drew in deep breaths until she regained her balance and stopped seeing stars.

"Darren!" She didn't recognize her own voice. It sounded gravelly. Chessa reflexively reached out for him as he fell backward, crashing onto the floor, choking now himself, unable to catch his breath.

After fully regaining her faculties, Chessa wildly searched for her cell phone, which she had left in her purse, and dialed 9-1-1, telling the person on the other end of the line that she believed her husband was having a heart attack.

The minutes spent waiting for the ambulance passed like hours. Chessa only left Darren's side to find a decorative silk scarf to wrap around her neck so no one would see the red marks which would soon darken into bruises that her husband's fingers had left there.

Once the paramedics arrived, time seemed to hurry past in a frenzied blur. After telling them what had happened, leaving out all but the part where he actually stumbled and fell clutching at his chest, Chessa rode in the ambulance with her prone husband, whose eyes were large with fear over the oxygen mask he wore. She couldn't look into them because of her own fear of the other emotions she would see if she did: rage, betrayal, spite, malice.

The torrent of activity continued once they reached New York Presbyterian Hospital. Doctors and nurses converged on the gurney bearing the Democratic presidential candidate and within seconds, Chessa was relegated to onlooker status and then ushered into a private waiting room.

She had called Darren's parents, asking them to call his sister, and then phoned Pete Connor, asking him to in turn to call Janine Secour. Then she sat and waited.

She gulped down a sob, feeling completely alone. There was one other person she wanted to call, but thought better of it. For some inexplicable reason, Chessa wanted badly to tell Leif what happened. But she knew she couldn't. He was still the "enemy." And if her instincts were correct, he would want to kill Darren for what he just did to her.

Before she had a chance to delve further into her wishful yet fruitless thinking, Darren's doctor commanded her attention. He came in to tell her that Darren had been stabilized and was headed into surgery.

Then Don and Dorothy Richards hurried in, and two minutes later, Deborah Richards and Pete Connor were in the room—all of them hurling questions at the doctor, who had to excuse himself when his pager went off and head back to the operating room.

Chessa greeted her in-laws, who, it seemed, looked at her with a mix of concern and accusation. *Don't wonder what they're thinking. Don't even go there*, she told herself. She repeated to them the same abbreviated version of what had happened that she had given to the paramedics and the doctor.

"Darren wasn't feeling well." *I won't tell them he was drunk.* "I had just arrived home from work and we were talking about the day." *I won't mention that I had told him I went to see his opponent Leif Mitchell the day before.* "Then he just started clutching his chest, turned red, and fell down onto the floor. He couldn't breathe. I called 9-1-1." *Oh, and he tried to strangle me first.*

When Chessa was allowed to enter her husband's room following his surgery, she did so alone and with much trepidation.

She tried hard not to feel guilty or to blame herself for her husband's heart attack. She was grateful that she at least had her Al-Anon tools to rely on—namely the phone numbers of a handful of friends in the program, some of the literature which addressed issues just like this with stories from fellow members who shared how to "detach" and remind her it wasn't her fault, and of course, the Twelve Steps.

While she waited for what seemed like an eternity, Chessa rehearsed steps one, two, and three in her head, realizing she was powerless over all that had occurred, trying to believe all over again that her Higher Power, whom she called God, would restore her to "sanity," and praying to have faith enough to turn her life and her will over to the care of God as she understood Him.

Still, when she walked into Darren's private room and stood by his bedside, all of that left her when the look he gave her nearly struck her with the force of its hatred.

He couldn't talk, with an oxygen mask covering his mouth, but his eyes told her everything he was feeling: that she was to blame for what had happened to him and that she would pay.

Chessa couldn't even find any words to say to him, knowing they would all sound shallow. *Of course I feel sorry for him*, she thought, knowing at that instant that he could read her expression, which only served to heighten the malicious gleam in his eyes.

And so she wordlessly stood at his bedside for what seemed like the right amount of time and then quietly departed his room to invite his parents in. Too afraid to cry, Chessa pasted a teary-eyed smile on her face and dabbed her eyes with a tissue as she passed them in the doorway, faking grief but not despair.

Darren's open-heart surgery was successful, the doctors said, but he would need to stay in the hospital for about ten days to recuperate and rebuild his strength.

With the election looming just sixteen days away, Pete Connor was in to visit daily and consult with him on press briefings. The eyes of the world were on New York Presbyterian Hospital, waiting on the word as to whether Darren Richards would retain his candidacy given his confinement to a hospital bed, while his opponent was healthily and actively campaigning.

Of course Pete did his magic and spun the stories to proclaim that Darren Richards had only had a very minor "hiccup" with his heart, that the surgery had gone extremely well, that he was otherwise in perfect health, and that the candidacy would proceed full steam ahead.

Meanwhile, Janine Secour became the newest media darling, outshining Darren and Leif in her showmanship. The public suddenly adored her. She debated Jordan Greene and won handily against the shy Republican vice-presidential candidate carrying the weight of his father's baggage.

News reporters who weren't camped out at the hospital or tagging along Janine's tours hung out at Leif Mitchell's campaign headquarters and the governor's mansion. However, they were dismayed when Logan Reese or Governor Mitchell gave them little in the way of a publicized reaction.

Leif continued to visit cities and towns across America. But instead of capitalizing on his opponent's weakness, he stuck to his platform, which bore the slogan: "Leif Mitchell: God. Country. Service."

Polls showed most of Darren's supporters remained sympathetic, but as each day went by, his popularity waned a little. Americans wanted a strong, healthy president, even if they weren't originally behind the renegade Tea Party candidate who had less experience in office.

Each day for Chessa was agonizingly slow as she forced her way through a charade of wifely visits. After their first "talk"—which nearly became a shouting match that ended with Darren having a coughing spasm, elevated blood pressure and Chessa calling a nurse, they agreed to mutually stay silent and do their own thing during their pretend "visits." He would often read over the daily news and press briefings, and she would read a good book that would take her mind away from this time and place to anyone else's drama but her own.

Darren's health continued to improve gradually, but the doctors told Chessa confidentially that her husband's heavy drinking had already caused chronic damage to his heart, as well as his liver and kidneys, and that as a result his progress would be slower than normal and a bit more complicated.

Being the dutiful wife, Chessa had to relay the message to her husband. "Darren, your doctor asked me to tell you the latest prognosis." She vowed to stick to the facts, not allowing her emotions to get the best of her. When he didn't say anything, she continued. "He said that you already have a lot of damage to your heart, liver and kidneys so your recovery from surgery might go a little slower than usual."

"Because of my drinking?" Darren sat up straighter in his hospital bed, glowering at her. "Go ahead and just say it. I'm sure you want to lecture me even now, when you couldn't care less how I am or how I feel. Why don't you just go back to Kentucky and be with that loser Leif Mitchell."

"Darren, that's not fair."

"Not fair? I'll tell you what's not fair." His voice seethed with anger but he kept it low so as not to bring in the nurses. "It's not fair that I'm married to a back-stabbing, nagging, ungrateful, selfish, spoiled brat of a wife who has never appreciated me. It's not fair that just as I'm about to win the presidential election I have a heart attack. It's not fair that Leif Mitchell, some nobody from the backwoods of Kentucky who only knows how to play a guitar and clean horse stalls and is totally unqualified, is waiting to take advantage of my condition and slide into office. I'm surprised you're not with him right now. This is all his fault...all your fault. You're probably hoping I just die here..." Darren put his hand over his chest and heaved a deep breath.

Chessa felt panicked and she drew closer to his bed, then saw Darren's breathing slow to its regular rhythm. The monitors bleeped irregularly for a few moments, then settled back to normal.

She reached out and put her hand on his. Darren didn't draw his hand away but turned his face sideways, away from her. She felt a stab of guilt and grief.

"That's not true, Darren. I'm sorry for all you're going through."
But I didn't cause it, she silently reminded herself. *His drinking did. He just can't see it. Or won't see it.* Suddenly Chessa felt genuinely sorry for him. "I hope you get better. And nothing happened between Leif and me."

Darren turned his head to look at her again, a mix of resentment and resignation in his eyes. He pulled his hand away from hers. "I don't need you to pacify me anymore Chessa. I can tell we're over. You're free to go."

"But…"

"Go."

Chessa slowly stood, and started to head out the door. She turned back in the doorway to look at her husband one last time before leaving. "Goodbye Darren." Then she closed the door behind her and walked out.

On his tenth day in the hospital, with just another ten days to go until the nation voted for their next president, Darren had another heart attack in the middle of the night. This one was fatal.

He died within fifteen minutes, with no one at his bedside except a team of doctors and nurses who tried their best to revive him.

When Chessa and the rest of the Richards family arrived at the hospital, they were too late. Dorothy and Deborah Richards wailed and moaned in their grief while Chessa quietly cried, mourning the loss of the love she had hoped for but never really experienced, and despite all of the self-knowledge she had gained through her Al-Anon program, the feeling of having somehow failed.

Donald Richards and Pete Connor worked together to make sure the coroner's report did not reveal anything other than that Darren had suffered another heart attack. The autopsy, however, stated that the patient's second attack was caused by the collapse of his aortal artery working overtime to compensate for all of his organs, which had deteriorated over the past few years due to acute alcoholism. But the autopsy would remain forever sealed in a vault.

Darren's funeral took place much like that of Ray Silas's just a few months earlier, although it was more understated, more private, and less populated at the request of his wife, who had the final say in such matters according to Darren's living will.

Chessa nearly had a shouting match with her in-laws over her decision to bury her husband quickly and without fanfare. Chessa conceded to an open casket viewing for one day at Washington National Cathedral. A semiprivate funeral would be held the next morning, to which only a handful of selected members of the press along with a few hundred family members, friends, colleagues and campaign staff would be invited.

Janine Secour automatically and seemingly effortlessly stepped into Darren's shoes as the Democratic presidential candidate, choosing the U.S. Senator from California who had come in second to Darren in the primaries as her vice-presidential choice.

It was an unprecedented event, a presidential candidate dying just days before an election, but just as in theater, the political show went on with the understudies waiting in the wings, ready to take the stage.

So, with just a week left to campaign between the funeral and Election Day, Janine and Leif went head-to-head in thirteen of the largest cities across the nation.

It was Democrat versus Republican, woman versus man, liberal versus conservative, right-to-choose versus right-to-life, increasing spending on the defense of government programs versus increasing spending on defense—and the two candidates, according to the polls, were like War Admiral and Seabiscuit, neck and neck approaching the finish line.

But there could be only one winner.

CHAPTER SEVENTEEN

Leif Mitchell was declared the next president-elect of the United States at midnight November fifth after Janine Secour conceded defeat.

Still officially in mourning, Chessa was thankfully allowed to abstain from showing up at the polls to support Janine, and managed to avoid the media's attention, staying secluded in her Manhattan home.

No one really expected her to do anything else. She was thankful that, for the first time since before she got married, she felt free and at peace again.

God really does work in mysterious ways. She smiled to herself as she watched Leif take the stage in all his glory at the University of Louisville, where thousands of supporters had gathered, waving signs that read "One Nation Under God," "Leif Mitchell for President," and "God. Country. Service."

With Vice-President-Elect Jordan Greene by his side, Leif thanked everyone gathered and was graciously congratulated by

Congresswoman Secour. Then, to growing cheers of "Sing! Sing! Sing!" Leif motioned for Logan Reese to bring him a guitar, which was concealed offstage, and to thunderous applause he sang. The song started out slowly, softly, like a ballad:

"I'd be nothing without Him, He gave me all I have to give,
He made me all I am, showed me why I have to live,
He helped me conquer all the dark, led me with His mighty arm,
Led me with the light of truth, sheltered me from every harm,
This win's for Him."

The song took off as Leif started strumming faster and louder, growing in momentum until it became a fast-paced rock song and had everyone on their feet loudly clapping and singing along with "This win's for Him."

"Thank you, America," Leif said into the microphone after the song was over and the room erupted in cheers again, red, white, and blue confetti flying as the country-rock singer clasped his best friend's hand and held it high in the air in a sign of victory.

Chessa stayed home from work at Safe Horizon for two weeks, pretending to be in mourning.

Secretly, she felt happy and free again and prayed for Darren's soul and that God remove any hidden resentments against him she still might harbor. She decided to go back to Al-Anon meetings and resolved to start over, focusing on herself. *I need to find myself,* she thought, *now that the alcoholic in my life is gone. For so long I was focused on him, his wants, his needs. I forgot what I wanted out of life.*

And she prayed to know what God wanted for her to do, to be.

While she enjoyed her work at the shelter, she knew deep inside that God wanted something more for her, because she wanted something more, and felt in her heart that this desire must be God-given. But the "more" did not take shape for her in her mind's eye as far as a career went. She did know that she was painfully lonely, and wanted to eventually find a husband and start a family. But it was a different, less painful loneliness, at least, than she had felt with

Darren.

And at least God never blessed us with children, she thought. *We would have probably argued over everything when it came to parenting, or I would have practically been a single mom while he was busy running the country.*

Stephanie called to ask if Chessa wanted to go out to dinner to celebrate her birthday. Although grateful her cousin-in-law and friend remembered, Chessa declined, saying she still didn't feel comfortable being in public. So, not taking 'no' for an answer, Stephanie planned to come over to the house and cook dinner for her.

Chessa was glad Stephanie was joining her, but dismayed she would not be celebrating her birthday with a mate. She was turning twenty-seven and felt her biological clock had started to tick, a feeling of which she had only started to be aware after Darren had died. She woke up late on her birthday, a cold but bright December Saturday, and was fixing coffee and toast when she heard the doorbell ring.

She was amazed when a deliveryman thrust a huge bouquet of red roses in a large glass vase into her hands.

Setting them on the granite island in her kitchen, she wondered who they could possibly be from before opening the tiny envelope attached and reading the card inside.

It read "Happy Birthday, Chessa. Thinking about you…Leif"

Chessa had tried hard to put the president-elect out of her mind since she had seen him on that fateful evening before her late husband entered the hospital.

But she had nonetheless thought about him from time to time, secretly feeling thrilled that he won the election and proud of herself for helping in her own small way.

Still, receiving two dozen roses from him on her birthday shocked her.

How did he possibly know it was her birthday?

No sooner had she pondered this question than the phone rang.

"So do you like the roses?" Leif's voice was filled with eagerness, and she could picture the look of anticipation on his face.

"They are gorgeous. Thank you. But how did you know?"

"Know you like red roses? I didn't; I picked them, of course, because of the Kentucky Derby. You know—'run for the roses'?"

Now she detected a bit of nervousness in his chatter, and Chessa felt a warmth clutch her heart. "I meant, how did you know it was my birthday?

"You forget how powerful I am now." His voice was rich with humor. "I'm kidding, of course," he hurriedly said. "I knew because I care about you, and I did some research."

"You mean had your people do research," Chessa jabbed back at him playfully. "And no, I didn't forget how powerful you are. Congratulations on your victory. I'm sorry I hadn't told you that sooner, it's just that—"

"You've been preoccupied, I know." He finished her sentence.

"As have you."

"That's an understatement. Still, I owe you a huge apology. I'm sorry I haven't called to say I'm sorry for the way things turned out when we met. I just wasn't sure…"

"That's okay, I understand. Besides, all's well that ends well, right? I didn't call you either."

"It wouldn't have been a wise idea anyway, since reporters seem to catch hold of everything and somehow might have heard about your call. And I know you're a very wise woman, well beyond your age." She could hear his broad smile.

"And what if they hear about this call?"

"I don't really care. Let them think I'm calling in sympathy for your husband."

"And that the flowers are sympathy flowers?"

"Okay, if that works. Although I'd be lying if I said I was sympathetic. I do feel bad for you that you had to go through all that. But I don't feel bad for him. It makes me realize all over again that God has a plan and that He was looking out for you. Still . . . would you rather they be sympathy flowers?" Now she could hear the nervousness back in his voice, and she didn't want to play games with him any longer.

"No, I love that you thought of me on my birthday."

"Then come have dinner with me. I'll fly you down to Kentucky. I'll make sure it's private. I want to thank you in person...for everything."

Chessa was tempted, but knew it was out of the question. She knew there was no way he could keep his affairs private anymore. *I took too much of a risk to help him win the election to tarnish it all now by giving the media hounds fresh meat.* She wanted to be coy and tell him that if he really wanted to see her on her birthday, he should fly up to New York, but knew that would be selfish and wrong.

"I can't, Leif. My cousin Stephanie is coming over to cook me dinner and help me celebrate. But thanks for the offer."

As if reading her mind, he said, "I'd offer to fly up to see you but I can't. I have to sit in on Congress and figure out what they're up to before I take office."

She could hear the smile in his voice. *He has a wonderful sense of humor,* she realized. *Still...it's way too soon.* "That's okay."

"I have a favor to ask you though."

"Ah . . . I knew there was a price to pay for the roses." Chessa didn't know why Leif Mitchell brought out her ornery side, but she enjoyed the fact that she could be playful with him. Even though they barely knew each other, they seemed to enjoy a certain easy humor and comfortable communication. It was as if they had become friends. *Politics makes strange bedfellows,* she thought with a smile.

"I would like you to be present at my inauguration. No—more than present. I would like you to accompany me there, and at the Inaugural Ball afterward. I do need someone to dance with you know."

"Are you asking me on a date?" Chessa was sorry she asked the question even though she had meant for it to be playful. If the answer was no, she would feel embarrassed. If the answer was yes... well...she would have to say no. She didn't wait for an answer. "Leif, you and I both know that even if I wanted to, it would not be a good idea for me to be there."

"Did you want to?"

"That's beside the point."

"Can you please answer my question?"

"If things were different...yes, I would have liked to have danced with you."

Leif was quiet on the other end.

Chessa finally broke the silence. "I hope everything goes well," she said softly. "Congratulations again. I know you'll make a fine president."

Doing the right thing was so hard sometimes, she sighed. *But as Stephanie would say, it's about what I can feel best about in the long run.*

President Leif Mitchell's inauguration was typical of presidents past with all of its speeches and swearing-ins, concerts, parades, and pageantry.

Chessa was working at Safe Horizon but, like most other Americans, watched some of the day's events through a live news stream on her laptop.

A gentle snow had fallen on the East Coast through the night, turning DC from a government building cityscape into a magical winter wonderland.

The wintry weather didn't hold down attendance, which was estimated at a record three million people. Those with tickets crowded around the Capitol steps to watch the swearing in, while millions more stood in coats, hats, and boots on the Mall watching the ceremony on the Jumbotron screens.

Jordan Greene stood at Leif's right and his parents were at his left. Martin and Carol Greene could be seen standing in the first row behind them as were Leif's brothers and their families. Chessa wished she could have been standing there, not to be visible but to be present, in his circle, by his side as his friend supporting him.

She had been formally invited to all of the ceremonies, as had Don and Dorothy Richards. They had respectfully declined, as had she.

Chessa hadn't spoken to her in-laws since the funeral. She knew they still thought she was to blame somehow for Darren's death, and they were as contemptuous of Leif Mitchell as their son had been.

Chessa watched as he took the podium, facing the masses gathered before him, who were waving American flags and chanting, "Leif . . . Leif . . . Leif."

Then a hush fell as the new president of the United States began his address solemnly, proudly, no longer the rocker cowboy but the dignified leader of a nation.

"My fellow citizens of this 'one nation under God.' " Leif began and had to pause as applause erupted and then silence fell again. "I thank you for your trust in me, and more importantly, for your faith in God, Whom I ultimately thank for guiding me here, to this place, to this moment in time, to lead you forward in unity. I first want to express my profound sympathy and condolences regarding my fallen countryman Senator Darren Richards, to his wife Chessa Richards, and to his family; may he rest in peace. Second, I'd like to remember my comrade also recently lost, the great Ray Silas; may he, too, rest in peace. Third, I'd like to thank President Martin Greene for his service to our country, and his son, Jordan Greene, who stands by my side as your next vice president." The crowd again applauded as Leif nodded to his best friend.

"This has been a challenging election, a difficult year, a time of tests. Our economy, while it did finally recover, still needs to be cultivated like a fragile flower; America may not have it in her again to weather another recession so we need to do much more to continue to create jobs, lower taxes, support American-made products, depend less on foreign resources, and remain the world leader in trade.

"Great strides have been made to achieve peace in the Middle East, but this tenuous peace is also still fragile, and we need to continue to protect and defend it, because peace outside our borders can ensure peace within them. And while our great country has continued to make progress in science and technology, we have made compromises in social justice and respect for human life, and changes need to be made.

"I believe, with the hand of the Almighty gently pushing us on, we can rise above and forge ahead into a new era of peace and prosperity. But we have to meet God halfway. It is our responsibility as a nation to reach out globally to those less fortunate: the poor, the oppressed, the abused. It is our responsibility as citizens to work together to grow our economy; it is our responsibility as children of God to temper scientific and technological progress with respect for all life, to ensure liberty and justice for all. When our forefathers crafted the Pledge of Allegiance, they did not mean to exclude the rights of certain members of society, including the unborn.

"Just as King David conquered the giant, a seemingly insurmountable opponent, because he had faith in God, we can conquer the 'giants' of poverty, global imbalances, economic insecurity and social injustice. Instead of cowering before them in fear, we can see them for what they really are—mere obstacles we can overcome and rise above.

"I know these ideals seem lofty, and possibly some may scoff that they are overzealous or overly religious. But I argue that they are God's will, and if we proceed without them, we will surely fall, just as people who turned from Him have fallen throughout history. We must act according to His principles, not our own—principles of compassion, forgiveness, fairness, and love. We must live up to His call to be our best selves and act with integrity and honor, to act from our individual and collective conscience instead of out of chaos, to make tough choices instead of taking the easy way out. God gave us our own free will, and I believe we, your leaders in government, must act accordingly, limiting our interference in your independence, in the people's rights to choose in matters of personal and religious freedoms. Yet we are called to live according to His will for us, to have faith that it will light our path . . ."

Chessa sat, tears in her eyes, feeling proud of this man, and proud of herself for believing in him.

President Mitchell finished his speech with a quote from a collection of excerpts from the Bible's book of Psalms:

"It is God who governs the world with justice, who judges the peoples with fairness. The Lord is a stronghold for the oppressed, a stronghold in times of trouble. The generation to come will be told of the Lord that they may proclaim to a people yet unborn the deliverance you have brought. For the Lord's word is true; all his works are trustworthy. The Lord loves justice and right and fills the earth with goodness. Unless the Lord builds the house, they labor in vain who build. Unless the Lord guards the city, in vain does the guard keep watch. The Lord is good to all, compassionate to every creature. The Lord supports all who are falling and raises up all who are bowed down. You Lord are near to all who call upon you in truth.

"Thank you, God. Thank you all. God bless America."

For the first time in history, the president thrilled the hundreds of thousands who lined the parade route along Pennsylvania Avenue from the Capitol to the White House by riding the entire way on horseback, sitting atop his favorite mount—Little Sally. Vice President Jordan Greene rode beside him on an equally stunning white gelding.

Marching bands played familiar military favorites as well as songs from the president's very own country-rock repertoire.

It had been a long day and Chessa was too tired to cook so she picked up some Chinese carryout from her favorite restaurant in Chinatown. By the time she got home it was nearly eight o'clock. She turned on TV for company and sat on her couch at a snack tray to eat.

She watched as the live program covering the inaugural balls continued from the Walter E. Washington Convention Center in DC. Guests crowded the main ballroom in front of the main stage chanting "Leif, Leif, Leif!" Then she heard a band strike up "Hail to the President" and loud applause as the president approached the dais. Strikingly debonair in a dark-gray tuxedo with a white shirt and red bow tie, he confidently smiled and waved to the crowd. Minus the signature cowboy hat, fashion announcers would comment that he looked distinguished with his hair cut short and his face clean shaven for the occasion. The chants and applause finally subsided as he addressed the crowd, thanking them again for their support, telling them he was honored and humbled, and promising to live up to their hopes in him.

Then it came time for the first dance.

Press Secretary Logan Reese had managed to keep it a secret, even from the press, who the president's dance partner would be at the Inaugural Balls.

Leif had decided to introduce her following his speech. "I know you are all probably wondering: Who is this guy going to dance with?" Laughter followed and then voices buzzed with anticipation.

". . . So without further ado, allow me to introduce my dance partner for the evening, my mother, Elizabeth Mitchell."

How sweet, Chessa thought. *What a great guy.*

Chessa watched, lying covered in a blanket on the sofa, as mother and son danced to a slow waltz. She was so exhausted she fell asleep with the television on.

Chessa woke with the sun, showered and was eating her breakfast with the morning news on when she nearly choked on the spoonful of cereal in her mouth.

She heard the female news anchor say, ". . .and President Mitchell left his biggest surprise   for the crowd of guests when he saved the last dance of the night at the Commander in Chief Ball for none other than Miss Kentucky, Rhonda Byrnes. . ."

Chessa swallowed, grabbed the remote and turned up the volume, watching Leif holding the gorgeous young blonde in his arms as they slow-danced to Leif's latest hit, "Brand New Day"—the last he had recorded before hitting the campaign trail.

> ". . .*Right here and now, in this place and time I choose to stay*
> *With you by my side I can see the light in this brand new day.*
> *All past regrets I leave behind like ashes strewn along the way*
> *The future's ours and it begins for us now in this brand new day.*"

Leif and Miss Kentucky moved fluidly together to the slow rhythmic melody, a blues song with a sax and piano blend he had recorded with some friends he had made on one of his campaign stops.

Rhonda Byrnes had chosen a floor-length gown designed by Versace that was a shade of midnight blue so dark it was almost black, contrasting with her light hair, which she wore pulled up and to the side in a matching sequined pin. The gown was made of a lightweight satin material that shimmered when she moved and had long sleeves made of fine dark lace.

Chessa stared, open-mouthed, at the screen watching Leif and Miss Kentucky stare into each other's eyes laughing and smiling. *What happened to his mother?*

As if to answer her, the female news anchor broke in. "President Mitchell danced with his mother at most of the inaugural balls last night, but obviously saved the last dance for Miss Kentucky." She turned to her fellow news anchor. "So Bob, do you think there might be something starting between these two?"

"One can't help but wonder," Bob said into the camera with a wink. "After all, he is the country's most eligible bachelor and she's his home state's beauty queen…."

Chessa couldn't help but feel jealous and turned the television off. *Thank God I have to go to work,* she thought, trying to keep her mind on getting ready and to erase any thoughts about what she had just seen.

But that was impossible. Everyone at work that day talked about the President's dance with Miss Kentucky the night before. "I think they're an item," one female co-worker gushed. "They looked fantastic together. She's the luckiest girl alive."

"He's not doing so bad either," a male co-worker said in response. "Miss Kentucky is a knock-out."

"Who's to say they're a couple?" Chessa interjected. The four co-workers in the room with her looked at her with puzzled expressions. *Never mind,* she thought. *They probably are. And why should I care?*

EPILOGUE

The next two-and-a-half years passed slowly for Chessa, but she focused on her work at the women's shelter, attending Al-Anon meetings and getting together with Stephanie and Amy whenever they were free.

Chessa had tried to keep in touch with her ex-in-laws, sending them birthday cards, calling to find out how they were doing, even inviting them to her new apartment in Queens. But she never received any responses, was never invited to any family gatherings, never received cards or mail back from any of them except Stephanie, and was told in no uncertain terms never to contact them again.

The Richards family's bitterness over Darren's death had only fed upon itself, and infuriated that, in their opinion, Chessa had not only probably caused it but had capitalized on it, they shunned her.

So Chessa heard about the cure for diabetes finally being discovered from her friend Amy when she went to cover the story for the *New York Times*.

And she found out through Stephanie about her father-in-law's death following the accident he had driving while intoxicated.

As promised, following the election Chessa had given Amy copies of the documents regarding the research RA had done toward finding a cure for diabetes. Donald Richards had tried to block the reporter's way, refusing any interviews and barring her access to the company.

Of course Amy could not be deterred, and she managed to talk to some scientists behind the scenes, who gave her information about the research telling her the cure was close but not confirmed. More digging on her part led her to discover that other pharmaceutical companies had caught wind that the cure was close and were working hard themselves to produce it.

In the end, RA Technologies lost the race to another major competitor, one that didn't make use of harvested human eggs for its research but instead used harvested eggs from other animals. In the *Times'* two-page spread about the cure, Amy had included a sidebar about stem cell research and the use of harvested human eggs. The story was objective and unbiased, but most readers would deduce from it that there had to be thousands of girls who needed to donate their eggs for the research RA and competing corporations had done.

Amy followed up with an investigative piece on this, interviewing girls in Eastern Europe, Cypress, Africa, the Middle East, and the United States, telling the stories of pain, suffering, and loss they experienced through the human egg harvesting and trafficking processes.

Meanwhile, Donald Richards had gone out with fellow employees to drown his sorrow that RA Technologies had not only lost the patent on the cure but—thanks to the *New York Times* articles— was being investigated by the US Food and Drug Administration for its practices. The FDA was looking into whether RA not only used but solicited harvested eggs overseas from impoverished and even enslaved young women. It was suspected that RA paid egg trafficking "pimps" to round up or kidnap fertile but underage girls as young as thirteen and fourteen to harvest their eggs against their request, often leaving them maimed or left for dead.

He had been driving home from a bar in which he had downed multiple double shots of bourbon on top of several glasses of wine and beer when he swerved to miss what he thought was an oncoming car and ran head-on into a telephone pole.

Chessa had attended the brief, closed-casket funeral and had sat in the back of the church quietly, heading out early and for the most part unnoticed.

It was a bright, sunny June afternoon when next they met.

Chessa had just gotten off work from Safe Horizon and was headed to meet Amy at a restaurant in downtown Manhattan to celebrate her friend's birthday. She was walking down First Avenue when she saw an entourage approaching her on the street. It looked like some celebrity was probably going to be performing somewhere nearby. Dusk was falling and Chessa couldn't tell who was headed her way; only that they were preceded by a lot of media reporters and cameramen, photographers and microphones.

When they got close enough that she could make out faces, she saw him.

Leif Mitchell stopped in his tracks, his Secret Service men almost stumbling over him, and stood a mere few feet away, looking right at her. A broad grin lit up his face and he slowly approached her, the media parting like the Red Sea before him.

He ignored the popping flashes and shouts from reporters and spoke directly to her. "Well isn't this a nice surprise Mrs. Richards. It's so good to see you." He shook her hand and held it for a minute.

Chessa was completely flustered, but managed to smile, nod and respond, "Likewise Mr. President," as cameras captured them for what would become the front page photo of every paper and news website the following day.

That next day brought with it even bigger surprises for Chessa.

While eating her breakfast, she read in the news that Leif had been in New York to address the United Nations and was headed to dinner at a nearby restaurant with some heads of state when he had run into her on the street the night before.

Chessa hadn't known that he had stayed in a hotel room in Manhattan that night, alone, and that he was staying in the city the next day for an anniversary celebration of the new World Trade Center.

So she was flabbergasted when the President of the United States of America showed up, literally, on the doorstep of Safe Horizon just minutes after she sat down at her desk for work that morning.

He was flanked by Secret Service men, who shielded him from the media. Because her office was so small, only Leif and one bodyguard entered the building to the astonishment of a speechless shelter worker who stuttered as she shook his hand and then ran to get Chessa.

Leif again shook her hand.

"Hello again. I'm sorry to interrupt your day unannounced but I was wondering if you could possibly go to dinner with me tonight if I stay in New York?"

Chessa stammered her response. "I…I…don't know, um, what to say."

"Say yes."

"But…isn't…doesn't….." *What about your girlfriend, Miss Kentucky?* she wanted to ask but didn't.

"I understand if you say no. But look, you do owe me since you didn't come to the Inaugural Ball to dance with me."

Chessa took advantage of the opening. "It looks like you had no problem finding a dancing partner."

"Oh, her. She was alright, but no Chessa Richards."

"I thought you were dating…"

"Who, Miss Kentucky and I? Not a chance. She's not my type."

Suddenly there was an impatient knock on the front door of the offices and an aide gave Leif some type of hand gesture in which he whirled his finger in the air.

"He's suggesting I wrap it up. I guess we need to get to the World Trade Center. But I'm not leaving without an answer."

"Okay, yes."

"That's great. I'll pick you up at six? I'm not sure where you live…"

"And here I thought you knew everything." Chessa teased him with a gleam in her eyes and he laughed. "I'll still be here at work."

The President's black limousine pulled up at precisely six o'clock in front of Safe Horizon. Only a dozen people worked at the women's center and, sworn to secrecy by Chessa, they all remained late to watch as the President, Secret Service agents in tow, picked up their famous coworker.

They clapped as he walked in the door. Only a few lucky reporters had caught wind of the secret plan and snapped pictures outside once the President and Chessa Richards exited and climbed into the back of the limo.

They went to a very tiny restaurant which had been cleared of other patrons and reserved just for the two of them. Following an intimate dinner, Leif had the limo take Chessa to her house and he walked her to her door, the bodyguards doing double duty keeping an eye on both of them.

"Thank you for a lovely evening," Chessa said demurely. She would have liked to have asked him inside for dessert and coffee but knew it would look inappropriate.

"You're welcome. Can I call you...and see you again soon?"

"Yes...and yes."

Leif kissed her on the cheek, a shot that was captured by some lurking photographers and displayed prominently in the news the next day.

Chessa's heart thudded in her chest as she sipped her coffee and read the news online the next morning. *Wait until Amy sees this*, she thought with a smile.

No sooner had the thought crossed her mind than her cell phone rang.

"I can't believe it!" Amy was nearly shouting. "You've been holding out on me again! "

"I take it you saw the news this morning."

"Only on every single network, in every major newspaper and on every online news source. You sure do have a thing for powerful men don't you?"

Chessa knew Amy was teasing but she took her question to heart for a moment.

Maybe I do, she thought. *Maybe that's not a good thing.* Perhaps it had to do with her parents getting divorced, or her father not being there for her much as a child and leaving when she was twelve. *Maybe I've been looking for a father figure.* After all, although the age difference was not as vast as it had been with Darren, Leif was still much older. Perhaps she was just blindly ambitious to make a difference in the world. *Or maybe it's my destiny. God has a plan*, she reminded herself.

And then her phone rang again, relieving her of her overactive mind.

It was Leif. He asked her if he could see her again the coming weekend.

Winter arrived, colder and harsher than usual in the Mideast states.

President Mitchell was cooped up that next January at Camp David to work with a few staff members on preparing his State of the Union address and going over his upcoming campaign.

Leif asked Chessa to join him at the camp after he and his advisors were finished their work, and had one of his most trusted drivers bring her to the camp that Saturday afternoon. The presidential retreat was heavily shielded by woods, guarded by armed security guards and could not even be found on a map, so they would have complete privacy.

With its stone retreat house, acres of woods and surrounding mountains, Camp David was beautiful in any season but it held a special magic in winter, especially after a snowfall. Chessa gasped in delight as they drove up to the entrance. Snow had clung to the branches of the trees, making the scene before her look like a picture postcard.

Even the Secret Service agents took a break that evening, leaving the President and his new girlfriend to enjoy a candlelit dinner that had been prepared ahead of time by the White House chefs.

After dinner, they sat side by side on the overstuffed couch in front of the lodge's fireplace, enjoying the warm glow of a roaring wood fire that Leif himself had started.

They had agreed Chessa could spend the night in one of the many guest suites and they would return home separately the next day, he to Washington DC, she to New York City.

Leif got up to stoke the fire as Chessa smiled contentedly.

Instead of sitting back down next to her though, Leif knelt on the big bear rug before her.

"They say behind every great man is a great woman," he said, looking boyish for a moment despite the fact he was the president of the United States. "And I know of no greater woman in all the world who I'd rather have behind me—no, beside me—on this wild and crazy journey I'm on." Chessa blushed as he took her hands in his. "Chessa, I knew from the moment I saw you ride up to me on that horse, hair flying and eyes wild with delight, that you were the woman I wanted to spend the rest of my life with. And I don't want to waste a minute more not being with you. I love you." Leif reached into his jeans pocket and pulled out a small velvet box. He held the box out toward her, and opened it. Inside was a ring bearing a rose-colored diamond cut in the shape of a budding rose. Chessa felt her heart leap and time stand still.

"Chessa Reynolds, will you marry me?"

Her eyes blurred with tears, but she could still see the sincerity and love shining in his. She didn't trust her voice, which stuck in her throat, so she blinked away her tears and nodded as he put the ring on her finger.

He got back up on the sofa next to her and kissed her tenderly, with abandon, sealing their fate with all the wondrous facets bound together in that kiss of a love God meant for them to share.

Chessa decided she wanted to convert to Catholicism and marry Leif in the Catholic Church. He hadn't asked her to convert; rather, she had decided she wanted to share in his faith, and if they had children, to bring them up in that faith together.

So she began the Rite of Christian Initiation of Adults process and would become Catholic that following Easter at the Vigil Mass. Then they could hopefully get married.

But first, they had to wait to see if Leif would be granted an annulment by the Archdiocese of Washington, DC. Since he had been married to Wendy Greene with the Bishop's permission, he had to ask the Catholic Church to annul the marriage, or declare it to be null and void – as in, it never should have taken place. According to his Catholic faith, marriage was considered a lifelong commitment before the eyes of God that could not be dissolved through divorce, though it could be annulled if invalidly entered into. An annulment would allow Leif to marry Chessa, not only lawfully, but sacramentally.

The ensuing year went by quickly. Of course Leif was busy from morning until night not only running the country, but running for re-election.

That November, he easily defeated his Democratic opponent in a landslide win to enter his second term in office.

Chessa kept just as busy at her new job at Catholic Relief Services, the international humanitarian agency of the Catholic community in the United States headquartered in Baltimore. She had moved into a luxury apartment in downtown DC across the street from the Metro station so she could take a commuter train to work and back. More importantly, it was located just two blocks from the White House so she could see Leif on some weeknights and weekends. Since he was the president, she realized she needed to revolve around his schedule if she wanted to see him at least once a week.

The more she learned about Catholic Relief Services, the more she was amazed at how far-reaching their programs were. She discovered that the agency, founded in 1943 by the US bishops, employed five thousand and provided assistance to 130 million people in more than ninety countries and territories in Africa, Asia, Latin America, the Middle East, and Eastern Europe, helping victims of war, natural disasters, poverty, disease, social injustice, ethnic conflict, and abuse.

Because she was poised to become the First Lady, Chessa became a spokesperson for the organization and began flying out to its satellite offices to see their services firsthand and help where needed. She had set up a tour schedule to eventually visit Bosnia and Serbia in Europe, Kenya, Uganda, and the Sudan in Africa, Afghanistan and Indonesia in Asia, Guatemala, Haiti, and the Dominican Republic in South America, and Egypt, Jerusalem, and Iraq in the Middle East.

Often Chessa was moved beyond tears seeing those sick and suffering with AIDS, children dying of malnutrition, people who had lost loved ones to violent murders, and young women who were victims of rape, torture, and abuse.

But she realized she was finally serving God's purpose for her life, and while she was often exhausted emotionally, physically, and mentally during and after these trips, she could sleep at night knowing that, having been blessed with so many riches, she was giving back in some small way to a weary world.

Chessa started with a campaign to help young women who were victims of human trafficking, and she had helped Leif draft federal legislation that would illegalize the practice of human egg harvesting in the United States and toughen once again the laws governing stem cell research.

She hadn't intentionally sought out to focus on this issue, but, she believed, God had not relinquished her from it. *There are no coincidences in God's world*, she knew now.

A little over a year after Leif had proposed, and just two weeks after his inauguration he received a letter in the mail from the Archdiocesan Tribunal stating he had been granted an annulment of his marriage to Wendy Greene.

Chessa and Leif had prepared for their wedding, having faith that God hadn't brought them this far not to see them through.

Once they received the good news, the only thing left for Chessa to do was send out invitations.

Needless to say, Stephanie was the only member of the Richards family invited to the wedding. And Jordan was the only representative of the Greene family.

Through extensive therapy, Wendy Greene had eventually healed emotionally, psychologically, and physically. She had moved back home with her parents to their new house in their native Savannah, Georgia, where the weather was usually warm and days seemed to move a bit more slowly than the rest of the world.

For a short time, the defeated yet still energetic Martin made the rounds like other ex-presidents, being paid handsomely at first to give speeches and make appearances to various organizations across the country. But after several months of harping on the same subject during those speeches—namely that his son-in-law had been his undoing and that he, Martin Greene, should have stayed in office, a subject no one really wanted to hear—he was increasingly seen as a disillusioned, bitter old man and was invited less and less to speak until, eventually, he was not invited at all.

Martin had regressed, his old resentments toward Leif resurfacing. But he was older and had no power anymore. So he, his wife and their youngest daughter mostly stayed home on their plantation-style grounds, and Martin took up writing a book about all the trials his ex-son-in-law had brought upon him. Meanwhile Carol hosted various book and bridge clubs and other such socials for her friends, and Wendy worked at the local insurance agency.

Jordan visited his family occasionally, about once every two to three months, having reconciled with his father and forgiven him for all he had done to his best friend, although his visits were normally kept very short. Jordan had to always get back to work with the administration.

When he learned of his father's book, coming across part of the manuscript on one of his visits—a part that depicted Leif as a deceitful, backstabbing son-in-law out to take the "kingdom" from his father—Jordan's trips became fewer and farther between.

Approximately three thousand people filled "America's Catholic Church," the Basilica of the National Shrine of the Immaculate Conception, that first Saturday in April. Leif and Chessa had chosen the date because it was during the predicted "peak season" of DC's famous cherry blossoms.

The pews of the massive church were filled with dignitaries from around the world, resplendent in their native garb including Israeli Prime Minister Abel Rozen and his family, ambassadors, soldiers dressed in military uniform, the members of the president's staff and cabinet, Chessa's coworkers, and many friends the couple had gained. Selected members of Congress and the media rounded out those invited, while members of the general public who managed to camp out for the remaining general seating filled the back dozen pews that weren't reserved. Thousands more filled the lower level of the church, where they could hear the service, and spilled out to the grounds outside where Jumbotrons were set up to show the proceedings. Millions more watched the Mass from the comfort of their living rooms.

Chessa was naturally a little nervous; she would be walking the same steps traveled by innumerable holy people including Pope Benedict XVI, Pope John Paul II, and Mother Teresa.

The towering Byzantine-Romanesque architecture, stained-glass windows, and mosaics of the largest Catholic Church in America were adorned further with thousands of red, white and blue roses.

The wedding was set for four p.m.; Leif and Chessa had also invited seven hundred guests to a reception gala immediately following in the Atrium at the Ronald Reagan Building and International Trade Center, a magnificent glass-enclosed ballroom featuring a contemporary grand staircase, marble floors, and a magnificent skylight soaring to 125 feet.

Chessa had asked both Amy and Stephanie to be her attendants, and Leif had asked Jordan and Logan to stand up for him. All had gladly accepted.

Amy and Stephanie kept Chessa relaxed prior to the wedding, although Amy had a hard time remaining calm herself as the three girls worked on last-minute touches to their hair and makeup in Chessa's apartment while the limousine waited to take them to the church.

"Whoever thought in a million years that my college roommate would be marrying the president of the United States?" Amy nervously chattered away, making Chessa laugh despite her own nervousness. "And that I'd be in the wedding! I mean, this is bigger than any Disney fairy tale movie . . . bigger than the Academy Awards . . . bigger than . . . well, I can't think of anything that tops this!"

"You're doing a really good job of calming me down, you know," Chessa said sarcastically. "Stephanie, can you shut her up?"

"That's beyond my control." Stephanie sprayed Chessa's hair, telling her to close her eyes, count to ten, take deep breaths, and pray.

"Great, now I have one of you totally out of control and the other talking Al-Anon program to me."

"I can't believe all of his brothers are already married. You'd think God would have saved one for me." Amy frowned at her reflection in the mirror, smoothing her dress.

Chessa laughed. "I forgot it's all about you."

Amy stuck out her tongue at her friend, and Chessa did the same back to her.

"Now, children, if you can't behave, I'll have to sit you in separate corners." Stephanie clucked her tongue, pretending to keep them in line. "I for one am grateful just to be part of it all. And I absolutely love my dress."

The three of them, now ready, looked at themselves in the full-length mirror they'd set up in Chessa's bedroom. Amy and Stephanie were dressed in floor-length satin gowns that were a shade of pink slightly darker than that of the cherry blossoms they would carry, with burgundy sashes and shoes dyed to match.

Chessa was dressed in a flowing creamy satin gown with a beaded brocade bodice and stunning lace train.

She chose to wear her hair down around her shoulders with waves cascading from a beaded tiara. Chessa had never felt more beautiful and fought to hold back tears, thinking, *I don't deserve all this happiness.*

"Yes, you do." Stephanie replied to Chessa's words, which she hadn't even realized she'd whispered out loud. "Now don't start crying; you'll ruin your makeup. Plus, it's time to go."

The whole world watched as Chessa strode elegantly down the aisle, following Amy and Stephanie to a string quartet playing Johann Sebastian Bach's "Jesus, Joy of Man's Desiring." When her eyes finally found Leif's, she could see he was fighting back tears and saw him mouth the words, "I love you."

Making love to Leif that night was an act so totally opposite to that which Chessa had become accustomed to with Darren that she felt like she was experiencing it for the first time.

Leif was gentle, reverent of her body and her soul. He didn't like to drink, believing it clouded his judgment and took away from experiencing the wonders of God, of life—and especially something as wondrous as love.

After the reception, they managed to sneak out a back door to a waiting limo, which took them to Air Force One, on standby to fly them to an undisclosed location on Guana Island in the British Virgin Islands in the Caribbean, where they planned to honeymoon for five days before President Mitchell needed to return to his affairs of state.

If heaven could be found on earth, Chessa thought, lying in her husband's arms in a hammock on the white sand beach and gazing out into water a shade of indescribable blue, *it would be here.*

Their time was all too short, but they would remember forever their days on the island, spent swimming, sunning, snorkeling, laughing, talking, dreaming, caressing, and loving.

And they thanked God together each morning and night for all the blessings He had bestowed upon them.

May arrived and with it, once again, the Kentucky Derby. Lil' Phil wasn't the favorite to win the Derby. He wasn't the long shot either, but rather was in the middle of the pack of three-year-olds running for the roses at Churchill Downs that mild spring Saturday evening.

He had grown strong and beautiful with a dark-red coat and a white marking on his muzzle inherited from his sire, Phillip's Pride, the colt borne of Little Sally and named after the man who had saved his life.

While he didn't win, Phillip's Pride had run a good race in the Derby several years ago, finishing sixth. He had also gone on to win several other purse races throughout the country before being put out to stud at Little Falls. Now it was his son's turn.

The President and First Lady, Secret Service and media in tow, strolled through the stalls to wish their horse good luck that morning.

Soon it was time for the President to briefly address the crowd before taking their seats in the owner's boxes.

"I am proud today to be part of a great American tradition," Leif began, standing on the stage in the infield with the Master of Ceremonies, local dignitaries including the Governor, his parents, his brothers and their wives, and of course his wife. "And I feel blessed by God in so many ways; to have been raised and to have served in the proud state of Kentucky ... Leif had to wait for a minute for the swelling roar of the crowd to die down... to be supported by my family, and most of all, to be married to the most amazing woman in the world. She reminds me every day that in order to find fulfillment in this life, in order to know true peace and happiness, we must look beyond ourselves and serve others." Leif put his arm around Chessa's growing waist as she waved to the crowd, which responded with even louder applause. She was six months pregnant and absolutely glowing.

"So may the best horse win, although I think I might have to place a wager on that horse from Little River."

Leif and Chessa sat in the box of seats with Henry and Elizabeth Mitchell and Hal Baker, the trainer responsible for training Little Sally, Phillip's Pride and now Lil' Phil.

Hal shook Leif's hand as the President and First Lady took their seats.

"I thank God every day that you saved Little Sally's life," Hal said to Leif in his soft, deep southern voice. "We wouldn't be standing here today if you hadn't."

The irony of it didn't escape Leif.

The story of how Leif saved Lil' Phil's sire, and in turn his dam Little Sally, from death had made headlines leading up to race day. Of course, Leif had always fought for the pro-life agenda. If a foal—or a child—were aborted and never had the opportunity to live, one might never know the greatness God had in store for them, Leif had always believed.

He blinked back tears now, thinking of his unborn children, praying that they were in heaven doing great things. And he sent up a prayer of deep gratitude for the child in Chessa's womb.

And then he focused all his attention on the racetrack, tote board, and pomp right in front of him, and said a little prayer asking that God make straight the path for Phil, keep him safe on his run, and give him the strength and speed to win, if it be His will.

The trumpet sounded.

"My Old Kentucky Home" started up from the Louisiana University marching band. This time Leif was one of the record crowd of 165 thousand people singing along in the stands.

Lil' Phil's jockey wore the Little River silks of red, white, and blue—a big white star on a navy background with red-and-white striped sleeves. If he wasn't anything else, Henry Mitchell had always been patriotic. They had received the favorable post position of seven in a field of nineteen.

The media were consumed with the story of Lil' Phil. After all, Little River was the place that raised a United States president, and now, possibly, a potential Derby winner.

There were other stories—how the favorite, Chosen Land, a thoroughbred owned by an Israeli magnate, was pitted against the second favorite, Sinbad, an Arabian stallion owned by an emir from Saudi Arabia; how there was a first "all-female team"—the trainer, the jockey and the filly, a white horse with a long light blonde mane named Rapunzel; and how, as usual, the nation hoped against hope that whichever horse won, it would go on to win the Triple Crown.

The horses were led into the starting gate. Although her hat shielded her eyes from the late-day sun, Chessa squinted and craned her neck to try to find Phil in the pack of horses being led into the gate. Both Chessa and Leif were dressed in red, white, and blue—she in a red suit with a navy scarf and white wide-brimmed hat with navy trim and red roses, and he in a navy suit with a white shirt, red tie, and white cowboy hat.

But now the "fashion show" part of the Derby was over, didn't matter; it was race time, the most exciting two minutes in all of sports.

And the words everyone was waiting to hear were finally belted out by the announcer: "And they're off!"

All of the horses got a fairly clean break out of the starting gate. Leif and Chessa strained to hear the announcer above the deafening din.

"...Sinbad takes an early lead out of the gate with Rapunzel right behind on the inside followed by Candy Apple, Chosen Land in fourth, and Lil' Phil in fifth . . . in the middle of the track here comes Rapunzel leading the pack of boys behind her, with Sinbad and Chosen Land neck and neck for second, followed by Candy Apple, who's fallen back to fourth on the outside and Lil' Phil is still in fifth . . . as they move into the back stretch, here comes Dennis the Menace coming up from the outside in sixth . . . Rapunzel has lost her lead and has dropped back to seventh while Sinbad and Chosen Land battle it out by two lengths as they race to the far turn with three-eighths of a mile to go . . . and here comes Lil' Phil racing ahead into third . . . as the field turns for home at the one-quarter pole, Lil' Phil is running past Sinbad and Chosen Land. . ."

The screams from the crowd nearly drowned out the announcer's voice, and Leif handed Chessa a pair of binoculars. He was too nervous to do anything except pray, his hands folded to his chest.

"Honey, he's winning! He's going to win!" Chessa heard herself shriek.

". . . down the stretch they come, and Lil' Phil is ahead by three, now four, lengths . . . it's going to be Lil' Phil . . . Lil' Phil wins the Kentucky Derby in record time!"

The Mitchell family and Hal jumped up and down, holding each other, laughing, crying, shouting with joy. Even the Secret Service agents flanking them smiled and cheered.

They all hurried down to the winner's circle, and after congratulating the jockey and patting Phil, who was blanketed with red roses, they climbed onto the platform. Hal spoke a few words into the network television microphones, and together they all held the gold trophy high.

The television news announcer held up the microphone to Leif. "President Mitchell, did you ever think you'd be standing here after winning your own race, to win the Kentucky Derby?"

"Actually, I knew this little guy could win the minute he was born. I had faith that since we saved his father and grandmother, God would have big plans for him. Sometimes we just have to let nature take its course, believe in God's will, and get out of the way." Leif looked over at Chessa and took her hand in his. "And sometimes it just takes a helping hand."

ABOUT THE AUTHOR

Michele Chynoweth (pronounced shun-ó-with) has worked in journalism, advertising and marketing prior to becoming a published author. She has won several awards for her work including first place in the drama category of the Maryland Writers Association fiction contest. She is a graduate of the University of Notre Dame, is remarried, has five children and lives in her native Maryland.

Michele believes that the stories in the Bible's Old Testament are compelling, but because they were written so long ago, readers today have difficulty relating to or comprehending them. She believes she has been called to "re-imagine" these Bible stories through modern-day novels filled with the same drama, suspense and romance, yet written so that today's readers can easily see themselves in the characters and hear what God is saying.

Her stories will not only grip you, taking you for a wild ride that will leave you hanging on until the end - they will inspire you to search your own heart for God's Will in your life and find a deeper faith in God's Plan.

Enjoy an Excerpt from The Faithful One...

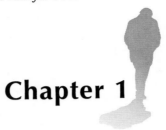

Chapter 1

Life is good.

Seth Jacobs reflected on the idyllic September afternoon outside as he adjusted his tie before the hallway mirror while awaiting his limousine. It was the type of day that made you grateful just to be alive – clear, crisp, with temperatures in the mid-seventies and puffy, white clouds billowing across a bright cerulean sky.

There, perfect, Seth thought, surmising his outfit. He still had a tan leftover from summer that contrasted nicely with the starched, white shirt collar around his neck and the charcoal tuxedo, which had been tailored well to fit his large, muscular frame, bringing out the golden highlights in his silver-flecked, light brown hair.

Hearing the sound of a vehicle approaching, Seth quickly shifted his attention from the mirror to the foyer.

The limo driver pulled the sleek, black extended Cadillac into the entrance of the Jacobs' estate, maneuvered up the long, circular drive and parked, letting out a soft whistle as he stretched his lanky figure out of the driver's seat. He had chauffeured many wealthy people in his time, but never before had he seen anything like the breathtaking home that lay sprawling before him.

Perched atop a manicured hill like a crown jewel was the Jacobs' mansion. The stone and stucco exterior and architectural lines gave it the look of a magnificent European chateau adorned with an arched entrance, floor-to-ceiling bay windows, and first and second floor verandas. The landscaped mansion was surrounded by a wooded backdrop as far as the eye could see. It was like a Hollywood dream home tailored to fit the more rustic look of Massachusetts.

The driver stood waiting, continuing to stare. Although he was six-foot-four, he had to crane his neck to view the entire forty-room mansion. He couldn't see what lay beyond, but it was public knowledge that the two-hundred acres behind the house sported an Olympic-sized swimming pool, several gardens, and forests that buffered the estate for miles.

Seth's approach startled him from his reverie.

"Ahem, you must be my driver?"

"Good evening, uh, Mr. Jacobs, sir." The driver recovered by clearing his throat, taken off guard by the impeccably dressed man who stood nearly as tall as he.

"Relax, what's your name?" Seth extended his hand.

The driver hesitated for a moment before shaking it, appearing flustered that the famous multi-millionaire had made such a friendly, down-to-earth gesture.

"James, sir."

Seth laughed warmly, sending slight crinkles fanning out from his sea-blue eyes. "Well, I might have guessed. Okay, James, let's go."

With Seth safely tucked inside, the limousine wound its way through the New England countryside and into downtown Boston, where it proceeded to get hopelessly snarled in traffic. James attempted to meander through it before he was forced to come to a complete stop, stuck just within the city limits.

Boston's highway system was once again under major construction and traffic was a nightmare.

It was already five o'clock and Seth was due at six. He was hosting the black-tie-only, thousand-dollar-a-plate fundraising dinner for U.S. Senator Robert Caine, a rising star in Massachusetts who was seeking the Democratic nomination for President in the upcoming election.

The dinner, of course, was being held at the Perfect Place, one of a series of now-famous restaurants owned by Seth Jacobs. With all of Boston's many fine eating establishments, it was still second to none, located at Rowes Wharf, the city's most prestigious waterfront district.

Seth checked his watch for the tenth time in two minutes. Traffic was at a standstill. *At this rate, it will take over an hour to get to the restaurant,* he thought.

"James, no offense, but I won't make it if we sit here much longer. I think I'll take the T."

"But sir, the way you're dressed, it might be dangerous," James protested.

Seth held firm. "Don't worry, I won't hold you responsible." He smiled and handed the driver a fifty-dollar bill. "Thanks, James."

Seth jumped from the limo and headed for the nearest stop of the underground metro, known in Boston as the T. *At least I'm moving,* he thought as he rounded the building on the corner of the next intersection and scrambled for the station. Seth boarded the Blue Line, which he calculated would get him to Boston Harbor in about ten minutes, just in time to make a last-minute check on everything before cocktails were served.

The Senator's dinner will be a culinary coup d'état, Seth thought proudly, taking his seat on the train.

Dining at the Perfect Place was always an occasion in itself, whether one dined alone, with family or friends, or with an intimate partner. One had to make reservations weeks, sometimes months in advance to get a table. But everyone knew the wait was always worthwhile.

Seth wanted his customers to enjoy their dining experience whether they were nine or ninety-nine. Each of his restaurants had a different decor but the same name - a name that Seth hoped reflected the experience within.

That experience included several signature attractions: a location on prime waterfront property, whether it be on a river, lake or ocean, a scenic indoor waterfall, paintings and sculptures by the finest local artists, a variety of appropriate dinner music from grand piano to string quartet, several strategically located fireplaces and the most important feature of all - the finest and freshest cuisine from around the world.

All of the restaurants in the Perfect Place family - Seth hated the word "chain" when it referred to his restaurants - were owned by Jacobs Enterprises, the company Seth formed when he was just getting started in the restaurant business at the young age of thirty. He had built his restaurant "family" one at a time and there was now a Perfect Place in every state in America.

There were no menus at the Perfect Place, which also made it unique, as well as both perplexing and delightful to first-time visitors. Daily specials were suggested by the wait staff, or patrons could order whatever they wished. Seth had decided people should be allowed to eat and drink whatever they preferred at the moment, whether it was lobster stuffed with caviar accompanied by Dom Perignon, or a good hamburger, fries and a shake. Everything was prepared to order by the finest chefs in the world.

Seth was by far the best-dressed and best-looking person on the train despite the fact his tux was disguised under his overcoat. He was forty-nine years old and felt at his prime, at the top of his game, and it showed.

Since he loved food in all of its wonderful varieties, Seth had to work to keep fit and trim for his size. He exercised early each morning in the spa in his penthouse on the seventeenth floor of the Custom House Tower, Boston's oldest but still premier office skyscraper.

He allowed his employees to use the multi-room suite and spa when they visited, or sometimes gave away private stays complete with airline tickets as incentives or rewards for jobs well done.

Seth valued his employees and believed he could always learn from them, especially those who were gifted. He also tried to be readily accessible to them, just to listen or to dispense ideas and advice even if it was by phone or computer.

Stories spread about how Seth Jacobs had helped various employees, building a loyalty among his staff unmatched in the restaurant industry.

There was the time Seth had been leaving the Perfect Place in New York City and found Billy, a frightened, black fourteen-year-old runaway, rummaging through the trash bin in the alley behind the restaurant. Billy had run away from an orphanage in the Bronx where he had been sexually abused by one of the wards. He would have been headed for life on the streets dealing drugs had Seth not caught him in time and offered him food, shelter and a job to pay for it after listening to his story.

He had found a foster home for Billy and offered him work after school as a busboy to keep him off the street and help him save some money of his own.

Bill Brown was now thirty, married with two children, and managed New York City's Perfect Place restaurant. He was one of Seth's most faithful employees and a good friend.

And there was Miss Carla. Raised in a mixed marriage by her alcoholic mother and abusive father and living in tenement housing in a Louisiana ghetto, Carla was neglected unless she was being beaten, and was ridiculed by other schoolchildren as a "poor little white nigger." She grew up tough and mean and ended up getting by on her own as a teenage prostitute. Seth saw her hooking one night in New Orleans and picked her up. But instead of paying her for her services, he asked her to waitress at the Perfect Place which he had just opened in the French Quarter. If she could stay "straight," Seth promised he could match her income and help her get her life together.

Seth helped Carla discover the beautiful girl with the café latte skin underneath the pancake makeup and rough street exterior. Carla started as a waitress, but Seth later discovered the girl could sing. The Perfect Place in New Orleans was now known for its famous Friday night musical entertainment featuring Miss Carla, who belted out jazz and blues in a sultry, sophisticated soprano that melted men's hearts. But if guys tried to pick her up, Miss Carla knew how to say no.

Seth also helped many an aspiring cook or sous chef become world-renowned culinary masters.

In return, his entire staff – now numbering more than nine hundred – admired him, and many loved him, even though they worked thousands of miles away. Seth made sure he met each and every employee at least once, which meant he did a lot of traveling.

But his wife and kids seemed to understand the sacrifice, and they loved him too.

Tonight I'll be back before they fall asleep, Seth hoped.

Unfortunately he had to attend the Senator's dinner without his wife Maria, who had come down with a stomach bug that day. *Too bad,* Seth thought. Maria loved to get out and mingle.

At least his teenage daughter Angelica had cancelled her Saturday night date to the movies and stayed home to play nursemaid to her mother. She hadn't seemed to mind much when her father asked her for the favor. He couldn't very well have asked his sons Adam or Aaron. Both were still at Dartmouth, hopefully celebrating Harvard's soccer victory. Aaron was just a sophomore at Seth's alma mater but was already a lead player on the varsity team. Adam, a senior at Harvard, had gone with his brother to the away game.

Adam never seemed to be jealous of his younger brother's athletic prowess, secure with his own academic abilities. Seth was proud that all three of his children seemed to have a healthy self-esteem.

I'm lucky I have such good kids, Seth mused as he looked out the T window and saw the late day sun reflecting its coppery light off the glass and chrome office buildings on the downtown horizon. Looking closer, one could see the scarlet glow cast on shorter, historic brick and stone landmarks, church steeples dotting the scene and majestic trees showing off their fiery autumn colors.

Boston never looks more inviting than in the fall, Seth thought while he watched the city speed by in his mind's eye as the T plunged underground.

Seth reflected on his beloved city and all its special attractions this time of year. He knew the large grassy expanse known as Boston Commons, the nation's oldest park, was full of squirrels gathering their harvest, college kids, joggers and a mix of humanity who sought to stretch their muscles or just get some fresh air.

It was still warm enough for boaters and fishermen to be out in the Massachusetts Bay and Seth smiled, remembering how his family was looking forward to next weekend's upcoming Charles River Regatta they attended together each year.

It was warm enough to still catch a Red Sox game at Fenway Park. And the perfect climate - not too hot or cold - for tourists and townsfolk alike to dine al fresco in Quincy Market or wander through its outdoor emporium filled with arts, crafts, souvenirs, and food vendors hawking everything from fresh produce to just-caught seafood to homemade fudge.

Schoolchildren from near and far would be planning trips to Boston's plethora of historic attractions, to experience the Boston Tea Party or walk the Freedom Trail and hear stories of the Battle of Bunker Hill, Paul Revere's ride and the Boston Massacre that had been told countless times.

Seth especially loved Boston because the city was always so alive and seemed to have it all – a fascinating and eclectic combination of old and new architecture, an All-American legacy and European flair, and so much history, culture and scenery. One could never get enough in his opinion.

He had so many memories, both as a child when his family would visit on weekends from their home in Providence, Rhode Island, and as a father who delighted in soaking in all of the city's events and attractions with his own children.

I'm lucky to live in this city, Seth thought as the T raced through the black bowels of Boston's underground, and then churned to a grinding, screeching, unexpected halt.